MAUREEN DUFFY was born in Worthing in 1933 and spent her childhood on the south coast, as an evacuee in Wiltshire, and in Stratford, East London, where her family comes from originally. She published her first poem at the age of 17 and wrote plays while at King's College London. She has continued to write for stage and television. For five years she taught in various schools in London, and subsequently taught creative writing at the City Literary Institute. She is the author of 15 novels including *That's How It Was, The Microcosm, Love Child, I Want to Go to Moscow, Illuminations* and *Restitution*. Her novels *Wounds* (1969), *Capital* (1975) and *Londoners* (1983) form a trilogy about the city. She is also the author of biographies of Aphra Behn and Henry Purcell. In 1972, with other writers, she formed the Writers' Action Group and has since been instrumental in writers' movements, in particular the foundation of a writers' collecting society (ALCS) and pushing through the Public Lending Right Act. Her new book, *England: The Making of the Myth from Stonehenge to Albert Square* (Fourth Estate) is published in 2001.

PAUL BAILEY is the author of seven novels, of which *Kitty and Virgil* is the most recent. His work has won several prizes including the Somerset Maugham Award, the E. M. Forster Award and the George Orwell Memorial Prize. His novels *Peter Smart's Confessions* and *Gabriel's Lament* were shortlisted for the Booker Prize. He is also the author of a memoir, *An Immaculate Mistake* and was the editor of *The Oxford Book of London*.

Also by Maureen Duffy

Fiction

THAT'S HOW IT WAS

THE SINGLE EYE

THE MICROCOSM

THE PARADOX PLAYERS

WOUNDS

LOVE CHILD

I WANT TO GO TO MOSCOW

HOUSESPY

GOR SAGA

LONDONERS

CHANGE

ILLUMINATIONS

OCCAM'S RAZOR

RESTITUTION

Non-fiction

THE EROTIC WORLD OF FAERY

THE PASSIONATE SHEPHERDESS
A LIFE OF APHRA BEHN

INHERIT THE EARTH

MEN AND BEASTS

A THOUSAND CAPRICIOUS CHANCES
A HISTORY OF THE METHUEN LIST 1889–1989

HENRY PURCELL

ENGLAND
THE MAKING OF THE MYTH FROM STONEHENGE TO ALBERT SQUARE

Poetry

LYRICS FOR THE DOG HOUR

THE VENUS TOUCH

EVESONG

MEMORIALS OF THE QUICK AND THE DEAD

COLLECTED POEMS 1949–84

THE LONDON FICTION SERIES

Maureen Duffy

CAPITAL

With an Introduction by
Paul Bailey

THE HARVILL PRESS
LONDON

First published in 1975 by Jonathan Cape, London

This paperback edition first published in 2001 by
The Harvill Press, 2 Aztec Row, Berners Road, London N1 0PW

www.harvill.com

1 3 5 7 9 8 6 4 2

© Maureen Duffy, 1975
Introduction © Paul Bailey, 2001

Maureen Duffy asserts the moral right to be identified as the author of this work

A CIP catalogue record for this book is available from the British Library

ISBN 1 86046 830 6

Printed and bound in Great Britain by Mackays of Chatham

Photograph of Maureen Duffy by Jerry Bauer

INTRODUCTION

There was a time, not so long ago, when Maureen Duffy's *Capital* would have been described as an "experimental" novel. The word was invariably used to account for those works of fiction that didn't rely on the customary sequential narrative, with the beginning, the middle and the end all safely in place. "Experimental" came to mean anything that wasn't completely naturalistic, a slice of recognizable life. It spelled danger, alerting the cautious reader to troubles ahead. It indicated – insidiously and wrongly – that there was no pleasure to be found in the book. It also signalled trickery, of the kind those clever-clever French writers indulged in.

The term "experimental novelist" seems to be virtually obsolete these days. In the 1950s and early 60s, it had the power to bestow pariah-like status on the wretched man or woman who persisted in telling stories from angles that varied from the conventional. People of discernment understand now that any novel which merits attentive reading is experimental in some form or other. The novelist is experimenting the moment he decides to set down the thoughts and feelings of someone who isn't himself. When Jane Austen took a scythe to the fiction of creaking staircases and things that go bump in the night, she was conducting an experiment on behalf of the quotidian, then more or less absent from the English novel. Henry James's lifelong refusal to fall back on the easy short cuts to character and incident of the picaresque testifies to his abiding brilliance as one of the most dextrous experimenters. The history of the novel is the history of experiment. "Novel" and "experiment" could almost be synonymous.

Capital was written with the intention to surprise and inform, and it succeeds in doing both. The surprises are constant, thanks to the anonymous dead who are brought back to vivid life as the author, and her unlikely hero, see fit. Maureen Duffy knows that every city is a city of the dead: they are there in buildings, in gardens, in the streets, in churches, in the great rivers that run through them. It is possible not to acknowledge those lively ghosts in the often hectic business of earning a living, but sometimes even an unimaginative soul will pause in front of a statue or a date inscribed on a wall and wonder about a life once lived and the significance of four numerals. Duffy knows, too, that the vast majority of the vanished have no statues or monuments or a page or footnote in a history book to celebrate or denigrate their existence, which is why she denies Wat Tyler his place in the limelight when she summons up the Peasants' Revolt of 1381. We meet a prostitute instead, a vibrant girl who has been rescued from poverty, thieving and nuns by Fleming Froe, an astute brothel owner well versed in the ways respected men can make despised women rich. In scene after scene, she turns the historical novel, much concerned with the habits of the famous, on its head by seeing the Battle of Hastings not through Harold's or William's eyes but via a nobleman and soldier fighting on the losing side.

The capital of the title is London. This is a London that is not specifically Gothic, in the manner of Peter Ackroyd, inhabited solely by nightmarish figures. Duffy invests it with light as well as shade, in many passages that dwell lovingly on its myriad charms. A city, by its very nature and diversity, cannot be categorized neatly or given a particular characteristic. (I have a Venetian friend who resents the fact that Venice is usually depicted in movies and novels as a darkly sinister place. All cities have their dark alleys.) Duffy's London has a past, a present, and a future. She mentions prisons and churches and noted sights that have gone forever. Hers is a London of empty skyscrapers and decaying tower blocks, of once humble terraced houses converted into miniature palaces. She never tries to pin it down, preferring rather to lose herself in its sprawling abundance.

The protagonist of *Capital*, the man who raises the dead, is called Meepers. Just that. At the start of the novel, he has made his home in a garden shed, behind the square where he was born and brought up. A rented flat in the square is beyond his modest means. Later in the story, he will move to a small lodge in Kensington Gardens, and later still to a washroom on the eleventh floor of an unoccupied monstrosity that resembles the notorious Centre Point. Meepers is one of the city's many outcasts. You can picture him as you read: walking the streets, the light of some mad mission in his eyes, muttering to himself, oblivious of passers-by. He is, terrible word, a loner. His madness, such as it is, is treated sympathetically, so that he doesn't seem to be so mad after all. He was wounded during the Second World War and remains in possession of a piece of shrapnel that causes him occasional pain and annoyance. Meepers is a visionary, a self-educated man with an imagination in tune with the Picts, the Romans and the wandering Jews.

Meepers is angry in the early pages of *Capital* because an essay he has submitted to a historical journal has been returned to him unpublished and, probably, unread. The person responsible for the rejection is a professor of history at Queen's College in the University of London. Emery, as he is called, is the book's other substantial character. He has decided to teach the summer school and not take his annual vacation. His partner, who may or may not be his wife, is in America where she stays throughout the narrative. He writes her long and detailed letters. Meepers has taken a job as a porter at Queen's College and sometimes has the insolence to sneak into the room in which the lecturer is lecturing. His involvement in *Capital* is in the form of an unanswered correspondent, writing to his beloved of matters both high-minded and trivial. He is an expert on the Eighteenth Century, the age of reason, and is scornful of the history that has to be largely composed of supposition. Meepers is passionately interested in the past that has no names or dates, when the winds howled and the sun shone and there were no chroniclers to record the passing time.

How these two men come together in a near-friendship is at the core of this genuinely unusual novel. I leave it to the reader to discover precisely how, since it is one of the book's surprises. What I shall do instead is to quote one of my favourite captured moments. Meepers is looking down the Thames and musing:

What were the gulls harrying? Something bulked and dipped as the tide pushed it along. His mother would never buy mackerel: she believed it fattened on drowned men's flesh. What was he thinking of? Something tugged at a memory of ragged boys mudlarking through the pockets of corpses stranded at the ebb. No, that wasn't it. The first bank of ooze was appearing with bubbles of gas and trapped air rising, freed from the weight to suppurate and pop in the soft wet skin. The dun-coloured mousse was full of treasures: flints, battle axes, shards, coins cast or fallen in, even whole ships . . .

Then, as he recalls that a bronze head and hand of Hadrian were retrieved from London's river, he remembers his childhood:

When he had gone for Sunday afternoon walks with his parents he had seen with horror and envy the slum boys leaping like froglings from the landing steps, and grown hot under his grey flannel collar at the typhoid that flowed coolly into their mouths, ears and eyes and ran down their sleek otter heads. If he was sick when they got home his mother called it heat-stroke and made him lie down in a darkened room. Statues of Aphrodite and her relations were drawn purged from the warm Aegean seasalt dip with the clean calceous tracery of marine worm and mollusc in their flesh . . .

I, too, experienced that same "horror and envy" watching the same spectacle when I was a boy. It is Maureen Duffy's achievement in this daring, not to say experimental, novel to merge the immediate past with the remote one; to succeed in reviving any number of credible Lazaruses, and to bring all these disparate events, characters and imaginings together into a satisfactory whole.

PAUL BAILEY

"Facturusne operae pretium sim si a primordio urbis res populi Romani perscripserim nec satis scio nec, si sciam, dicere ausim, quippe qui cum veterem tum volgatam esse rem videam, dum novi semper scriptores aut in rebus certius aliquid allaturos se aut scribendi arte rudem vetustatem superaturos credunt . . ."   LIVY, *Ab Urbe Condita*

"O beauteous queen of Second Troy
Take well in worth this simple Toy"

Prologue

The island was overcrowded; that much was clear. They spilled off the land into the sea like the fringes of a chenille tablecloth, first from stocky blunt-nosed ferries, then from the hovercraft that coyly gathered up their skirts and ran down the beach, maidens from the vast bathing machine the island had become. On package tours they wafted further, voyaging gossamer the wind had got hold of and drifted in seemingly lethargic radiants boxing the compass. What had begun on the pebbles of Brighthelmstone when the first striped boxes on wheels were pushed into the water and become the far-flung bounds of Kipling's Empire, an immense warp and woof of British tweed that covered the earth as surely as longitude and latitude (not for nothing was it Greenwich meridian and mean time) was now a lemming rush off the white cliffs from the hordes pressing behind.

It was a wonder it didn't sink under the waves with the sheer weight of human flesh. Only Taiwan was more heavily burdened and they were mere bags of bones, fly and feather-weights with the thin hollow skeletons of birds. Now the Empire no longer carried away the surplus the island's only relief was at the annual migration when seven million took their mistcoloured flesh to ripen in the sun and came back in summer plumage of red legs, striped oatmeal and tan bodies and the blanched polls of white-crested cockatoos, to their nesting boxes wedged side by side along suburban roads or stacked neatly in towerblock batteries.

It sat map flat in the water like a toddler with arms and

legs stuck out in front, or a Velasquez dwarf heavy headed, in the once silver sea that roiled with the iridescence of a starling's back and excreted its pitchy droppings on the pebbled stones until the toddler was tarred and feathered with the stained corpses of oiled seabirds. Among them, and among the black gobs of tanker shit and the jetsam of immortal plastic arte-facts, picked those thirty millions who hadn't been able to get right away from it all, taking deep lungfuls of the fumy ozone.

The cities seemed half empty, plague stricken under the dust-veiled sun, trussed by the flat tapes of motorways that bound them to each other and to the hedgeless fields of monotonous cereal where no insect wings burred in the sun-light except for a cropspraying mechanical locust raining megadeath on the larvae below.

Along the highways to the capital itself the land was pocked by abandoned diggings and scarred with decaying commercial buildings, hastily run up in concrete with metal fittings that had wept rust down their façades. As you drew nearer by road or rail they thickened into industrial estates and suburbs still with the same temporary appearance, put down from a child's toy box without foundations and as easily toppled, until sud-denly there were no longer patches of dusty stubble between them, the greenbelt was behind you, the head high jungle of cowparsley dropped away as the road rose on its stilts, treading down the clustered roofs, and began its last run down to the river.

I

The City of the Dead

He couldn't help it if the bones poked through the pavements under his feet; plague victims, there was a pit hereabouts he was sure, jumbled together, massacred Danes weighted by their axes to the river-bed, the cinders of legionaries in porphyry and glass urns gritting beneath the soles of his thin shoes. It was the living who passed ghostly around him, through whose curiously incorporeal flesh he moved without sensation while the dead pressed and clamoured, their cries drowning out the traffic. As he passed below, long buried noblemen looked down at him from the portrait gallery of street names enshrining their riverside mansions and estates above his head. Well he had kept his while most of them had lost theirs, one way or the other. He looked up at them without envy. He would have raised a glass if he'd had one but it was too early in the day for that, the streets still chilled and the burnt diesel of the double-deckers sharp in his nostrils. They had found mammoth bones here, he remembered, when they were digging the first underground in the 1860s. He lifted his leg to step over a monstrous tibia. An archaeopteryx flapped like a garish broken parasol from the tower of St Mary's blotting out the clockface. He scurried through the arch into the courtyard of Queen's, raising a hand to the outside porter. Through the columns at the far end he caught a glint of water among the tossed coarse salad of plane leaves. Sweet Thames was running out with the tide. No ships strained against its bosom, only the police launches skittered, waterboatmen under the bridges. No sirens called in the New Year or mourned

17

through the fog, guiding the strung corks of lightermen. Commerce had quickened it, killing off its natural life, and when it was no longer profitable, after nearly two thousand years, commerce had abandoned it. The sea trout were creeping back. A seal had got as far as Dartford.

He climbed the two shallow steps and pushed open the swing doors set into the classical portico. The head porter was already stationed behind the curving desk, first as he always was but then he lived in.

'Good morning, Mr Meepers.'

'Good morning, Mr Emery.'

His eye would have flicked automatically to the clock above Queenie, the students' mascot, a tombstone bishop who presided over the entrance hall, her or was it his, two fingers raised in doubtful blessing, one having been chipped away by a rival college, mitred, crooked and draggle-tail. Meepers ducked away to the porters' staffroom beyond the hall to assume the jacket of his disguise. Today he would try again.

Perhaps she was too tired to get up. They had made a bed of leaves for her behind the windbreak before they went off to hunt the herd of elephant that had come to bathe in the Thames that morning. They had put the baby beside her where it grizzled hungrily. She looked down at it. Its head lolling in the crook of her arm was too big. That was the whole trouble; that was what had torn her. How could its puny body bear such a head? At the darkest point of the year they had piled up the fire, jumping and dancing to keep warm, even, as it sank a little, leaping through the flames. During the day they had happened upon another group that had come down from the upper cold and after appeasements, exchange of presents, they had squatted down together to eat. The strangers had given two strong yew spears with fire hardened points and received a pearshaped stone, chipped to a cutting edge on both sides, carefully trimmed to the hand. One of the strangers had opened a folded skin bound with a thong and showed his collection of pebble fragments. She had turned them over with a finger so that the light caught the jagged edges. They had no finished shape, unlike their own tools, but they were very sharp. He showed them how the spears had been pared, stripping an alder branch expertly and whittling it to a point. Then as the fire softened the winter darkness they had begun to chant and dance, intoxicating themselves with sound and movement and the mesmeric flames. The females of both groups who weren't nursing children had presented themselves, calling and beckoning with their buttocks for the males to mount, burrowing their faces into a pile of skins so that the thick animal smell was part of the excitement, along with the splutter and reek of bones among the embers. At last, exhausted, they had huddled beneath the skins to sleep. In the morning when the sun came up late and low, tracing a shallow trajectory along the horizon they had begun to move across the landbridge towards Holland and Germany before the cold came. The strangers had already gone. By the time the ice began to crack and the green creep up the grass stalks she was already heavier, slower. Soon she no longer joined the hunting party but took a handaxe to forage among the thickets of oak and hazel for roots, grubs and honey. When the hunters came came back with haunches of aurochs or fallow deer, or sometimes only the skinny corpse of a pine martin if the day had been bad, she exchanged some of her harvesting for meat. She worked the ground methodically, sometimes alone, sometimes with a suckling mother and child, watching for signs of what lay under the surface by the shoots that thrust up through the earth and turning the piles of leaf mould for insects or parting the branches for nests with new eggs. There were snails she gathered among the sedges in the shallows and marshes, and young green frogs. Sometimes she fished from the bank, lying patiently in wait with cupped hands, until her belly grew too big and it was easier to gather shellfish in the shallows. The temperate airs of the Great Interglacial lifted her lank greasy hair as she sat on the plateau beside the Thames and waited for the nine months to pass, and the foliage swelled with her. It was her third child. The first, a boy, was old enough to go with the hunting party; the second she had weaned but it had sickened and died. A new baby would give her a brief importance when they all gathered round to look at it. Gradually the year had ripened until there were wild seeds to gather to pound into an edible mush. She needn't be afraid of having nothing to barter when the hunters came back. By the time it was autumn and the old man's beard straggled white over the thickets she would be free of the weight that made her sweat in the August heat. One morning, she woke to the pre-birth restlessness that drove her beyond the camp to hollow out a cave for herself in the undergrowth where the grass and small weeds were softest, to be alone with the pain. Her other children had come easily but this one fought her for its life as the day passed until at last it lay bloody and moist on the grass. Her fingers barely had strength to cut the umbilical cord with a sharp flint. She forced herself to make a sponge of dock leaves and clean its nose and mouth so that it could breathe, and then the rest of its body. It cried like a seabird. Her exhausted muscles just managed to eject the afterbirth before she sank into a dazed sleep with the child held to her breast. She woke to the face of her eldest child peering between the leaves down at her. He had brought meat and water. She was too tired to chew but she drank greedily from the skin bag. The next days passed in one long twilight broken only by the baby's mewling and her first child bringing food. Then she had crept from her hole to the camp, grateful to see the flames again and the others squatting over their work, scraping skins or pounding roots or splitting open the long bones for the succulent marrow pâté. They had left their jobs and come to stare at her fingering the baby gently. She had been received back to the fire and fell asleep in its warmth. But in the morning when she woke her limbs wouldn't move; they were too heavy. Two of them lifted her on to the leaves her eldest had piled for a bed and he wove her windbreak of alder branches for shelter and camouflage. Then he left with the others, looking back over his shoulder. They all had something to do; only she was forced to lie there drifting between lucidity and hallucination with the purposelessness of the clouds. It was then in a moment of clarity that she realized the baby's head was too big. The day began to darken. Swanscombe Man, who was probably a woman aged about twenty-five, was dying beside the Thames. Three bones from her skull would be found a quarter of a million years later. She would never quite reach London. Unnourished the big-headed baby would die too although its elder brother would try to tend it for a few days. Perhaps he would survive, and his descendants, to be gradually pushed back into Europe as the icesheets moved south again, pressing down the earth.

I wonder if I'm going mad or is it just that I miss you so much. Do you remember (why should you except that I must have told you since I tell you everything) a lunatic called Meepers who wrote to me some time ago with an article for the magazine. When I sent it back saying the usual things about 'extremely interesting but next issues filled, rarely accept uncommissioned pieces and so on' as one always does, he insisted on coming to see me to argue and explain. I got rid of him in the end but only after he'd accused me of being timid and conventional and of suggesting that he wasn't academically respectable and all sorts of things that I'd thought but hadn't of course said. I pointed out that it didn't really count as history; that certain periods when historical records cease belong in a sense to pre-history or to some category of ex-history as yet undefined, more properly to archaeology. The Dark Ages, which always seems to me a term that works on several levels in characterizing that untidy period, is less accessible than the Egypt of Nefertiti if you see what I mean, even though comparatively it's so recent. I'm sorry; you probably don't want my lecture on historical relativity, my darling. No doubt you've heard it anyway often enough and perhaps that's why you're there and I'm here, sweating through an extra term. What I began to tell you is that either I've got a touch of the sun or I saw Meepers in the corridor of Queen's, going away quickly so I suppose I could have been mistaken, and in porter's uniform. By the time I'd gathered myself together enough to go after him and see, he'd gone like some niebelung – I've always thought the corridors in the basement had a touch of Götterdämmerung about them, perhaps because the music society practises in one of the lecture rooms and since they play rather slowly, and spend a lot of time tuning up, everything tends to sound like Wagner. But if I did see him, and I'm almost certain I did, why is he here? It really comes down to either (a) I didn't see him but am fantasizing in which case I'm mad or (b) I did see him and he's mad. At the time, when he came to see me I mean, I thought him merely eccentric. Lots of historians (every historian?) get bees in the bonnet. No doubt my colleagues titter over the sherry about my passion for the eighteenth century. But suppose he's decided to blow the place up because of my recalcitrance in not accepting his wretched piece? If I see him again I shall ask him what the hell he's playing at. You'll think I'm making much ado, and I suppose I am but I feel curiously menaced. It's partly that the building's so empty, just a few of us going doggedly on almost talking to ourselves. I feel if I open one of the doors I might find myself face to face with myself across empty desks and the voice I'd heard from outside turn out to be mine. Why did I let you go? Why did I stay here? When I agreed to do this extra course it was so far away I never really believed it would happen. It's supposed to be what makes us different from the other animals: the ability to look before and after, and yet back in the winter dark, when the old man called for volunteers, I simply couldn't imagine this end of the tunnel. And tomorrow I give my first lecture. Already I can't be bothered to cook. In a minute I shall go along to the Indian delicatessen and bring back one of those foil dishes of curry and rice. It seems appropriate to the weather and to my fantasy that you've gone off to the hills for the hot season while I soldier on in the plains. Then

I shall go out for a drink. I feel myself slipping into bachelor-dom. I daren't think what you're doing. My mind veers off, favouring a sore place: if I lost you the eighteenth century would collapse.

He pushed open the door into the porter's room. Whoever was first put on the kettle. Dutifully he crossed to the sink and gas ring. The porters could have tea in the refectory any time they liked but they preferred to brew their own. It added to the atmosphere of sergeants' mess, thickened by blue smoke and tales they couldn't have told in front of youngsters of both sexes. In there they could retreat to a sieged existence, the castle guard chamber in the gatehouse smelling of serge uniforms dipped in tobacco and sweat away from the popinjay young aristocrats and their rose girls, who were somehow different from their own sons and daughters glimpsed across the teatable between hometime and date.

'If a kid of mine turned out like this lot I'd tan their back-sides til they was blue,' Mr Emery would mutter as the students surged through the front hall bearing Queenie head high to her annual dip in the Trafalgar Square fountains on bonfire night. As a newcomer Meepers had already been warned what he might expect if he stayed that long. 'It's quiet now, gives you a chance to get used to it, but you wait til the real term gets started with the freshers all wandering about like lost sheep and the great hall turned into a fairground and dances til midnight.' The complaints had a tinge of admira-tion, like blitz mythology in the mouths of survivors. Meepers took his uniform jacket from his locker, hung up his own coat after transferring the contents of the pockets, and buttoned himself in in spite of the August warmth. He made tea when the kettle boiled, poured himself a strong mugful and went to the window to look out on the flurrying cars of the Em-bankment already flashing helios from their sunlit skins. Had there been a river wall there further along out of the obliquest corner of his mind's eye through the arches of Waterloo

Bridge where the bank curved like a dropped skipping rope? He would go up now before there was anyone about and before his official duties could begin. If anyone asked he was just checking that all was well. After all you couldn't be too careful with valuable machinery. Someone might have been careless and left something running. He rehearsed his face into a disarming stupidity.

Leaving the porters' room he went along the empty dim corridor, past the principal's office and the staff common room, all deserted in the early August morning, and began to descend the basement stairs. Two main staircases curved up from the front hall, with Socrates and Plato comfortably encircled by the final curves of the balustrades where they could admire the young in constant peripatetic. But there were insignificant back stairs too that led down to a jumble of dark windowless lecture rooms that seemed as if a century of dust had filtered down from above and was held in suspension in their unmoving air, never to be swept away. Here too the walls were lined with the original grimy students' lockers in institution dark oak, now far too few for the increased numbers, and the students' lavatories, carefully apart from each other like the entrances to nineteenth-century school playgrounds. Through an outer door he stepped into a prefabricated cloister. But instead of a green central garth under sky the blank walls, pierced by functional oblongs, that were the Department of Cybernetics shut out the view. Inside the air was still and dustless as if a deliberate attempt had been made to create an ideal modern business environment of antiseptic efficiency in contrast to the traditional academic fustiness. The laminated surfaces gleamed. Even the chemistry labs weren't as clean as this. A flavour of alchemy still clung to them, compounded of mercury and mummy. Here there was almost nothing to see, even when he penetrated to the inner room where the machinery lived. Yet machinery with its overtones of steam, of metal muscle and iron voice was too coarse a term, Meepers thought, running his palm over one of the disc units. There were four of these and four tape units, a line printer, a console typewriter and the C.P.U. (he was proud of these initials) the brain, or perhaps more correctly central nervous system since it couldn't make decisions but only respond to the correct stimuli. 'You are the inheritor of the abacus, the quipu and Sumerian astronomy,' he said aloud. 'There are lots of things I want to ask you but even I know you can only summarize and analyse what I tell you and first I have to be able to give you all I know, and I can't. I have to learn how to use you or find someone who will.' He had stayed too long. He felt his head singing with concentration and frustration as he used to feel when he knelt at the foot of his bed in a gethsemane of adolescent meditation straining to leave his body, to be lifted up and look down on himself, emptying his head of everything until the warm gush of conviction should flow through him bringing an exhausted but triumphant peace that would allow him to scramble into bed. He had always had that facility for auto-hypnosis. It transferred readily from god to the shining angles of the central processing unit. Now he was older he knew it for self-indulgence not grace, a form of psychic masturbation that differed most from its physical counterpart in degree of harm. The man who masturbated in a context of other relationships took a necessary meal between banquets. Psychic masturbation was a withdrawal upon the self with the illusion of a contact that could bring a dangerous access of pride and isolation: the belief that god partook of one's orgasm as in the locked fantasies of a consistent masturbator to whom reality had become unreal and unsatisfying. Perhaps it was one of the chief evils of prison, Meepers considered as he turned away. They did these things better in other countries were wives came visiting with open baskets of food and love. Had he lost touch with reality in his pursuit of the dead? It was all done in honour of the living but he too might be falling into the pride of isolation. The prison that locked thousands away in enforced but unenforcible chastity was a nineteenth-century invention. He thought of earlier imprisonment which had been harsh and rough but still kept contact with reality. The fort-

25

ress prisons of the Victorian system removed that, made it part of the punishment that prisoners should be dehumanized. Men ate when they were hungry and fucked when they were hungry for that. And if they couldn't they died. How had he led himself to this point? He shook his head. What was he trying to tell himself? That he was too much among the dead, that the capital he walked was a city of bones. He had to talk to someone. He had to explain. But he had tried. They wouldn't listen. He had written it all down for them and then the editor, damn his ignorance and courteous insolence, wouldn't accept the piece. Meepers trembled and sweated in his blue serge. And he was here. At any moment he might round the corner and meet him. Why couldn't he have gone away for the summer like all the rest?

It was that first visit, after he'd determined to have it out, not meekly accept rejection, that had put the idea into Meepers' head. He would go to university; he would study and then he would prove he was right, irrefutably. But he had to get in and to do that he had to be able to reconnoitre first. That was why he had taken the porter's job. The uniform was a passport to anywhere in the building and now it seemed as if it was all the entrance qualifications he needed. From the door he looked back at the silent metal furnishings. He had wanted to see them. This had been the day set aside for that. And now he had. Was he disappointed? Was that the origin of the slight sinking he felt now? They squatted about the room, locked magic caskets he might never unfasten. He was aware of his own shifty disreputableness standing there in borrowed clothes. The room seemed airless and claustrophobic as if he had come out of sunlight into a chambered tomb. Meepers closed the door quickly.

Neanderthalensis stood shivering in Whitehall. It was perishing cold in spite of the declining summer sun. He twitched the woolly rhinocerus skin closer about him and adjusted the pouch, with its lump of iron rations that he had cooked the night before, to lie more comfortably as he plodded on. It would have to last him several days while he looked for another group to join in their hunting. His own had all sickened and died, one after the other, including the woman whom he had mourned and dug a shallow grave in the cave floor, placing a circle of stones about it and providing her bound body with meat and tools. That was an unlucky shelter. When they had arrived the ashes of the last squatters' fire had been still warm and their smell had hung in the air. Their leavings and excretions lay on the floor. But his group had been glad to get in out of the bitter rain. Now they were all dead. He had wandered along the southern bank of the Thames looking for a place to cross. He had a good supply of weapons but would waste them trying to hunt alone. At Battersea he launched a log across the current and, although it drifted quickly downstream, by paddling hard with a leafy birch branch he was able to land at Millbank where he shook himself and leapt up and down to restore his legs numbed by the chill water. As he moved up towards Piccadilly he pulled handfuls of black crowberry fruits and stuffed them into his mouth. They had little flavour but they dulled his belly and quenched his thirst. He must be as sparing with his food as he could. Away from the river bank with its fringe of stunted willow and birch the tundra stretched open before him rising gently. He was glad of the pink cushions of thrift under his feet that would be soft to sleep on later. At the corner of Glasshouse Street on the site of the Regent Palace Hotel he paused to lean on his flint-tipped spear and look about him. A man alone was vulnerable to cave lions and bears. A few feet below, the sharp handaxes of millennia before lay quietly together on a bed of London clay. Earlier he had seen smoke rising from higher ground to the North West but it had gone, dissolved in the mizzle. Still he made in that direction. He must find shelter and company before the dark. His slightly bent stance made it easier to lope along than to walk and he was soon at Hyde Park. He climbed the heights of Kensington for a better view and looking directly West saw the hover of smoke about six miles away. The weight of fear lifted from his belly. He would run on with the setting sun; his shadow running behind him. As if in answer the clouds broke ahead letting him see the beacon he must reach towards. He was right to go West. He began to rehearse what he would do when he found the smokemakers. Soon he was through Shepherds Bush and, pausing on Acton height, snuffled at the smell of fire below. Now he must be careful. He didn't want his brain eaten. They must believe he was strong and lucky but better alive than dead. A man's brain divided among them gave them each a part of his strength and skill and luck. He took the lump of meat from his pouch, impaled it on his spear and crept forward until he could hear the sounds of a camp behind a clump of dwarf birch. Then he stood up and began to run shouting and calling, sometimes leaping high in the air and thrusting up his spear. The sounds ceased, he was in the middle of the camp, the people were standing up. Slitting his round eyes he focused on a woman alone with no child beside her and running up dumped his offering at her feet. As she stretched out eager hands towards it he took up his place behind her with his spear held ready. Now the others would have to kill them both.

Later he lay stretched out by the fire with his head in her lap while she searched his head for lice. Sleepily, for he had come a long way, he heard someone begin the song of the mammoth, how he scrapes away the snow with his swinging tusks and his breath is like firesmoke in the air, and how he falls only to the bravest and cleverest hunters. Then the woman began to sing as she picked at his scalp. She sang of the golden age of sun, the dreamtime of naked innocence when every day was warm, the streams flowed like honey before the glaciers stalked over the land scouring away the trees so that men and animals fought together for survival and men took the skins of beasts to wrap themselves in and the blood of beasts to feed the warmth of their bodies. From his special place by the fire an old one-armed man took up the song. 'Who is he who shall drink deep of the blood of the mammoth, who shall not be afraid when the cave bear wakes? It is the man who carries sharp weapons, who has tipped his spear with ridged flint, who is patient and skilful to strike sharp flakes.' Falling asleep he heard the hyenas howling a few miles away on Hampstead Hill as they hunted through the night.

The day began badly waking without you. Then going up the Strand I noticed that they'd almost finished knocking down the North side, the last of the Nash, just the two pepperpots forlorn on the end and the middle of that beautiful building sliced out like a fillet from a dead fish; the windows whitely opaque too with the sky open behind them more dead cod, calcined eyeballs in the façade. They're letting that stand til last so that the public has a chance to adjust gradually to the shock and won't complain too much. But they do complain, only no one takes any notice, any more than they did when his Regent Street was torn down in the twenties to make room for neofascist art deco. And all I do is stand on the kerb like Cassandra crying woe or the old tramp with sandwich board saying: Repent, the day of the Lord is at hand. Last night I happened to look out of the window before it got dark and the old woman went past with her pram, you know the one we've often noticed who's like a great rag bundle with boots at one end and a beret at the other and her pram full of god knows what. You said once she was actually the understudy in a Beckett play who was never called but liked to keep in costume and in practice. Such people don't exist nowadays, in theory at least, and yet there seems always to be a shadowy chorus of them in the background saying, Beware the ides of March, or mouthing something one can't quite catch. Are they waving or drowning or both? Or are they waving to warn us as we go under? The city this morning was a drowned Atlantis under deep waves of mugginess and fumes as if the dew had been drawn up from the pavements not to be burnt off by the sun but hang in a damp ocean shroud over the streets. There's a dreadful ballad I learned when I was at

school about a city drowned in Semmerwater because it
wouldn't give the poor traveller food and drink:

> By king's tower and queen's bower
> The fishes come and go.

It's been running in my head all day. I never had much fellow
feeling for the disguised prophet or whatever he was who
cursed it down 'the brant hillside' but the 'city proud' always
gave me a lump in the throat like Wordsworth's 'sight so
touching in its majesty' even though I'll never forgive him for
what he tried to do to poetry. What he saw was the eighteenth-
century London: 'Ships, towers, domes, theatres and temples'
in the smokeless air of early morning (you see I've been reading it again) looking down towards St Paul's from the bridge.
How is it that our air is so much cleaner than it used to be
and yet I still get the drowned feeling? Perhaps it's because
after that moment that he caught on the bridge, and Blake
caught too, the air got darker and thicker down through
Dickens til we were groping for the hand in front of our face
and it's left a perpetual smirch. Or perhaps it's that although
we can't see the muck so clearly now we know it's still there.
The deadliest fume is invisible. I passed Adam St. and suddenly thought that I didn't know whether it was Robert Adam
or the old Adam or some other political Adam. However since
he, Robert, built the Adelphi the chances are it's his street
which cheered me or at least diverted me (you would say that
should be spelt with an 'a', divarted, and that I'm coming
over Wishfort, which is true as long as you're my lady and
wishfor't too). Would you accept me as a compound of
Adams, old and new: the primeval father adorning his lusty
nakedness with elegant classicism. I know I'm posturing in
the mirror of my own prose but it's to make you laugh, to
make you think of me that I become the organ grinder's
monkey. Pat me, pet me. Are such tricks ridiculous in a
middle-aged lecturer? I suppose so yet I don't seem to care as
long as they hold your attention. I said it was a bad day in
drowned London, began badly, went on worse and is ending

now a little better with me sitting in our flat closed to everything except your fantasy presence I address formally on paper, though sometimes I break out aloud and speak to you. I'll stop chivvying you with love and tell you happenings. This time I have seen him: Meepers I mean. I went to my first lecture this morning and there he was. I didn't see him at once of course, you don't see anything for some time except a frightening blur when you start with a new group, but when I'd settled down enough to pick out individual faces I saw him sitting at the back with his head down. For a moment I really thought I'd gone mad or that I was mistaken and then he looked up and smiled at me. It was almost a relief. How did he get in? Being a summer school it's a very motley class: visiting Americans, some postgraduates, assorted external students so that at first I wasn't sure that he shouldn't be there, hadn't enrolled legitimately. But I checked the register afterwards and he's not on it, at least not under the name he gave me before and that was on the wretched article. Now I don't know what to do. Am I afraid of him, afraid to challenge him openly and ask if he's got any right to be there? Today's was just an introductory lecture to ease them in gently and hand out reading lists. When I asked for questions at the end there was the usual American who wanted to tell me and the rest how much he knew already and that I hadn't impressed him with my chatter about sensibility characterizing a period and that what they meant to themselves should be as important to us as what we think they meant in the chain of historic cause and effect. Wrap it up and deliver it, that's what they want. Give us all the little facts in order and tell us what to write so we can get our little diploma to hang on the wall at the end of it. And the natives? What do they want? They seem to want nothing; nothing impresses them, everything bores them. 'Those old stones and bones have nothing to give us.' Is it a reaction from lost empire, lost world importance that makes them turn up their rather pale faces with glazed eyes that my words fall on like rain on bare skin, brushed away or simply left to dry but without any power to penetrate the surface? At least a duck's feathers get wet in the end if you push it under often enough. Drip, drip I go on through the hours and their marble is untouched. The first day is always bad.

They were disappointed. After all it was a local society and he had given them no delicious titbit of local information, piquant as village gossip, to fasten on. Finally the stout figure in the front row that brought the word bombasine irresistibly into Meepers' mind shifted on the hard chair and wheezed out: 'Nuzzing, nuzzing at all.'

'I'm afraid not,' Meepers smiled uneasily wishing he wore glasses so that he could take them off and wipe them while he looked down and gathered his resources to answer the accusation. 'As far as I know there isn't a chip of evidence that Advanced Palaeolithic man ever passed through the area. There isn't much for the British Isles as a whole but for the Thames Valley not a weapon, not a fragment of carved bone or figurine, no burials, nothing.'

Their disappointment was like a sigh in the room. He had denied them the first accepted homo sapiens, handsome upright homo, artist and hunter, whom he had created in that room for them and then whisked away with the cruelty of a conjurer. Now in France and Spain dogs fell into holes to show their masters the way to underground caverns smoking with bison in rich pigment and flowing outlines. Horses snorted on the walls and deer came down to drink, flinging delicate nervous heads over their shoulders at the imaginary hunters who had drawn them. Carved spear throwers spoke with engraved mouths, salmon ran and serpents twined, spirits and men danced, hunted or climbed cliffs for honey. 'That isn't to say that they didn't come here. It's always dangerous to draw negative conclusions from a lack of evidence but there might be reasons. Perhaps what evidence there was was swept away when the river rose as the ice melted or perhaps it was the last home of earlier people, a refuge for them from the waves of newcomers. Perhaps this was as far North as they could retreat in that last bitter cold.' He remembered now: the name of the bombasine woman was Tildemann. He smiled at her. 'Perhaps early on this was asylum, sanctuary.' But she wasn't to be placated.

'And the people who were here, who then were they?' If she had added a 'pray' her meaning couldn't have been clearer.

'No one knows. They have left no bones. Our soil isn't kind to the prehistoric dead. They dissolve.' Meepers realized this wouldn't do. Something more must be attempted. 'It swallows them up.' He wanted to say 'engorges' as a boa constrictor digests but he knew that was beyond his audience. 'However we can make an informed guess based on the nearest evidence, geographically nearest that is. In Belgium and the Channel Islands there are the remains of what is popularly known as Neanderthal Man and we would probably be justified in concluding that the people who left their flints but not their bones behind here are of the same stock.' He had shocked them again. Beatlebrowed caveman had shambled into the room at his suggestion, artless and regressive as a mongol child, and our apefather, the clubbed giant of fairytale, an unloveable Wilmer Flintstone, shaggy as a hearthrug and fit only to be trampled on by lissom upright true man.

'Isn't there some mystery about his end?' a nervous man in a shiny blue suit offered.

'It used to be thought so,' Meepers said. 'Nowadays it's considered more likely that the less extreme forms were absorbed into later stock.' They shifted uncomfortably on their hard wooden seats, each trying not to examine his neighbour for traces of hairy Esau in a thick neck and deep-piled pelt below clean cuffs and to conceal his own bow-legs under his chair.

Sensing that the meeting was ending badly the chairman stood up and began his grateful epilogue: 'to Mr Meepers who has so generously given of his time and such a stimulating ... ' They clapped to reassure themselves. 'Can I give you a

33

lift to the station?' The chairman was trying hard to make up for the frost that had suddenly dewed the summer night.

'Kind, most kind.' He felt exhausted, content to sink into what turned out to be a surprisingly opulent car though since he was no good at such things the make eluded him. It would have some grandiose reach-for-the-stars vision embodied in its name or the fiction that cold metal wrapped round an internal combustion engine was a supple hide and bunching muscle about an athlete's heart. This year there was a new image of tycoons abroad, the jet set, the good life embodied in names with a Romance flavour: the Corrida, the Bravo, the Palma and its baby version, the Minorca. There was no need to go. It was enough just to read the names as he did in the café where he sat sipping his second cup of tea, work and a helping of pie and chips safely behind him. Meepers devoured the paper with his supper, even those indigestible morsels of things he would never buy, like cars. This year, he noted too, there was a boom in estate models with every man his own white hunter on safari in Surbiton or gentleman farmer overseeing his backyard.

The chairman tipped him out at the station, his thanks mouthing into the roar of the engine as he shot away. Alone Meepers fumbled his return ticket from his wallet and set out across the grimy floor of the ticket hall smelling of trains and echoing as if it was St Pancras itself instead of just a suburban halt. He held out his ticket to the big uniformed Negro in his upright glass and wood coffin who clipped it, a black eunuch on guard at the harem door, and went back to the sports page and his halfdrunk mug of tea. The arrow indicating London pointed Meepers towards a pedestrian bridge high over the track. He climbed wearily. If the train came now he would have to run and he was already sweating flabbily in the close night air. Now he was up on the bridge, his shoes clanging on the bare boards, looking anxiously down through the windows in case the train should come swimming out of the dark, blazing its headlamps like the luminous eyes of deepwater fish and he a Jonah still suspended in the air miss his trip in its

34

belly. But he might have been alone on the station, in the world, and no more trains coming ever. For a moment he was tempted to run back and take comfort from the presence of the ticket collector. He began to mutter to himself; the words driving him on.

Travellers accustomed to the formalities of Continental railway-officials may perhaps consider that in England they are too much left to themselves. Tickets are not invariably checked at the beginning of a journey, and travellers should therefore make sure that they are in the proper compartment. The names of the stations are not always as conspicuous as they should be (especially at night); and the way in which the porters call them out, laying all the stress on the last syllable, is seldom of much assistance.

He neither saw nor heard the two silhouettes squeeze themselves out of the dense blackness under the footbridge. Only as he lay across the bottom steps, his face in the mingled dust and blood from his nose did he realize there must have been two: one to cover his face from behind with both hands so that he was blinded and suffocated together while the other ripped the briefcase from his hand and fingered his wallet out of its inside breast pocket housing before throwing his discarded body down on the stairs. He heard himself cry out as he hit them, faintly before he lost consciousness.

It must have been the train coming in on the other platform that had brought him to. Meepers scrabbled himself into a sitting position, retching at the blood that trickled into his mouth. The London platform was empty again and he was glad. Footpads, he thought. They'd be disappointed in the briefcase with its lecture notes and slides. He must get up. If anyone found him there they'd think he was drunk and fallen downstairs. He raised himself by the handrail, sobbing a little with pain and breathlessness. He must clean himself up before he could get on the train. How badly was he hurt? His fingers shrank from touching his nose to see. He must find a mirror and water. The dim lights were still on in the general waiting

35

room. He opened the door and peered round. It was empty. Slowly he made his way to the foxed mirror and looked at the unrecognizable face that must be his own. Barrault, bleached with shock and painted with dust and blood: a clown's face but a clown that had fallen from the high wire and been broken, as indeed his nose might be as it began to puff into a doughnut. Meepers eyed the door to the Ladies room in the corner. In there, if he dared, there might be a washbasin while in the men's urinal behind the partition on the platform there would be nothing but the trickle down the acid stained tiles. He put his hand on the brass doorhandle, his ears singing with the threat of losing consciousness again, and went in. Once inside bravado took over. It was quite simple. He would say that he was ill, which was true. There was a washbasin and mirror, a metal dispenser with a grubby cotton towel that no longer flowed and an upending closed chrome pot of liquid soap. Beside the mirror a firm hand had scripted: I like it any time, any way, and a phone number, in lipstick so fresh he could see the moisture of the mouth it would decorate. To wash away the blood and dirt made him whimper and his eyes run. His face as he stared at it was even more alien without its clown's makeup but that, he reasoned, was shock and inevitable. Now he must make himself go out into the waiting room. He'd heard no one come in but then the sound of the running water might have muffled any other noise. No faces turned towards him in astonishment. The room was empty. Meepers went as quickly as he could out on to the platform. A tide of sickness welled up in his throat and for a few moments he leant against the outer wall of the waiting room. The continuing emptiness of the platform disconcerted him. Had there been anyone else or had he just tripped on the bottom stairs and fallen, hallucinating the attack out of shock? But his wallet and briefcase were gone. What should he do; cross the bridge and explain to the ticket collector that he no longer had a ticket? The thought of the high dark echoing bridge slung swaying in the air over the canyon of track with its gleam of spinesnapping rails terrified him. He couldn't drag himself along it again. He must think. He drew in deep breaths of warm tired air through his mouth. His nose throbbed, distended across his face like a horned toad on a lilypad. He still had some loose change along with his keys in a trouser pocket. He would get on the train if it ever arrived and if he was asked for a ticket at the other end he would give his name and address. Everyone was entitled to do that. As if this resolution had called it up, suddenly his train appeared out of the dark, its caterpillar mask with the luminous window features sliding past and drawing its lit segments tantalizingly beyond his grasp until it relented and let a carriage door come to rest opposite him. He was almost too weak to turn the t-shaped handle and saw himself slipping between train and platform. Inside he found an abandoned evening paper which he raised as a fanshield from curious glances when the train drew up on other lit platforms to take on other passengers and hurry them towards London. No one got into his compartment. He found himself muttering the rest of the passage begun before the mugging to keep himself awake.

The officials, however, are generally civil in answering questions and giving information. In winter footwarmers with hot water are usually provided. It is good form for a passenger quitting a railway carriage where there are other travellers to close the door behind him, and to pull up the window if he has had to let it down.

But what about summer? Were there water-ices for the traveller with heat prostration and ice packs for a nose that threatened to engulf the rest of the features, a rampaging tropical succulent of a nose whose suckers of pain ran into the eye sockets and wrapped in steel tentacles around the skull. Let the officials be civil or he might weep. Thank god he still had his keys. He tried to remember everything that had been in the wallet but couldn't, at first, get beyond the few pounds and, the greatest loss of all, his ticket to the British Museum Reading Room. Behind his paper he trembled with misery and weakness until he was forced to put it down and lean his head on his hand so that his nose looked back at him from the window pane. At London Bridge he resumed his paper mask when a trio of spruce young navvies, loud from a night on the beer, got in swearing and pushing at each other. Would Charing Cross ever come? He wanted to be sucked into the obliterating city where he would be supported and comforted by its very presence and continuity, by its millions of ant bodies busying around him.

'I've lost my ticket. Somebody stole my wallet and briefcase.'

'Bash you about a bit did they? You don't look too good. We'll forget the ticket. You'll have to make a complaint though.'

'Tomorrow. I'll come back tomorrow. Not tonight.'

'You should go to the hospital. Could have broken that nose by the look of it. See here, you never spoke to no one, when you come to make your complaint, just walked straight through the barrier. By rights I ought to keep you here but if I do you'll be here all night. You get off to the hospital and pretend you never saw me and I'll pretend I never saw you. Have you got any money? I could let you have a couple of bob.'

'I had some change in my pocket. I've still got that.' Meepers pulled out his handful of coins, among them a sevensided 50p piece, reassuring in its bizarreness.

'That's alright then. Now you get along and get that poor busted conk seen to though now Charing Cross is gone I don't know where the nearest casualty is.'

'I'll call in at St George's on my way home. Thanks, thanks very much.'

'You look after yourself mate; no one else will.' Meepers drew himself away from the dangerous kindness that threatened to destroy him into the safety of a sudden cascade from the next platform that swirled him out of sight until he was level with the left luggage where he retrieved his holdall. He examined his change again, adding painstakingly like a child because the sums wouldn't stay in his head. There was enough for a taxi to the square. He prayed the driver wouldn't be in a mood for talk but would let him sit in a stupor in the dark with the breath dribbling in and out of his mouth.

The driver put him down at the corner so that he could walk the last few yards to the stall. It was a bus with one open side that served hot dogs and drinks. Every night his Thermos of tea was put up for him but tonight he was late.

'I was just going to shut up shop. Gawd and all his angels, what happened to you? Walked into a wall?'

Again he wanted to weep. 'I can't pay you for the tea to-night.'

'Pay me. I should think not indeed. Just wait there a minute.' The shutter concertina'd down with a clatter that made him wince. Then the back opened, letting out the light. 'Come on up if you can make it.' Meepers no longer had the will to refuse. The holdall was taken from him and he was almost lifted into the steamy cell of the bus and dumped on a stool.

'Don't tell me to go to the hospital; I'm too tired for that.'

The woman set a cup of tea carefully in front of him. 'Does it hurt still?' she asked, smoothing the front of her apron where spilt tea had stained a continent across her belly. He identified it as Africa, recovering suddenly the ceiling of his bedroom when he was a child patched with damp into Mercator's projection of unknown lands, a whole world above his head. He mustn't stare, and anyway now she was reaching in a drawer, Africa creasing across the equator of her tie belt, and handing him two aspirin-shaped tablets. 'Get them down you and you'll soon feel better.'

He gulped at the tea whose steam was Christmas pudding rich from some spirit she had surreptitiously and generously laced it with, washing down the tablets with its glowing flood. His blocked nose made him slurp noisily. The woman patted his shoulder encouragingly. 'Feel better?'

He nodded.

'Do for yourself do you?'

'That's right.'

'If it's not too good in the morning you take it to the

39

hospital.' As if it was a dog. All noses should be kept on a lead in traffic. Meepers gathered himself to stand up.

'Thank you, you've been very kind.'

She passed him the flask. 'I put a bit of something in that too. Now I don't want to hear no more about paying me for it. If you can't do a good turn once in a while ... ' The clichés of kindness as comforting as the fortified tea or old shoes slopped over him. He must get away or he would fall asleep where he sat. The woman stood at the top of the steps watching his descent and set stirring a very faint memory that he was too tired to retrieve as she leant from the lit frame of the door.

Passing under the fringe of trees that spilled over the railings of the garden in the middle of the square, Meepers carried his weariness away from the traffic and the lights, round two sides and through a connecting lane of tall white-painted houses with their finely scripted numbers picked out in black and their solid doors lit with elegant overhead halfmoon fans. Now he was in an almost identical square, quieter than the one where the coffeestall stood but also with a hedge-fringed garden in the middle whose iron gate he unlocked after a quick look round.

Not that he shouldn't be there. After all he was the gardener, mowed the lawn, dug the beds and snipped off the deadheads. Now that he'd become a porter too the gardening was relegated to weekends and the long light evenings. He followed the familiar path under the trees to the hut where spades, the mower and spare pots are usually kept. The hut gave off a reek of hot creosote. Meepers unlocked the door and let the air rush out from the sun-fuelled oven. He would leave it a few minutes to cool and sank to the threshold where he unscrewed the Thermos top and poured himself a tot of laced coffee. Through the trees he could see the house where he had been born before the square had become fashionable and priced him out. Clerks' terraced cottages they had been once and now they were desirable residences for designers and television script editors and advertising men. If he had been strong and not alone he might have resisted the pressures that had finally forced him out, an undesirable hard pip extruded by the squeezer before the juice could be bottled off for sale. What broke him was the fair rent set by the tribunal, fair to the landlords and by current prices but unfair to his war-pension. Meepers had shrapnel in his head, fine metal fingers that had left his mind sharp but severed his emotions so that the wires that should have governed and connected them led nowhere. You depressed the usual key but no response followed. Yet sometimes it was as if an emotion deep inside him triggered itself letting an eruption of hot feeling burst up through a crack in the external surface of his personality, the neat façade he presented to the world. Like that business over the article when he had found himself arguing, refusing to take that polite typed no for an answer, almost shouting.

The ache in his face was localizing itself into a nose shape at last though he still had to breathe through his mouth. He stood up and went inside, unzipped his holdall and got out a big rubber torch. Then he bent to the floorboards and heaved up two short sections revealing a black cavity under the hut from which he took a single rubber mattress and a bigger battery lamp. He dropped the sacking curtains before he switched it on. From the holdall again he took a travelling alarm clock, a book, his pyjamas and washbag. Blowing heavily he undressed and hung his suit on a coathanger from a nail. It was still stuffy in the hut and the smell of tar penetrated even his mashed nose but a slight breeze stirred the sacking at the open windows. Switching out the rubber torch, he set the alarm, poured more of the liquid from the Thermos and stretched himself out on the airbed. His experience wasn't unique or even ususual. He flipped open the book and began to follow the soothing phrases.

We need hardly caution newcomers against the artifice of pick-pockets and the wiles of imposters, two fraternities which are very numerous in London. It is even prudent to avoid speaking to strangers in the street. A considerable degree of caution and presence of mind is often requisite in

41

crossing a crowded thoroughfare, and in entering or alight-
ing from a train or omnibus. The 'rule of the road' for
passengers in busy streets is to keep to the right. Poor
neighbourhoods should be avoided after nightfall.

The forest must have grown thick as pubic hair clustering the
banks. The night before they would have passed the smooth
stone shape from hand to hand. It was polished to a dark
patina by the sweat and grease of years of palms until now it
was wet seal coloured. No one knew who had shaped it or
whether it had been thrown up by the river as a sign that they
were to take and kill every year when the seal people followed
the salmon up stream past the village. A wall of nets had been
strung across the river above where the Brent spilled into it.
It had taken the women weeks to check and repair it, singing
together as they sat with their legs thrust out in front of them
rebuilding the meshed trap, renewing the bark floats along
the top and the stone sinkers that would keep it upright, an
invisible barrier the salmon would fling themselves against in
flight from the harrying seal people. Then the seal people
would fall upon them, plucking them from the meshes and
in their turn, while the seal people were harvesting salmon,
they would fall upon them from behind with their fish
spears. Every year it was the same: the long days of preparation, the nightly incantations above the sound of the river,
telling old stories of the seal people, of drowning and escape,
until they were warned by the lookouts down stream that the
two waves, one of flashing green scales, the other of blunt
dark heads and roiling svelte backs, were on their way up.
During that day they laid the net, paddling hard against the
current in a small fleet with the net between them so that it
shouldn't tangle and anchoring it at both ends to two trees
that overhung the Thames.
  The rain fell incessantly, as it did nearly every day, so that
their waiting bodies were as wet as those of the seal people; it
was the rain that curled the forest down to the water's edge.

With their Thames picks they cut down the trees to build the village above the water but the rain made the trees and bushes spring up again so quickly it was hard to gain a footing on the land. The trees pressed them down into the water and the water threw them back towards the trees when the flood tides rose. So they perched between the two, building themselves a ledge and then the huts on it between land and water. Yet they were still the forest people, even though their young swam like frogs and their boys and men hacked treetrunks into dugouts. When it came to the struggle with the seal people they were out of their element. The seal people were strong and they didn't want to die. Therefore they passed the grey stone from hand to hand asking forgiveness and that the grey seal women shouldn't take the men down with them when they plunged. It was the men who needed to build their courage. The women laughed and sang together as they mended the nets or pounded roots with their children clinging to them. They were never lonely. The children were theirs; they had no need to compete for them or for attention. When a child died or a woman was in labour they keened together as if it was one voice. But the men's voices were raised separately, arguing, in competition with each other. They were the ones who faced death in the river because they were expendable. It must have made them anxious and lonely, boastful and rash. The women's society was natural and easy; the men's an artificial construct making its own rules and divisions.

On this day everyone would be there: the men in the dugouts; the women and children silent along the banks. They would make a noise if any of the seal people tried to escape up the Brent. They would drive them back by shouting and slapping the water for the men to have a second chance and later still, when the bodies of the seal people were brought on to the banks and the long wall of net hauled in with its captives, they would help with the skinning and carrying. Nothing would be wasted: pelt for covering, blubber for food and lamplight in winter, fresh meat, bones to shape and carve, the leftovers as bait for more fish and shellfish, the bladders

43

for bags and floats, the sinews for stitching. The dogs ran from group to group trying to snatch a piece of offal. Then they would be flung their share for although they didn't help in the seal hunt they went everywhere else with the men finding and picking up snared or bowshot birds and flushing game from the undergrowth. In the village pack they guarded the approaches, keeping off intruders, protecting the territory that belonged to the men their pack leaders and was therefore theirs too, and leaving their small skeletons for the museum glass cases to catafalque with their label epitaphs: the first domesticated animal.

'Where is your lady?' The short one asked this evening when I went for my ritual tinfoil handout of curry and rice. 'She's away.' They are African Asians which caused me to wonder as I walked to the lights on the corner of our road in a short procession of first a tall Ethiopianly exotic American Negro with busby hair and the most elegant slimcut clothes in sight, second an Asian mother and schoolgirl daughter both with fat shining black plaits and coloured robes and me bringing up the rear with my supper held like a presentation silver casket in front of me while alongside suddenly a chrome, pink and plum chara full of Japanese businessmen, grey suited and black camera'd, on their way to Heathrow looking down on us without expression (they'd read about inscrutable Orientals) whether this isn't the most poly metropolis since the Rome of Trajan. But we no longer have a style. When I crossed the road I passed a boy and girl in the blue sackcloth of denim, workman's bib and brace, prison gear cut from mailbags or woven from oakum whatever that may be, and limp as boiled flour sacks and it seemed to me that whoever was losing their cultural identity it wasn't the West Indians who all look as imperious as Haile Selassie or the Pakistanis, Bengalis and Sikhs who all look as Governor-General as Pandit Nehru but the runt of Western civilization which seems in full guilty flight; by that I mean it seems to be attempting to recess it-

44

self into an unnoticeable shadow. Let us keep our heads well down or someone will shout imperialist rapist or environmental polluter. It doesn't much matter which. Any name is strong enough to break my bones since I no longer wear any stylistic shield to protect my damaged ego. How I long for some positive assertion of identity like a clothcap and neckerchief, preferably redspotted. And now you're not here there's nothing to offset the sheer dowdiness of the city. Everywhere I look there's the same imitation of 'thirties, 'forties, 'fifties fashions that were hideous in their day and have gained nothing by regurgitation with a touch of green and mauve camp. Is it our own lost and mythical innocence we're nostalgic for? Or should I say 'they' and be honest about it, not pretend to an identification I don't have as I prink about like the last of the dandies in ruffles and velvet still while everyone else is in bags and tweed. I won't apologize for being alive. I wasn't responsible for the slave-trade. Not a drop of slaver blood runs in my veins. My ancestors died of the diseases of industrial poverty or were ridden down at Peterloo. As a rational being I reject the superstition of collective guilt which is merely a latterday manifestation of original sin, a post-Christian detritus. I will not have the sins of other people's fathers bowing my head. I must stop this.

(Continued later.) I think I must have had the spiritual gout while I was writing that so testy and choleric. Forgive me. Today there was no Meepers and I was thrown, of course, back into my dilemma of whether I had invented him and all my fine openings: 'Now look here' (a touch of the Blimps); 'What about a cup of tea in the refectory?' (the chaplain); 'Could you spare a moment?' (the don courteous) will have to be taken out and dusted when he comes back, if he ever does and I didn't invent him. There are two students who seem intelligent and promise more than the rest but it's too soon to tell. Talked today about craftsmanship: the combination of elegance and utility seen in a Hepplewhite pedestal and vase for instance, Palladian plate racks and funerary urns of iced water for the diningroom. Why is it we can only produce the brutishly useful or the frivolously ornamental was what I wanted them to consider; that is, why could they still pull it off superbly in the eighteenth century and is this part of the period's attraction. In a crash course there's even less point in spewing up figures than usual. They must get all that for themselves from the text books. I think they're beginning to get used to me. Went along to the common room for the first time to see if there was anyone else about or if I was holding the fort alone and there was Wandle sunk in an armchair with *The Times* as if it was Boodles or one of those other hideous stuffed leather clubs. A kind of greenish sparkle came through the windows from the leaves and water outside making his white hair almost halo. He must be nearly seventy. You met him once I think. I said wasn't the city hot and other bits of nonsense and was he going away. 'Not yet,' he said, 'I'm busy writing an apologia for my generation,' knowing that would mystify me and I'd have to ask for more, a trick of lonely people to spin things out so that like Oliver you have to keep coming up for another ration. So dutifully I asked. 'There have been several grave attacks of hindsight lately suggesting that those of us who joined the Communist Party between the wars were party to Stalin's camps and purges. I feel I have to explain before it's all fogged over and no one can see inside anymore. Silly perhaps and it might be better to keep a dignified silence but I feel that would be a betrayal.' Again that morning I was thrown, as if he'd taken his clothes off or told me he was dying, and very relieved when the door opened and Ponders came in. Him you haven't met. Head of Cybernetics; in a curious way not an academic at all but almost a businessman. It's something all the technologists veer towards or maybe assume; a bustling no-nonsense practicality. I suppose you need it if you have to build a department from the ground in anything as traditional as Queen's with its flourishing dog-collar department, legacy of our pious founder and our initial raison d'être but owing more to faith than reason. Ponders is pink, polished and jaunty, not crass but wearyingly energetic. You know he will win whereas Wandle has lost. I like him though. I like them both in spite of my embarrass-ment. I asked Ponders the same question. 'George is having some improvements,' he said smiling. 'George?' 'Our com-puter.' 'Why George?' 'One has to call them something if one's going to have a day-to-day relationship. George seems to fit, perhaps because of automatic pilots on aircraft. We're updating him. The field changes so fast there's almost an Alice quality about it. You know, nothing staying the same for two minutes together. All the different commercial firms are in such fierce competition that they come up with some-thing to scoop the market every six months.'

'The caucus race,' said Wandle, 'with everyone starting and stopping at different times.'

'That's it exactly. I've put off giving George a face-lift as long as I could because I know it'll take me six months to a year to get the bugs out of him afterwards.'

'Running in, please pass,' I offered.

'I'd like to meet George some time,' Wandle said, surpris-ing me.

'Why not. But there's nothing much to see: some metal boxes and a console, a couple of over-elaborate typewriters and telescreens.' His pride was obvious through the throwaway.

'As a dedicated Leftwinger I have a duty to be interested in the future.'

'Oh George isn't the future. He's here and now.'

'You mean he can't write a sonnet yet,' I heard myself wanting to prick all this ebullience that seems to me a danger-ous emotional, and probably practical too, South Sea Bubble.

'I don't think he ever will. But he may be able to tell you who wrote an existing one.'

'The end of academic criticism,' said Wandle. 'How re-freshing. No more of those donnish whodunits and que-ruling in the letter columns of this.' He shook the pages of *The Times*. 'What an enormous benefit to mankind. But how will they all be employed when you've settled Shakespeare versus Bacon? There will have to be a government retraining centre where they can learn bricklaying.' He was playing the rogue elephant, the role of elderly maverick that still endears him to students, while he skitters about on the edge of the herd tempting authority or runs down reputations like grass huts. 'Or you could train them to programme computers.'

I decided to catch a bus home. The underground would be stinking and steaming. I climbed outside and got that remembered shipsdeck sensation from childhood. Looking down I could peer through the leaf waves of St James's Park and see the drowned flat on their backs on the grass under a wash of sunlight and the true waters of the Serpentine rococo with enamelled ducks and the pencilled embellishment of fountains done with thin precise strokes. It was like the gardens I made in an enamel bowl when I was eight, with mossy slopes and a broken mirror pond for the one lead swan under a willow pattern match-stick bridge. Time and distance so diminish things, even the spurious height of the top of a bus. I look through the wrong end of the telescope at my eightyear self and at the people in the park and they both make a perfect encapsulated picture I can study. Yet if I get off the bus and walk about among the tanning corpses I shall feel the prickle of heat and grass, I shall puff going in the slow motion of all walking up a knoll, faces will rush hugely, Hogarthianly at me, dogs bark and children scream; all pressing in the gates of the senses like a panic rush for the fire exits. An Irish conductor wound out my tickets, pale mauve ink that smudged my fingers but was still unreadable, from the miniature lavatory roll hanging at his waist and I had a sudden total recall of the clip of tickets, the board with the little mousetraps all the way along that imprisoned the perfect oblongs of thin coloured card with the white badger stripe through them and the last of the art nouveau lettering. You remember? We used to try to collect a full set of all the fares and colours but the expensive ones were very rare. Every time I got into a bus I searched the floor and the seats for a discarded one even though I knew it was dirty to pick them up, that 'you didn't know where they'd been or who'd been touching them'. And today I longed for their variety and elegance as for a set of Bow figurines. We always tried to get them in as perfect a state as possible. They were in blocks with a wire holding them together and when the conductor ripped it out in a hurry to put them in the mousetraps sometimes a great V was torn out of the tickets that spoiled them for collecting. They must have been hell I can see that: inefficient, timewasting but they were pretty and infinitely desirable. Where too are the clippies of yesteryear? Gone North like summer swallows, tinging the bells in Bradford and Manchester and forsaken us, gone with the barmaids now the young micks have driven them out.

The alarm woke him at 7.00. Even that was a risk. One of the key-holders might have decided to exercise the dog early or to commune with dewy urban nature and heard the brassy cricket chirr of the little travelling clock. Usually he set it for 6.30. He had never known any of the residents be up and about that early. Usually too he slept lightly and woke fully at once but this morning he had to dredge himself up into half consciousness. Forgetful he shook his head to clear it and almost shouted with pain. That was it: his nose. All night he hadn't been able to breathe properly and now his blood and brain were starved of oxygen. Meepers opened his mouth and yawned and gulped deeply. He imagined the bubbles of oxygen straining through the pulpy lungs into the bloodstream, pumping through the central generator of the heart, swirling through the flexible pipe-lines of the arteries up into the skull where the atoms of oxygen sparked by a million minute electric charges burst into energy and began pulsing thought messages about the body. He felt better already. Carefully he stood up.

Carefully he lifted the edge of the sacking curtain and peered out into the garden. Thrushes and blackbirds ran through the wet grass on clockwork legs stopping suddenly to cock their heads, listen and stab down among the roots. Nothing else stirred. The birds would warn him. He dropped the sackcloth and began to dress. When he was ready he took a bucket from the corner and unbolted the door. The bolt was a giveaway if anyone bothered to question it. Why should a gardner's hut have a bolt inside? The garden was cool and dazzling in the morning sunlight. The birds chattered into flight as he made his way to the standing pipe that was used to water the lawn and beds.

With a careful look at the blank windows around he stepped behind a dense blue hydrangea, put down the pail, unzipped his flies and peed into the bush, the stream falling loud on the broad leaves and dry ground. Now he was at his most vulnerable so late in the morning and he was glad when he was done up and on his way back again with the bucket filled. Every flower stood out with hallucinatory clarity in the morning light. Their sharp colours and details made him feel a little sick and lightheaded as if he had been watching a colour film in oppressive close up. Every globule of drying dew flashed its heliograph up into his eyes. For a few minutes back inside the hut he could see nothing. He had to steady his trembling before he could begin to wash and shave. Taking the mirror that he had used all through the desert from his holdall he braved himself to look into his face. He hardly recognized it: it seemed as garish as the flowers in its wreck of pummelled flesh in which two small fiery eyes were impressed, red currants in a child's doughman before baking. Meepers began to dab at the suburbs of his face with a soapy flannel. He soaked it in cold water and laid it tenderly across his eyes, hoping to reduce the vol-au-vent cases they were set in. But even this was painful. He shaved his chin; his upper lip was out-of-bounds. Then he dressed himself, looked finally in the mirror to comb his hair and returned his night's lodging to the hole under the floorboards and his holdall. There was nothing more he could do to make himself presentable.

The pain and his inability to breathe properly made everything impossible; so too did the quick curious suddenly averted glances. From a unit in the ant-heap passing anonymously through the streets he had become remarkable. His nose stood out in the crowd. Over breakfast, snuffled and gasped through laboriously in the ABC, he made up his mind. He would go to the hospital and first he would phone Emery to say where he was going. Emery disliked skivers, the unreliable, with an N.C.O.'s passion. His answers were short and sceptical. Meepers sighed as he put down the receiver and then catching sight of himself in the kiosk mirror he was cheered a little. No one seeing him could think he was sprucing; not even Emery.

He must get some money before he could do anything more. Most of his remaining coins had gone on the scrambled eggs he had forked gently into his mouth, leaving their raft of toast for which his stomach yearned but which his breathlessness rejected. Enough for a bus took him to his bank where he would draw some money. It was only inside the swing doors, confronted by the cashiers behind their protective shields, that he remembered the chequebook in the wallet. He would have to buy a cheque.

'Have you some identification, sir?'

Meepers had chosen one of the bright girls. When he had first opened his account here there had been only men. It had been unthinkable that there should be this row of butterflies perched on their stools, though the image perhaps did them an injustice. They were smart as paint, more efficient than the men had been, their slightly cockney voices brisk but cheerful. This one smiled through the glass fence at him now, waiting for his answer. 'No, I'm afraid I haven't.' Everything had gone except the 1911 London Baedecker in his holdall. He must say more. The butterfly was looking doubtful. 'I lost everything yesterday. If I could perhaps see Mr Clark. I've been coming here a long time. I'm sure he'll remember me.'

'What name is it?'

'Meepers.' He spelt it out from long experience with its strangeness.

'If you'll just wait over there please the assistant manager will be out shortly,' she waved him into a comfortable cubicle where he sat down on the padded plastic bench. He no longer had an identity. But it was only for a few moments. Clark would make it alright.

'Mr Meepers?' The face at the doorway was that of a stranger. 'Sorry to keep you waiting. Would you come this way? Mr Clark's on holiday I'm afraid. Now what can we do for you? Do sit down.'

He stood there like a bobby, ready to sob.

'Cigarette?'

Gratefully he sank into the armchair that wrapped itself around him, holding him together. 'No thank you, I don't.'

'Lucky man.'

'I gave it up during the war when I was a prisoner.'

'Must have been the only benefit.' The young man was easy, not hurrying him, more like a psychiatrist than a bank manager. 'Wish my father could have said the same. Smoked like a chimney; lung cancer got him. Said he smoked more after being a POW, some form of compensation.'

'It does affect some people like that. I was lucky.' In fact he had spent so much time while they probed for the shrapnel in German hospitals, barely conscious or simply sick to death, that the habit had died on him. Perhaps he could get the words out now: 'Not so lucky at the moment. You see I had my chequebook stolen last night. It was in my wallet with everything else. My briefcase too. They took that. I've got nothing to prove who I am. Except this,' he pointed to his nose. It seemed time for the apologetic joke against himself that is the English forestalling of ridicule.

'Good Lord! Well it's certainly rather distinctive.' The young man took up the telephone receiver and asked for Meepers' file. 'Now if you'll just give us a couple of signatures. You'd like a new chequebook and we'll cancel the old one; put a stop on all the cheques.'

Meepers signed with a shaking hand but it seemed his efforts were like enough to his usual signature. 'The same address?'

'For the time being. I'm hoping to move soon.' Since he had been squeezed out of his home he had used a rented forwarding address that sent his infrequent letters on to the nearest post office where he collected them.

Outside, with money in his pocket and a chequebook stamped with his name to prove he was himself again he felt more cheerful until he remembered that before he could take his nose to the hospital he would need a paper from his doctor whom he disliked and feared because he had known him all his life and knew he wasn't quite right. He would be asked if he still had headaches.

'It's just my nose.'

'I can see that. What were you, drunk?'

'Not at all. I'd been giving a lecture. Two footpads.'

'Two what?'

'Footpads, muggers, whatever they call them now.'

'Two?'

'I think there were two; it was dark.' The doctor thought he had been drunk or having a fit. Why couldn't he just give him a paper?

'You'd better have an X-ray. They'll send you back to me for medication.'

'Can't you give me something now; then I won't need to bother you again?'

'Alright then. You can come back for a check-up next week. I'll be on holiday. See the locum.'

Meepers escaped thankfully. His doctor belonged to the old brusque breed who ran the village with the squire and the parson and was bracing with the panel patients that hacked miserably in his dingy waiting room under one sighing gas light whose delicate mothwing mantle showed a rent through which the flame stuck out a tongue. He was a sawbones who only believed Meepers wasn't malingering when he mentioned his headaches because he had seen the plates with their black splinters. He took pleasure in stabbing them out with his blunt forefinger for the patient's benefit. 'You're lucky to be alive,' the finger said and also, 'You're not quite right in the head.'

They wanted him to complain he remembered as he crossed to the prefabricated annexe to the gothic main building that

53

was the out-patients department. The traffic thundered unceasingly outside the forecourt. A few dusty roses, more thorn and twig than blossom, wilted behind the railings beside the bubbling tarmac. He remembered the cool lush pine groves of the Asklepion at Epidaurus where he had wandered among the ruins during a lull in the fighting, tracing the cells where the sick had fallen into drugged sleep waiting for the dream visitation of the god to expound their cure. It had seemed possible in that healthful sauna shade, watching the butterflies planing over the ranks of tall flower-threaded grasses ahead of a mower with his scythe, to be cured of anything. Perhaps one day he should go back there to fall asleep in the narcotic sun and wait for a vision to tell him what to do. He pushed open the glass doors and crossed to the clinically overalled receptionist.

There was no shade here even from the eyes of passersby. Two walls were of glass. For some, no doubt, Meepers thought, that was an advantage. The haggard woman with her two small children could look out at the sunlight and the familiar traffic passing beyond the railing bars. She wasn't cut off; not yet. At any moment she could get up and be out in the street going home. He gave his letter to the receptionist who filled up a card and told him to wait.

An ambulance drew up beyond the glass. The back opened, a stretcher was taken out, put on a trolley and wheeled in, accompanied by a policeman and a girl. Another girl's face, white with blank closed lids, lay on the pillow. There was a sudden bustle. Those who'd relapsed into the apathy of waiting looked up. The policeman began to whisper to the accompanying girl. Attempted suicide, appendicitis, accident, backstreet abortion, the audience speculated. The girls were foreign; their eyes large and dark as their hair; their skins sallow.

From time to time a young houseman, white coat flying open in soap opera caricature would appear and call a name from a card and one of the waiting sick would get up to follow him. When it was Meepers' turn at last he was led into a small consulting room where he told the story of his nose again. Holding his card carefully in finger and thumb to get as few sweatprints on it as possible he pursued the X-ray department through intestinal corridors until he was halted by a shoal of people too tired and lost to go any further, more receptionists, more stretchered trolleys and doors with glowing warnings above them to the uninitiated. The priestesses wore green robes and rubber aprons and issued from the darkened rooms. A child with the local elf-face, too thin, too sharp, too pale, hopped on one leg, swinging the other. The swung foot was bare and mottled with plaster itch. An old woman lay as light as a starved bird in a nest of blankets on a trolley, her sparse hair a scattered handful of bleached grass, her features pared down to the skull, plucking at her coverings and muttering incessantly. Eventually a passing nurse bent an ear over her lips and patted the blankets. He wouldn't come here to die, to be called grandpa and left alone to murmur with mummy's mouth. He would die with dignity when he could no longer live with it, alone, preferably in the open air. He must see to it. He had almost forgotten his nose.

Two middleaged men in pyjamas were brought in wheelchairs and added to the dump. Then the trolley with the foreign girl, Greek, Spanish, Italian, accompanied now by a dark boy in bright shirt and trousers as well as the other girl, was brought to join them. She was conscious, perhaps she had been all the time. The boy, brother, lover, held her hand and whispered to her and she whispered back with closed eyes, the lashes lying like black silk fringes to the smooth vellum cheeks. Meepers had seen such faces on late Hellenistic sarcophagi.

Something of his old terror came back to him when he was called and his head positioned under the metal boom. 'Hold very still.' How often had he heard a voice calling that out of the darkness behind him when he wanted to jump up and run from the menace of the metal contraption being gently lowered towards his head. But it was only his nose this time, nothing else, and in a few minutes he was being shown out to await development of the plates.

'Nothing broken,' said the houseman cheerfully. 'Just have

55

to wait for the bruising to subside. It'll go all colours before it's back to normal.' Meepers felt a fraud beside all the real cases, the life-or-death atmosphere hospitals always engender. He thought of those who were being told a different story in other cubicles or told nothing. The only vision the god vouchsafed him when he stepped into the loud sunlight was that he was glad to be there and he was hungry again. He drank soup and ate ice cream in small melting shavings. People still looked at him covertly but he no longer minded as he sat in the underground train to Russell Square. Before anything else he must get back his Reading Room ticket. That was his true identity card. The pain had caused reality to recede from him for a while but now as he crossed the square, student-free for the summer, the living dead began to nudge and jostle him again. He would go round to the main entrance and straight to the Director's room, avoiding the temptations to stop and marvel at every case of ravished Imperial booty if he went in by the Edward VII gallery.

'Are you really very old?' asked the boy as they turned their ponies eastwards along the track.

'Older than you'll ever be,' the bundle of sticks beside him cackled. The boy had grown used to the ambiguous answers but he went on with his questions because there was no other way to find out.

'And did you really build the great temple?'

The stick body shook with laughter like a winter gale through scrub. 'Even I'm not that old. I built the last part, the best part, the unbroken ring of the goddess. But her temple has stood for hundreds of seasons before our people came here. When we first crossed the narrow water the island was already holy, the site of the mating of sun and moon, but the people who lived here knew her only as the earth mother into whose belly the sun struck fire every year. Before that there were those who worshipped her in darkness as mistress of the dead, going down into her womb to sacrifice.'

'I don't understand,' said the boy. It was hard to follow a theological argument and govern the pony at the same time.

'Let him find his own way. He'll do it better without you keep tugging at his head.'

The boy flushed but slackened the reins. He was proud of his riding but today he couldn't even guide his horse right. He'd be falling off next. Fretfully he cuffed the sweat from his forehead. It had been cold when they'd started and he'd been glad of his wool cloak but now the sunlight poured over the high downs in a molten blue and gold stream. He would have liked to stop and take the cloak off but that would have been to admit a weakness that the shrivelled figure hunched beside him was no longer subject to. Larks jumped out of the grass and bubbled high up into the air, tossed spindles whose throats unreeled a thread of fine sound as they stoned down again. Ahead and behind the trackway dazzled like a strip of moonlight on water where centuries of use had stripped the turf down to the chalk. Small blue butterflies fluttered on thin linen wings over the parched grass. He mustn't let the heat and the old man rouse his anger. That way he could make mistakes and he knew he was being tested again. On the sightlines of the downs the round white breasts of barrows thrust gleaming into the air. They rode directly into the eye of the still climbing sun, steadily hour after hour until he was dizzy and the sweat from the pony's belly mingled with his own to trickle down his bare legs and put a dark stain on his new soft buskins.

The track dipped between two banks of downs. Hunger was added to the dizzying heat as the hours passed. Soon they would have to rest the ponies who were beginning to labour. Suddenly the ears in front of him pricked, his pony's head came up and the foam flecked nostrils flared, scenting water, Now he had to hold him back.

'Let him go,' called the old man. Could he do nothing right today? The ponies cantered down the path, their hooves thudding on split logs that paved the way to the water's edge, shrunk now beyond cracked plains of mud that would bog down in winter. 'Like an old man's gums,' he thought fiercely as he slid from the pony's back, kicked off his boots and followed him barefoot into the river. He found a spot where the hooves hadn't churned the water milky and scooped up clear handfuls to drink greedily and dash over his face. Then he undid his belt and the thong that held his cloak and tossing his clothes on to the bank plunged into the water, letting it carry away the sweat and the ache together. As he lay on his back and looked at the bank he could see the old man perched on his pony like a great hoodie on the back of a sheep searching for ticks. His own pony had followed his example and wallowed in the shallows threshing its hooves and throwing up spray. He would show the old shaman something. He whistled. The pony righted himself and came stepping daintily through the water towards him until he could grasp its bridle and be drawn to the bank, a smooth brown fish on a line.

'So you can swim too,' the old man cackled, looking down at him. 'Weren't you afraid?'

'Afraid? What of? There might be leeches ... '

'Out there the current is strong. The lady might sweep you away. This is part of her river, the dark water, although here she is gentle for her because it is summer.'

'Why should she harm me?'

'She doesn't harm. She only tests. If you don't survive it's because you're not worthy to.'

'Is she greater than ... ?' he named the goddess of the Severn where he had learnt to swim.

'They are all names of the lady. Whatever she is called she is the same. But this is priest's knowledge, not for shepherds and digging women. They believe each one is different and they love their own best. Let's eat before we cross.'

Relieved the boy took the bag of barley cakes and the skin of beer from the pony's neck and left both horses to crop under the trees that edged the watermeadows. As long as he could keep the old man talking they could rest. But the old man was tired at last, or the beer made him drowsy. Ordering the boy to keep watch, he pulled his cloak over his face and slept. Under its black cover the body was so slight it might have been nothing but a dropped cloak and a pointed skin cap. The afternoon heat began to close the boy's eyes. He jerked awake. There was no real danger. The wild animals, bears, wolves and boar were probably asleep too. But robbers might steal up on them. Lordless men lived in bands in forests and preyed on travellers. Smiths in particular with their valuable booty were often victims unless they travelled in company, several strong together. Why then had they come so defence-lessly? The old man had only to murmur and any lord would have ridden with them with his people. Was his magic strong enough to keep mishap away? If so why had he told the boy to watch? Perhaps the sleep was a pretence and he was listening all the time under his cloak. Almost the boy wished himself back in his mother's house, a child again. The old man's years seemed to rub off on him the further they rode together. He fingered the whetstone on his belt and considered sharpening his dagger to pass the time, but the small rasp of metal on stone might wake the sleeper.

He was proud of his dagger. His mother had given it to him for his twelfth year. The little stone knife he had used til then had been broken and buried with his childhood. He moved so that the row of small gold studs in the hilt caught and threw the sunlight into his eyes. And now there was that other, the longest dagger he had ever seen, that he had won, that had brought him there.

They had gone up as they always did for the festival of the harvest moon when she was at her fullest and hung low and heavy and milky over the still warm downs. There was always a faint wind up there, a voice perpetually whispering over the short grass, some said the voice of the many dead lords under the barrows clustering round the temple, others the voice of the earth herself and that it was by listening to it that the old man knew when to plant and to sacrifice, others that the stones themselves talked together. But the boy thought that the old man knew what to do and when by the movements of the moon and sun as his mother did, keeping their household

59

calendar in their own temple. Once when he was very small they had made a special journey to the great temple on a heavy overcast day. That night there was no feasting and drinking as before harvest and the next morning they had gathered silent on the downs while the old man moaned and keened within the great ring and he had seen in terror the moon begin to eat the sun. At the moment of darkness when only a red-bronze halo glowed from behind the black disc there had been a sudden cry from the heart of the stone thicket and then miraculously the moon had let the sun slide out from under her.

The boy had thought about it a lot afterwards. The white moon had turned black and quenched the sun until she was fed blood to appease her. The god of fire and light had bled flame until the sacrifice bled for him. He was used to sacrifice. Sometimes it was a lamb or kid but at the great festivals it was man, woman or child. At harvest libations were poured before the great barley straw figure of the goddess. The feasting and barter went on for days. All the lords gave potlatch to their own people and to each other. His mother put on her finest jewellery.

This year was different. The Artor was growing feeble and there was to be competition among the youths for who should succeed him. He had asked his mother for her blessing to take part. A sarsen block was set up in the middle of the camp with the pommel of a dagger sticking out of it. But first they went in procession to the cursus where the elimination foot and pony races were run between the crowdlined banks. The boy did well. At the end there were only five of them left. Then they returned to the camp. The next day they would try to draw the dagger from the rock.

There was magic to it he reasoned. Otherwise the blade would slip from its stone sheath at a touch. When the rest were asleep he stole up to it in the starlight that followed the setting of the ripe moon.

The huddle of clothes unnoticed before beside the stone suddenly spoke to him. 'Shall I tell you how it is done?'

The boy wanted to run away. The night was a stifling

blanket thrown over his head. He gasped for breath. What should he answer? He knew it was the shaman and forked his fingers into the night. He had been a child then, he thought now beside the river. For the first time he had heard that irritating cackle. 'Not merely strength makes the Artor. He must have daring and cunning. He must know when to retreat before attack. Go back and sleep.'

He had half obeyed, to lie awake in the hot night almost until the early dawn. The lords and their people gathered at noon for the assay. Two others were before him, the sun highlighting their muscles. Each in turn spat on his palms, tugged and sweated and fell back. The boy stepped forward, conscious of the silent crowd and the pommel above the stone winking at him. Now that he saw it close to, his eye measured its height above the block. It must be longer than any dagger he had ever seen. The others hadn't moved it a thumb's height but already it showed the length of his own blade as if it had sprouted there. 'To retreat before attack.' He picked up a boulder the size of his cupped hands and called on the goddess by their familiar name for her. Quite clearly behind his closed eyes he saw his mother's lodestone amber necklace. If he was wrong he would die. He brought up the rock and smashed it down on the pommel driving it right into the stone. There was a great shout from the crowd. The boy put his hand round the dagger and drew it easily out of the sarsen block, and it was longer than any dagger he had ever seen. He had held it up so that the sun leapt on its blade while the people had shouted again.

The old man stirred and sat up. Perhaps he really had been asleep. They mounted and let the ponies find their way across the stream, swimming strongly in the middle where the current ran fast. Then they rode on with their shadows lengthening ahead of them.

'How is it done,' asked the boy 'the dagger in the stone?'

'That isn't for you to know.'

'Why did you tell me what to do?'

'I told you only the nature of the Artor. You had already

61

proved yourself by coming in the night to see while the rest were snoring.'

'What does it mean, the Artor?'

'The father, the chief of all, leader and sower . . . What more do you want?'

'And you?'

'What is my name?'

'You are called Murddin,' he said bravely.

'That's right,' the skin cap nodded beside him. 'Which is to say: the slayer.'

As the sun arched at their backs they had to stop more often to rest the horses. Sometimes now they passed flocks of sheep and goats above them on the hills with herd children in charge or a cluster of round huts set in a hollow. One track led away between the hills to the North; theirs kept close beside the river where the forest drew back. Loop after glistening loop it unfolded between the trees until they seemed not to be progressing at all but merely to rock on their horses through the close hours with the river pouring through their heads and the same branches plucking at their clothes as the sweat-darkened ponies plodded under them. Once a blue and green faience kingfisher arrowed the water.

The sun went from the sky and they rode through a fiery twilight, plashing across summer low streams that flickered the pink and blue and green of the sky round the black hooves. At last they came to a plain whose far edge was fringed with pale whiskers of ripe barley, already reaped in places. The night wind rustled among the standing bedstraw and rubbed the uncut ears whispering together. Through the falling dark he caught the smell of a settlement: woodsmoke, dung, roast flesh and meal, the exhalations of men and livestock. He did not dare to ask if this was their destination but let the old man take the lead.

Now he could see a large cluster of huts, as many as in his mother's domain, and the large one that would be the lord's. 'We will rest here the night,' said the old man. Thankfully the boy almost fell from his horse while a servant gathered up the reins. He ducked his head to follow the shaman under the overhanging eaves through the small door into the round house that was almost as big as a small barrow. Inside it was at first as dark and heavy as though he stood under a huge inverted beaker until his eyes accustomed themselves to take in the firelight at the central hearth and the figures around it but most the tall queen who stood at a loom on which was the finest web of cloth he had ever seen, straightening the hanging warp with a bone white comb. On her smooth pale breast and neck lay a crescent net of jet beads where the firelight flashed like the desperate tails of small silver fish.

They were expected, the boy realized at once. The harper who had been accompanying her song while she wove ended his cadence. She put aside the comb and shuttle and turned towards them. 'So this is the new Artor.'

'My sister,' cackled the old man, in pleasure at the boy's confusion and disbelief.

'I hope my brother hasn't ridden you into the ground.'

'He'll survive. Give him something to eat and drink. Make a man of him.' The spit was withdrawn from the fire and the haunch passed round for them all to cut a slice with the daggers at their belts. Wooden plates were brought too for this was no herd's hut where you crammed a piece into your mouth and bit off a chunk but a lord's house where you cut and speared your meat decently. Murddin's sister took a fine blade from her waist and as she carved her slice it seemed as if she slipped the yellow bronze into his body and shaved a piece from his heart. When she raised it to her lips and the white teeth sank into it the pain twisted in him again.

They were brought barley beer to wash the dust from their throats and honeycakes after their meat. He was so busy with his food that he didn't see her go until he was suddenly aware that the harper was playing again, a low continuous strumming that stopped the voices of her people under the dome. She had taken off her tunic and was naked to just below her waist where a band gathered a fine lawn skirt about her hips. The jet web lay over the white flesh: a tracery of winter branches across the moon. In her white hands she carried a cup carved from a single lump of magic amber. Behind came a young man with a goatskin bottle and others with sweet-smelling lamps whose smoke dizzied the senses. A golden stream of mead poured into the cup. She raised it to her lips: 'To the Artor, lord of all.' She was drinking to him. His eyes dazzled as now she held the carved cup towards him. For a moment he thought he heard the dead leaf rustle of a laugh behind him but it was drowned in the flow of sweet spiced liquid that burned through his body as he had seen smiths pour molten bronze into a dagger mould. He felt it concentrate and begin to harden. 'Let us see how our lord is armed.' Her hands unhooked his belt and let it drop. Then she took the cup and refilled it while he drew his tunic over his head. Now he was naked as a warrior and his dagger of flesh stood up firm and strong. She loosened her skirt to spread in shimmering ripples round her feet. 'The lord will sow his Spring harvest.' He had had women about his mother's domain, scuffled affairs in the fields, but not a lord in her own right and from her speech a priest of the lady. Yet he wasn't afraid only eager as he moved towards her. They would all see that he was indeed the Artor.

They left Heathrow in the morning long after the sun was up. He'd been slow to waken and when he did he was surprised to find himself in one of the smaller dwellings alone except for the old man shaking his shoulder. His nakedness brought back something of the night before and the weakness in his head and legs as he tottered into the stunning light. Gingerly he cupped his sore balls in his hand and peered at them through half closed eyes almost expecting to see the visible stain of bruising.

'My sister is resting,' the stick laughed. 'You did well. She has sent you presents to remember her by.'

A slow stream meandered outside the stockade they had passed through the night before without his noticing. The Artor plunged himself again and again into its cool body until his head began to clear. Then he drank a beaker of goat's milk, ate some barleybread and dressed for the journey in the cool new tunic and amber armlets he had won. This morning was different. He would make no mistakes today. Only his buttocks and thighs wincing against the pony's heaving back reminded him of the boy who had set out yesterday morning.

'Where are we going?' he asked.

'You'll see,' was the expected answer.

'Good,' and he began to hum as he rode, making in his head his own saga to sing in his mother's hall if ever he got home again.

They rode through thick forest now whose laced leaves kept off the sun but made a warm humid gloom smelling of leafmould, toadstools and the river swamps. Mosquitoes zoomed in on sweaty flesh and horse flies threatened the ponies' flanks til he cut leafy switches for himself and the shaman whose magic seemed useless against the throbbing insect world.

At Kew they plashed through the Brent then on through the thickets where the river looped up to meet them more swollen than before. He would have been afraid in the heavy groves if it hadn't been for the old man, though not of the animals of flesh and blood. The river when they came on it again ran glittering towards them so that he knew that like the Severn it flowed from the sea. The ground was rising gently. A fleet of narrow boats swam into sight heading for the bank below where there must be homes and small fields but Murddin made no move towards them. The boats were twigs on the dark belly of water under its flexing skin of light. Leaving Hammersmith they crossed another small plain by a much used track and then a strongly flowing stream. Beyond was a small hill. 'And beyond that is the water of wailing but that is not for us today.' They turned their ponies' heads towards the bank and when they reached it, dismounted. The old man began a long incantation to the goddess of the black water. A wind blew off it, streaming his hair and clothing like ruffled crowfeathers. Then he took the long dagger the boy had won from the stone and put it in his hand. 'You must give it to the lady as far in as you can.'

For a moment he hesitated. It was a good blade, the longest he had ever seen. The face of Murddin's sister swam into his mind and her hands offering him the cup. He took the dagger firmly by the point, whirled it round his head and sent it curvetting over the water in bounding flashes until it stabbed down through the muscled waves. 'Nothing happened,' the boy said. 'It just sank.'

'What did you expect? A white arm dressed in fine linen?' the dry bones cackled behind him.

II

New Troy

It's very late. I sit here above the city feeling it breathe round me in the dark and the ether even more full of radio chatter than it used to be. I read in the paper that the allnight programmes may cut the suicide rate, particularly the phone-ins. Shall I ring them up and say I'm lost, that we're all lost? Call us and we'll keep you from going over the edge, keep your fingernails digging into the ledge or whatever high station you're tuned to. I impersonate them in their bed-sitters bleak with someone else's furniture, the tall bottle of gin and the squat bottle of pills to hand and the electronic confessionals, telephone and radio, plastic priests whose faces don't change as the pitiful fantasies are poured into them. Oh they're the just moderators for this city, anonymous as itself. Somewhere out there Meepers is lying alone listening perhaps, for he's back and I didn't invent him. But changed, battered by something or someone; a fight or a fall. There he was today in the back row trying to hide his wound behind a copy of *The Times*: a great nose, Bardolf or Punch, streaked with blue and yellow bruising so that again I hadn't the heart to challenge him.

Today was the South Sea Bubble. That is, it should have been but it took off somehow from that most unlikely ground. I began as usual trying to explain (it's always a tough hard coconut to split and get at the meat and milk of it) and as I went on the whole thing became shoddier and more inexplicable, beginning with that monstrous amorphous amoeba the National Debt. Suddenly I stopped because I could see complete puzzlement on their faces. What can you liken this enormous symbolic construct to: this finance? Commerce is easy: you can draw girls in cotton dresses spinning cotton, weaving cotton, cutting and stitching, slaves in cotton dresses picking cotton, ladies in silk on the arms of plantation owners and mill owners. But finance is algebra, abracadabra, an image, a bubble. Where do you begin?

'With coin,' said Meepers, lowering his newsprint mask. 'The first coins in this country were minted by Belgic Kings before the Caesar came. Before that it was barter, the exchange of one or more tangibles for another: labour for eggs and milk, military service for gold and land. Then the symbol was invented that could represent them all and be exchanged for any of them. Coin came to symbolize not only the things but their relationship to each other and then relationships between the people through whose hands it passed. Because it is a symbol not a reality money can be inflated or depressed not only by realities like famine or a rich harvest but by illusions, imagination, falls in confidence, alarms, jobbery.' I could see he was trembling with excitement; the voice coming thick and breathy because of his beaten face. But I was grateful to him for his rescue.

'Exactly,' I said, 'and finance goes further than that because it deals in notional money not even real coin.'

'The difference between keeping your savings under the mattress and putting it in the bank,' someone suggested. 'A symbol of a symbol?'

'That's crazy; that's losing touch with all reality'; beard and sandals.

'What did they do? How did it happen?'

'They dreamt of the South Seas, of Southern and Latin America and what they could buy and sell there, of gold and timber, spices and slaves, tobacco and cotton and in return for a monopoly of this dream the company offered to take over the National Debt.'

'How much was that?' A boy in a neat suit.

'Just over fifty-one million.'

70

'But where had it come from and what was it for?' a blue denim ingenue.

'Mainly it had been raised to fight wars. People lent money to the state and in return they were paid interest on it as an annuity.'

'So how could a company take it over.' Neat suit again.

'By persuading all those who were getting annuities to take stock in the South Sea Company instead. It was a gamble. If the company prospered the shareholders should get high dividends.' And then I tried to sketch the whole mad bingo of it, the fever of speculation that floated dozens of companies, 'to design a wheel for perpetual motion', 'for a scheme to be promulgated hereafter', and the South Sea Stock itself swelling faster and faster, credibility stretched thinner, the evanescent rainbow lure of riches while underneath its dome fortunes and frauds were compounded, court and commons all paddling together, the king's mistresses dabbling ringed plump fingers, the chancellor of the exchequer up to his elbows in corruption, the panic and flight when the run began and the bubble burst.

The boys and girls are deeply puritanical about money. This first disastrous example of laissez-faire capitalism shocked them. It's as obscure and disgusting to them as nuclear physics. Is this new? I think so. Before the war many of those who went to university would have had a daily familiarity with the smell of power and money at their parents' dinner tables. Think of the Waugh diaries and compare their world and experience with our middleclass and artisan children whose highest flight of economy is the weekly wage or monthly salary. The Stock Exchange is a temple of Mammon they barely know exists. You have to begin at the very beginning with them, assume nothing. The most abstruse theology is easier for their minds to take hold of, I suppose because they get a grounding at school. I don't know whether I find their innocence refreshing or irritating or indeed whether I care for the image of myself in this droit de seigneurial role breaking their illusory maidenheads. They live in the money market of the world as ignorant of its meaning and workings as New

Guinea natives bartering with Cook for knives and bits of mirror. I shall go to bed and keep my thoughts on you and my hands off myself. Moloch-mammon Manhattan has swallowed you and no letter come yet.

Lludd took Llyr by the arm and helped him down from his chariot. 'It's good to see you, and your two girls.' Privately he thought they looked a fierce pair in their horned helmets but he liked the old man. The sun leapt back smartly from their enamelled shields slung over the chariot bows.

'You're building again,' said Llyr as Lludd led him into the hall. The noise of hammering and cries of workmen were cut off sharply by the thick walls. Lludd almost sighed aloud at the implied criticism. Soft and luxury loving Llyr thought him, he knew.

'One must do something. I don't spend my substance on squabbling. I prefer to keep peace with my neighbours. Try this,' he handed the old king a cup of wine. 'Just off the boat last week.'

'Not bad,' Llyr swilled it round his toothless gums. 'I still prefer mead. A man's drink.'

That was because he'd lost the trade, thought Lludd. Nowadays the Armorica merchantmen preferred to come round and up the Thames where they could anchor in safety to discharge their cargo rather than ride in one of Llyr's exposed bays where they were always in danger of running aground or being battered to bits on the rocks. It put them further inland too so that other tribes hadn't so far to come. They brought their hides and corn and water-proof cloaks and great hunting hounds from the North to his caer and made a flourishing market of it.

'What are you doing about the Belgians?' he asked to change the subject.

'Fortifying the walls. What else can one do. I've strengthened the gates with watch towers. These days I keep a permanent lookout on the cliff.'

'You're lucky in your girls, both fighters. My Creudylad thinks of nothing but sex. She's got two of them quarrelling over her now: Gwyn and Gwyrthr, both fine lads if she'd only make her choice. Your girls didn't come in with you. Let's go and see where they are and I can show you my improvements.'

Llyr found himself wondering why he had come. A visit to Lludd was always better in anticipation. He talked too much that was his trouble. He always had. There'd been no need for the druids to teach him eloquence.

'A bigger temple,' he was saying now. 'To Lleu and Ogmios. After all in times like these it would be foolish not to make the gods feel wanted. They might withdraw and leave us to the Belgians or send a fog of sickness up from the marshes. I've been working on our fortifications too. What I fear most is an attack from the river of course so I've strengthened the rivergate and called it after my father because his name means war,' he went on with a Celt's passion for false etymology.

It was Llyr's turn to sigh quietly. As if they hadn't all been to school under the oaks when they were young and anyway he remembered Belinus. He had been a good warrior, a good swordsman and bowman and able to run along the chariot pole with the horses going at full tilt. Lludd wasn't a bit like him. A bad choice of foster father had done that no doubt or too long at school. He'd have made a better bard than chieftain. Nowadays Llyr thought youngsters spent too long with the druids. Theology and composition and astronomy were fine in peacetime or for lulls between local skirmishes but these were new threats. The Belgians were tough and well-organized and behind them pressed other waves. The few traders who still came to his shore told him stories of the fierce Teutons and the Romans who moved Northward with the precision of the banks of oars that drove their galleys. The trouble with all Celts was always that they talked too much. Ogmios might bind men with the golden chains of speech but they would end up in iron fetters if they weren't careful. Thank Lleu for his daughters. There they were now. They

73

had taken their chariots down to the strip of clear river bank and were racing each other: Gonerilla a nose in front but Regan cunningly taking the inside of the bend. Fortunately the wheels hadn't got their war trim on or they'd have cut each other to pieces. Their charioteers had been left to cheer at the start and they held the reins themselves in their calloused brown hands. He was getting old but his girls would defend him.

Lludd followed the race with envy. If only his Creudylad had been like that. Still he was lucky. If the Belgians overran the South he could hold the ford against them and if they came up the Thames he could shoot fire into their ships. But if only none of it had to happen. If only he could go on enriching his caer, trafficking for beautiful things, listening to the stories of the traders and making them into barddoneg in the evening. Hadn't he built Lleu the finest temple in Britain on the hill where the rising sun would strike it, with a ceremonial way from the second gate? The hub of Regan's wheel caught under Gonerilla's left and lifted it enough to overset and send her sister sprawling. Maybe there was something to be said for Creudylad after all. If only she would make up her mind.

The smooth leaden face of the new padlock looked smugly back at him, its little pursed oblong mouth locked fast with the tongue behind. It reminded him of a face urn he had seen recently, dedicated to Mercury with eyes and nose and a raw round scab where a mouth might have been. Dug up where? He couldn't remember. That was bad. Meepers tried to shake his head clear of the hallucinatory sunset colours in the garden but it still throbbed too painfully for that. He musn't even try to catch the memory. He must think about the padlock and the meaning of its closed mouth. Someone had seen and reported him was his first explanation, soon rejected because wouldn't they have done more than simply lock him out, wouldn't they have lain in wait to catch him? Meepers looked round nervously. He should reconnoitre the garden so that if

74

they were hiding, waiting to pounce he would know, not be caught off guard and lash out like a cornered animal. He must be free to use his reason.

The garden was empty. Meepers investigated the back of the hut. The sacking still hung over the window. Later he would get in through there. He knew the catch well. Unless they had changed that too. Had they found his things; taken up the floorboards? No, it was much more reasonable to suppose that some administrative process had caught up with him. Perhaps they had appointed a new gardener on finding that he no longer answered to his old address. Yes that would be it, not personal malice but the inevitable trundle of the system overtaking him as he tried to dodge between the tracks. Civilization was a great marshalling yard where you were safe as long as you sat in your compartment and were taken from line to line, platform to platform but let anyone get out at the wrong stop or try to walk and the carefully timetabled, signal-boxed juggernauts would run him down.

But he must find somewhere else quickly. They had at last succeeded in shutting him out of his childhood garden. He looked round at it as sunset advanced over the grass with the trees, elongated daguerreotype shadows stirring a memory of black cut-out figures moving behind a paper scrim at his push or pull and the unfolding story. Because he was being shut out it had never seemed so vibrant and desirable since he had been allowed to come into it alone as a child. He watched a pollen powdered humble-bee honeying from flower to flower as if he was to be hanged in the morning.

Long ago he had given up the advertisements in tobacconists' windows. The evening papers catered for a different world. '4th girl to share £7 p.w.' 'Luxury bachelor flat £25 p.w.' For a few days he might try a bed and breakfast at £1.50 or even the little wooden cubicle of a city dormitory for 80p but the army which should have inured him to communal life had made it intolerable to him or perhaps it was the camp hospital with the groaning restless sick and the knowledge of guards outside. Meepers shook himself mentally: these were only personal underlinings of a basic primate need. Chimpanzees built their lone leafy nests each night in the tree-tops within knowledge of each other but a little apart.

The sound of the gate drove him away from the hut. The first of the evening dogs set out along one side of the circular path while he made his way round the other and let himself into the square of untouchable houses. He needed space to think, where he was allowed to walk about freely. Later, when it was dark, he would come back for his things. A bus took him to Kensington Gardens where he could stroll anonymous among the tourists, the handful of sad, shabby men who had come to smack their lips over passing girls, and the odd meths drinker waiting to be moved on until he fetched up with others on the Embankment or stumbled across the river to a South Bank demolition site where there would be a fire. Meepers straightened his shoulders and stepped out away from the Round Pond and its ducks, turning his back on Dutch William's country cottage. Among the trees of the Flower Walk by the Albert Memorial were benches he might have rested on but each already had one or two occupants, quarrelling or cuddling lovers; a couple of young soldiers, redfaced above their prickly serge collars, whose curly napes made him brush his palm with his own bristle of short back and sides; and a middleaged woman who addressed the uncaring air in a loud monotone. Not that, dear god, not that yet or ever. In control of himself Meepers strode on and crossed the torrent of traffic that separated the gardens from Hyde Park. A file of horses with hard-hatted riders, the last of the day, passed stately down through Alexandra Gate, a Stubbs in motion. Meepers strolled along the carriage way, still thick with the fumes of homegoing commuters although the bowlers on the baize-smooth green would soon find it too dark to play. A sharp smell of horsedung and grass clippings mixed with the car exhausts. And still he couldn't think. He would strike up towards the Serpentine and its comforting ducks. It was then that he saw the lodge.

*

A button loose on my shirt yesterday morning came away in my fingers as I tried to do it up. Here hath been dawning another blue day/Think wilt thou let it slip useless away. A thread breaks and civilization falls to the ground because a tie won't hold a collar together with that necessary appearance of crispness or a cuff flaps ungoverned out of a sleeve. But worse, when I looked there was no cotton, just a naked reel that I would once have notched and turned into a tank with half an inch of candle, a matchstick and a rubber band but now is useless except for an exercise in nostalgia. And where in the land of the Asian delicatessen can one buy cotton or get shoes mended or buy a newspaper? These are the real inadequacies and tragedies of life as Jane Austen knew when her girls deliberated as much over a length of muslin or a pair of gloves as some nations have over whether to go to war. Think of Catherine's terror, turned out of doors with no money to pay for the stagecoach to get her home to her parents and jolting through a day and a half of misery before she was safe at their doorstep again. So my button isn't negligible and my failure to buy cotton locally because all the little shops that used to offer such services can no longer make a living or pay the inflated rents in this area is a symbol of a wider loss.

Fortunately I hadn't got a lecture. I just wanted to look up a few things in the library and therefore my state of dishabille didn't matter so much. After a couple of hours' browsing I was driven again to query whether the nineteenth century was responsible for any real invention or discovery or merely for the exploitation of those of the century before. I must ask the students what they think. Those inventions led to the horrors of the nineteenth century, horrors because they were on such a vast scale, and the twentieth century: mass pollution, poverty, uniformity, exploding population, exhaustion of natural resources. At the end of the eighteenth century the population of these islands was less than that of today's London. Could we have done anything to prevent what's happened, that's the point. Are we elements in an unstoppable historical process or can we foresee and redirect? You'll say I should have thought of all this before; that that was what you were trying to make me see.

Went to the staff diningroom for lunch. Wandle waved me over to his table and I couldn't refuse. He is of course a vegetarian as well as his various other fads which is another reason why the young like him since they're still all on the health food kick and whenever one goes into the refectory there are little bowls of mixed chaff and chopped morsels of fruit and nuts and pots of yoghourt instead of tinned fruit cocktail with custard as there used to be. I asked him how his Apologia was getting on. The extraordinary thing is how he manages to shift with the wind, professionally I mean. Some of the old boys, I think I've told you, have been quietly weeded out, persuaded to take their pensions off to a cottage in the Weald, but for some reason Wandle's become more and more indispensable. There's never any lack of people wanting his courses. In fact he could teach twenty-four hours a day if he wanted to. I said in one of my letters that I like him. Do I? For some reason he makes me envious. He refuses to grow old gracefully, to moulder in silence. When Black Power came in he was there with a course in Changing Attitudes to other races in Western Consciousness or some such; then it was women's lib. No doubt he's got something cooked up for the winter: pop culture yesterday and today I expect. And he can sail them all under the flag of the radical conscience, undisciplined privateers that run in on the coast of a subject, snatch a few bright eye-catching fragments, and run out again. 'The swollen sheep look up and are not fed.' But they come back for more; like that blown-out feeling I suppose.

Ponders joined us and at once Wandle was on to him. When could we see his magic box as promised? Later that afternoon? Why not. I said I had some shopping to do first and walked out, down towards the full tide of human affairs. There seemed to be more people than ever about and I realized I'd picked the worst possible hour of the day. It's so quiet in college that nothing reaches you from the world outside. You think the torpitude seeps through the walls on to the pavements until you step through into that noise of people and traffic that makes you feel you have to shout not to be absorbed or smothered by it, a constant subdued tumult like a wind tunnel. The pavements were choked with girl clerks in summer dresses and men in shirtsleeves with half moons of sweat under their armpits queuing for sandwiches, interlaced with every nationality of tourist making for St Paul's or just lost. I wonder if there's some pound for them somewhere that every consulate or embassy has to go to each week to reclaim its own nationals and pack them off home or on their next sightseeing leg. They come to gape at the remains of this vast tel that's like a highdressed wig, powdered and bejewelled but where the mice have nested, undermined, heartless and the lice run among its remaining hairs and drop from the thin ringlets on to the dirty tidemarked neck, the suburbs.

Where would I find a reel of cotton in this flume of swirling people? I looked into Woolworth's but its window was dauntingly filled with bathing costumes, suntan lotion, buckets and spades though I doubt if any children ever go along the Strand to tug their parents in to buy them, waterwings, candystriped garden furniture, sprinklers, little rubber swimming pools and all the other appurtenances of the fake rural life that the city workers are spewed homewards to in the evening, leaving these streets entirely to the tourists. And then I had a terrible hallucination. I thought I saw you turn down Carting Lane beside the Savoy and was held back by a swooping taxi waved on by their commissionaire out of that glittering gullet and couldn't get to you. When I reached the corner of course you were gone since you'd never really been there. I looked down towards the river and at that small shaded garden that lies back on the right. The bark is stripping from the plane trees and their leaves are heavy with a kind of resinous sweat the dust clings to. It was very quiet although I didn't leave the corner but just looked into the little square where a couple of pigeons were flirting, fantailing and bowing to each other on the grey stones yet I seemed to be in that garden although all the time half my mind knew it was illusion.

I went on along the Strand and crossed over to the Civil Service Stores. Surely here would be reels of cotton. Civil servants must want it all the time. They seem the kind to patch and make do rather than buy afresh. Inside I looked for haberdashery and was carried on the escalator through the layers of the treasure chest. Unlike most of the other emporia it still has a nannyish air of rubber sheets and stout shoes (the window was full of umbrellas and reticent suitcases on one side and the white sale on the other, a drift of cool sheets for sunburnt skins), an end of empire touch. They probably sell topees if you know what to look under although that sun has long set (sportswear, menswear, hats?). I got into the men's gifts after passing somehow, up or down, the swathes of rainbow materials from the ends of the earth that are like a Victorian painting of Salome's dance, and found myself going from case to case of gold cuff-links, cigar cutters, calf wallets. Suddenly I found myself wanting to steal something, just to take it, slip a wallet or a pair of cuff-links into my pocket and walk casually away and I saw the whole scene of accusation and denial, the emptying of pockets, the arrival of police. I backed away quickly, not sure that it wasn't already too late and that I hadn't done it unconsciously, was remembering rather than foreseeing. I felt as if I'd become Meepers and yet that's quite unfair. I've no grounds at all for thinking he'd steal even a beermat and yet it was Meepers I thought of. I was shaking with fright as if I'd nearly been run over. I didn't want any of those things. I just wanted to take something. I almost wanted, I think, to be caught and accused. Had anyone seen me? I tried to saunter as nonchalantly as if I was guilty while getting out as fast as possible. Then I wondered if I'd find something in my pocket and had to resist the urge to feel. There were the doors. They always stop you trying to leave the store, I've read somewhere. But men don't shoplift, only women. They wouldn't suspect me. I walked out with my ears roaring and turned back towards Queen's. I would be safe in there, away from madness and temptation. So ended my attempt to buy a reel of cotton.

To my father. Honoured sir, greetings. I hope that my last letter written in Gessoracum before we sailed for Britannia reached you. I would not have you apprehensive for my safety. We had a fair crossing and landed surely at Rutupiae, the gateway to the North, with our veterans in good heart and order. You get a sight of the great arch that marks the port from far out to sea which frights the barbarian pirates so that as yet they have not dared to attack the port itself but land at other less well fortified places along the coast. Here Theodosius addressed the men before we set off to march towards Lundinium. The roads in Britannia are as good as around home, but the weather not so fair, and everywhere the barbarians have destroyed villas and farms, crops and animals, carried off plunder and slaves. We passed the still smoking ruins of several homesteads. Theodosius split the army into units to scour and cleanse the countryside. The barbarians are the Caledonii, composed of two peoples, the Picti and the Scoti, who come from the far North beyond the wall built by the Emperor Hadrian and restored by the great Constantine, and the Saxones, a tribe of the Germanii who sail here to plunder and destroy from the mouth of the Albis.

On the second day from Rutupiae we heard that a large band of these was drawn up on the bank of a river which lay across our road and that they had in their midst many captives and much spoil. We engaged and routed them, freeing their prisoners. Then see the magnanimity and wisdom of this general, for some of the spoil he divided among the soldiers so that they should be content but the rest he returned to the unhappy owners among those recently freed so that all blessed him. We stayed some days in the town of Durovernum, which is the capital of the Cantii where Theodosius received reports of the success of those troops he had sent out. So we marched slowly Northwestward pacifying the country and restoring order until we came to the great river Thamesis on which stands this city. It is not a gently flowing water like our Mosella with 'the vintage swelling in the crystal waves' but full and dark under shifting clouds. The city is not as large as Treveri but that is not to be expected. It is, I believe, bigger than the capital of the Parisii, than Arelate or Massilia, and is the capital of the province of Maxima Caesariensis and the seat of the Vicarius. Its walls are well fortified with bastions added by Constantine. As you approach from the South you must cross the river to reach the city though a little of it has spilt upon the nearest bank about the bridgehead. Here a strong guard is kept but when the citizens saw the dust of our approach they threw open their gates and flowed out to meet us.

The inhabitants claim that their island was peopled by Brutus, son of Ascanius, and from him they are called Britanni but whether that Brutus was indeed the descendant of Aeneas or another of that name is not clear. Nevertheless from this the tribe about Lundinium are called the Trinobantes which they derive from Troia Nova in support of their claim to be considered descended from Aeneas and thus equal kinsmen with the Romans. But this Lundinium I would rather think to be another Lugdunum as we have in Gallia, named from the Celtic Apollo, since the Britanni and the Galli, as both Caesar and Tacitus have written, are one people.

However it may be, it is a prosperous city with many fine public buildings and well-laid-out streets. The basilica alone is one of the largest I have seen in the North and the forum teems with shops and merchants as in the time of Tacitus. There are many temples, baths and all the appearances of civilization though a little reduced by the attacks of the barbarians which have made some traders fearful to come here. Yet when we reclined at the governor's palace we ate off fine silver dishes and, in my honour, drank a clear green mosella. The river about the bridge is lined with wharves and jetties where in more peaceful times many ships tie up, and our troops found good lodging in the excellent fort which defends the landward side of the city and its gates. When all is calm here we shall march out through one of them to Eboracum, the capital of the lesser province. There I expect more breeches and fewer togas on the streets. Here I might almost be at home in Treveri if I half close my eyes.

In acknowledgment of the citizens' courage in defending their walls against the barbarians the Emperor has graciously permitted the city to assume the title of Augusta as the last civilized centre of the Empire upon its borders.

It was a small, oblong classical building like a little temple with columns and pediment, crumbling, shrouded by trees. There were others sited about the park. Meepers supposed keepers or their families lived in them. But this one was empty. No nylon lace hung at its windows, only a veil of dirt. He sniffed the air like a dog. There were few people about at this hour on this stretch. Soon they would be locking the gates. He had never been in the park at closing time but he could imagine the cries, like a childhood street game of hide-and-seek in the dusk with the high drawn out call: 'All in, all in,' at the end. He looked quickly up and down the road before darting into the shrubbery and worming his way round to the back, a technique the army had taught him. Hidden by a laurel he peered through a back window, his eyes pressed close to the pane to bring the room into focus. It was quite bare. Through a door he glimpsed a litter of gardening equipment, tools and flowerpots. He made his decision, took a penknife from his pocket and went to work on the catch. It gave easily but then he was an expert. The sill was low. With a further quick glance round he put a leg over and squeezed himself into the room which smelt of stored tubers and the damp of disuse. The roof was sound enough it seemed. That was settled then. In the morning when he went out he would wear his porter's cap and no one would question but that he was some official with a right to be there. The keepers would think he was from one of the services: gas, water or electricity. Tonight he would go back to his old hut for the last time and put his things together. In the morning he would clear out early. He was moving into danger and every dawn and every evening return would be hazardous yet he felt quite calm and even rather pleased about it. It would be an almost regal lodging with Kensington Palace on one hand, the barracks, whose brutal bloody boxes mirrored its function, along the road and acres of ride and parkland before him. The twilight had deepened by the time he was back on the path. Perhaps they didn't call time at all but blew a whistle or rang a bell. He would soon find out. On his way to the Albert Gate he must look for a keeper and study his cap.

Meepers left the hut very early carrying his possessions snail-like on his back. The chances were that he would never see the square again or the house where he had been born. An ageing hippie, he deposited his bedding roll at the left luggage where they were used to him. He had sweated under the weight of his worldly goods and now he carried his holdall into the public baths, soaked himself gratefully and put on clean clothes. As he combed his thin wet hair before the mirror he prided himself on his nomadic cleanliness. Many men would have let their standards slip; Meepers remained shabbily spruce. Even his face was reassuming its respectability. He collected his forwarded mail now from the Trafalgar Square post office: an invitation to address a local historical society; a request to renew his subscription to the *London Archaeologist*; an income tax form. Over breakfast in a coffee house he reviewed the day and composed a letter to *The Times*.

His chosen early shift allowed him to change and be in his place before the lecturer came in. Last time he had been forced to speak, to draw attention to himself and his nose. But the man wouldn't challenge him or turn him out. In some way Meepers had frightened him; made him a party to his conspiracy. Because he wouldn't listen, wouldn't publish the truth when I presented it to him, he decided. A tramp passing the window on his way to the Embankment arches looked in at Meepers, at his steam-wreathed cup and plate of toast, with eyes in which not even envy sparkled. His beard and hair flowed wild like a prophet. In spite of the heat his raincoat was bound tightly with a string belt and bulged with innumerable underlayers. Meepers watched him stop a girl in flowered trousers and gauzy white blouse who fumbled in her handbag for a coin. What was the meaning of clothing? Not just for warmth surely, or rather, he corrected himself, not merely a response to external temperature. A man's, or girl's, internal climate could dictate dress too.

The two promising ones are a boy and a girl. I don't think they're lovers yet but I feel they will be. The girl's hair is marginally longer than the boy's, otherwise they might almost be twins with a mother determined to dress them alike. Meepers was there and sat quietly at the back. They wanted to talk today, touched off by my mention of Malthus, about the population explosion. I shall soon find myself outbidding Wandle in the popularity stakes. This afternoon there was no escaping the computer visit. Ponders would have been hurt. Yet what was there to see when we got through the sentry box of glass doors?

'Of course it's not working at the moment,' Ponders apologized.

'Ah, but what would it tell us if it could speak?' Wandle asked. 'Can it speak by the way?'

'Not exactly. It can write. Here. This gives a printout on continuous stationery. Like a telex machine you know.'

'The business man's private automatic news-sheet.' He was clearly enjoying himself, bouncing a little on his toes and clasping and unclasping his hands. Probably Voltaire was just as irritating, certainly Johnson was: think of the wheeze and whirr of grandfather clockwork, while one waited for the aphorism to strike.

'There is a sense,' said Ponders, 'in which it can't tell us anything we don't already know – except that we don't know we know it.'

'That's metaphysics. I thought computers were supposed to be unthinking robots.' I wanted to kick the thing and see all its discs and metal innards go rolling about the floor.

'Let me put it this way: we know if we add two numbers together that we can find their sum. All the computer does is do what we can do more quickly than most of us can. Now if the problem is more complex, stocktaking in a supermarket for instance, it's still something that we can do by a laborious process of calculation. To arrive at a world prediction on the rate of consumption of natural resources we have to tell the computer all the known facts, plus the variables that will modify trends and the trends themselves, show it how to proceed, what lines to follow, what calculations to make and so on. This is simply what we already know and inherent in it is the conclusion that the computer will come to if we've programmed it correctly.'

'It's what man has always been after in astrology: to take the uncertainty out of the future by a combination of mechanical, unarguable facts, in that case star combinations, something that isn't affected by human will or emotion and must be accepted.'

'As long as you accept the premise.'

'Oh the premise doesn't matter. It's the process that's important, or rather the search for a process, the handling of the concept.'

'So Aztec ritual murder was alright and led to the computer?'

'Did I say that?' He appealed to Ponders. But he wasn't to be drawn in on either side.

What could the computer have told the kids about the population explosion in the nineteenth century? Nothing that we haven't come to by human reason. Perhaps that was what Ponders meant. It couldn't have told us how to stop it or the exploitation and misery it made possible, inevitable. Or could it? By forecasting, by the Cassandra warning words. But then would we have known what to ask it in 1780? Another twenty years and Malthus had worked it out of course. So Ponders is right again.

This has spilled over on to Sunday night. This morning, when I went out to buy a paper, I had such a déjà vu, not even my own but MacNeice's, that I found myself making up some lines as I walked to the corner. When I got in I wrote them down for myself and for you as a kind of progress report, my temperature chart or a piece of pokerwork over the bed: Thou goddess seest me.

> Someone drops
> round pebbles of sound
> from a horn into the street.
> A blackbird competes
> among the rightangled metal branches of aerials.
> Forty years on they are still washing their cars
> each making a Sunday oasis
> a dark wet patch in the dusty street
> though the skullbells have clappered
> their harsh tongues through wars.
> They find their glistening dream
> of chrome and glass that can fly
> with its four wheels barely tacked
> to the tarmac
> though the afternoon will inch by bumper to bumper
> and tomorrow gets up just the same
> to be clocked in.
> Hindhead was a peak I remember
> on the road to windy Troy.

Does it explain itself? I'm out of practice with verse. I wanted to say that we didn't (this morning) seem to have progressed on a human level or perhaps I mean on a domestic level. It's a kind of urban *In Time of the Breaking of Nations*, you know where Hardy suggests that the lovers and the men ploughing are rural verities that will survive war and political upheaval; but stood on its head. MacNeice was justifying the escapist weekends of daily bread-earners. I wanted to say that, in spite of the cataclysms that should have taught us something, we aren't offering most people any more than we were forty years ago (leave aside the depression) except that now even their Sunday afternoon attempt to catch a little freedom and excitement has been curtailed by the simple fact of their all wanting it at the same time. What is to be done? On their way to the coast for cockles they pass the Ford plant at Dagenham, that Detroit moonscape where every man's car is processed out; they inch past it choking each other to death with their fumes. The dream of the bright young things, fast and furious whirling through the countryside, twists round all our throats like Isadora Duncan's scarf. The lady and the motoring veil: there's a dance macabre for a brave choreographer.

Meepers sat up in bed, his shoulders propped comfortably against the wall, making notes as he read. It was still quite early. Last buses growled by on their run in to home garages; cars kept up a ground continuo. The lodge had a sink and running water. It was almost a palace in itself. He turned the page in the torchlight and pounced excitedly. 'Gold fremisses of c.640 stamped Lunduniu,' he noted, 'but episcopal succession, after expulsion of Bishop Mellitus and reversion to paganism, not resumed till 653. Therefore pagan mint? Why no King's name on coins, only city? *Citizens* expelled Mellitus (Anglo-Saxon Chron.) Even when King converted didn't let bishop back.' He thought of the acres of park beyond the wall. Were any other warm-blooded mammals awake out there, treading delicately over the grass and among the trees to dip their snouts in the Serpentine or was it sanctuary only to birds? Probably there were rats and mice and hunting cats of course. A fox would have been good if it could have been persuaded to leave the waterfowl alone. In his mind a great owl planed under the branches. Were there squirrels? Meepers couldn't remember. He was falling asleep.

Fragments from the Berkynge Chronicle, probably spurious.
839 In this year there was great slaughter in London and many
    dwellings burnt by the pagans.

851 In this year 350 ships came up the Thames and stormed Canterbury and London and then went South over Thames into Surrey and King Noblewolf fought against them and made the greatest slaughter of a heathen host we have heard tell of and he had possession of the place of slaughter.

870 In this year was the Abbey of St Mary burned to the ground by the pagans and all the nuns put to the sword or carried away together with the abbess no man knows whither. Then King Elfcounsel succeeded to the Kingdom and in the course of the year fought nine times against the pagans to the South of the Thames and at last made peace with the Danes and divided the Kingdom with them and ceded to them Berkynge and all the Abbey lands and the heathen camped in the holy place which St Truepower founded and gave to his sister Noblefortress. And she was our first abbess. All the land beyond the River Lea was ceded to them.

871 In this year went the heathen host from Reading to London and to our shame the Mercians there made peace with them and paid them immense tribute and they took up winter quarters in the city but did not burn it because it seemed to them (the host) more profitable ...

879 In this year a band of pirates took up quarters at Fulham on Thames and the sun was eclipsed.

886 In this year the host being gone oversea to the city of Paris because of the might of King Elfcounsel the King came again to London and occupied it and all the English submitted to him. Then he rebuilt the walls and added defences and set up a mint within the city and gave all into the hands of his kinsman alderman Noblecounsel to rule to whom all the Angles and Saxons who had been dispersed everywhere voluntarily submitted.

889 In this year the abbess had twenty-eight houses in London.

894 ... then they put the host to flight and stormed the fort and seized everything inside it, goods, women and children and the citizens conveyed them all to London. The ships they either broke or burned or brought to London. One that was

taken was the son of the Danish King Haesten and godson to alderman Noblecounsel and because of this King Elfcounsel restored the boy to his father.

898 In this year died Bishop Highstone and Wolfstone was consecrated Bishop of London in his stead.

899 In this year King Elfcounsel rebuilt the bridge across the Thames.

901 In this year died King Elfcounsel six nights before All Hallows and his son Richprotector succeeded to the Kingdom.

910 ... Bishop Wolfstone ...

912 In this year died alderman Noblestone and King Richprotector took over all his lands and the cities of London and Oxford.

919 ... in the borough of Southwark.

926 In this year Godcounsel the Good, Bishop of London, went on pilgrimage to Rome in the year of his consecration.

927 ... eight moneyers in the city.

953 ... Brighthelm ...

961 In this [year] ... and a destroying fire burnt down St Paul's but it was built again the same year. Then also the Bishop of London, Hillstone, was consecrated archbishop of Canterbury and Elfstone succeeded him as bishop.

989 In this year was held the Great Synod at London.

994 ... Anlaf and Swein came to the city with ninety-four ships intending to set it on fire but God and the holy Mother of God be thanked who showed mercy to the garrison and delivered them.

996 In this year by the goodness of God King Richspear endowed the new Abbey and restored to it all its lands in Rainham, Ingatestone and Dagenham under the rule of St Benedict and ... Wolfstone succeeded to the bishopric.

99? In this year a woman was convicted of witchcraft and drowned at London Bridge. ... men from Rouen, Flanders, Ponthieu, Normandy, Liège, Huy and the territories of the Emperor ...

1009 ... they made frequent attacks on the borough of London, but praise be to God, she still stands safe and sound, and the Danes always suffered heavy losses there.

1010 In this year King Noblecounsel took refuge in the city from the Danes and all was done badly and worse than ever before.

1012 ... was Bishop Elf ... pelted with bones and the heads of cattle and one of them drunk with wine struck him on the head with an axe and his blood stained the ground. Then in the morning the citizens received his body from the heathen and brought it to London where it is buried in St Paul's church and many miracles are manifested by the holy martyr.

1013 ... a great part of the host was drowned in the Thames because they did not look for a bridge. The citizens held out against them because King Noblecounsel was inside.

1016 In this year Prince Happyprotection called Ironside began to gather levies and when they were assembled they demanded that the King should be with them and they should have the support of the citizens of London but the King heard that it was intended to betray him so he abandoned the levies and returned to London. Then on St George's Day the King ended his days and the citizens and the councillors chose Prince Happyprotection as King. The Danes came in their ships to Greenwich and on to London. They dug a deep channel on the South bank and dragged their ships round the bridge. They built earthworks and blockaded the city and attacked it again and again but the citizens resisted courageously ... At Ashington ... flight, betrayed his royal lord and the whole nation ... and all the flower of England perished there. Then the citizens came to terms with the host and they brought their ships to London and took up winter quarters there. King Happyprotection ended his days on St Andrew's day and is buried at Glastonbury.

1017 In this year ... C ... Alderman Richruler was slain in London very justly.

1018 ... seventy-two thousand pounds in addition to that which

the citizens of London paid which was ten thousand five
hundred pounds tribute for our sins ...

One should make use of the amenities I told myself. Music,
painting, theatre are all there to be enjoyed. Go out and
enjoy them. So I went to the opera, well almost. A concert
performance of *Dido and Aeneas* as part of the proms. I
queued, something I haven't done for centuries, in another
country with a dead girl. Or maybe I'm dead and sunk down
to shades of underground like Euridice or the girl who trod on
a loaf or, indeed, Aeneas, for surely he died for a time ex-
piating his miserable conduct of the Dido affair. And who
should be in front of me in the queue but my lovers and kind
enough to speak to me just as I was feeling my age had no
right to be there. They are called, believe it or not, Jenny and
Robin. There's a vogue among the young for sackbuts and
krumhorns but Purcell I'd thought wasn't really on their
beaten track. The queue was reassuringly long though and
motley enough. The building is just as ridiculous as ever
perhaps a little more so now that it's been cleaned and one
gets the full terracotta and ochreous plaster effect. It was more
decent in a veil of grime though it's almost the only building
I'd say that of. But inside it's a marvel, no other word for it, a
plush hat box of a building that becomes infinite and mysterious as you look up as if there was no roof, just tier upon
tier going up to some darkened Tiepolesque apotheosis of
clouds and sky with cut-out bits for stars lit behind by a giant
baroque stage designer. Now they've hung the modern
equivalent of clouds, white plastic moonglobes, under the
roof, I suppose to improve the acoustics which they un-
doubtedly do. Do you remember the cannon on the seashore
effect? There's no harm in the globes. For some reason they
fit in perfectly and don't interfere at all with the heavenly
balustrades from which gods and putti lean to hear the music.
At first we were grouped round the fountain and its attendant
grove of house plants. As usual the programme was too long
and we had to drone through several bits of makeweight be-

fore we got to the Purcell. In the interval I was privileged to buy the lovers a drink, the least I could do in return for their courtesy. Robin stood for the music while Jenny and I sat, she drooping her head forward so that her face was hidden by a fall of hair. I began to feel sorry that I'd intruded on them and wondered if they resented it without seeing any way to resolve the problem. Eight million people in this city and we are forced up against each other like that. My drink buying was an apology. For something to say I asked if they knew Meepers. They knew no one and anyway I couldn't describe him, not in any neutral tones. For them I suddenly saw the city as a series of anonymous concentric rings each further and further from the centre point which is always I or in childhood me: department, faculty, college, university, city, each increasing the depth of anonymity and isolation, wrapping the gauze layers tighter and tighter until all sound and sensation are padded away. Only the eyes are left free to blink and water as they stare at a world that they can't make meaning of by themselves.

After the interval I excused myself from the well and climbed up and up to be among the fates. There are no gods in this story, Tate's and Purcell's I mean. I suppose that's obvious but I'd never realized it before. There's just an embodied malice that can't bear to see human beings happy. What I mean is we've already entered the world of lifesize proportions and no more that's usually attributed to the Age of Reason. Hecate and her girls could just as well be a spiteful faction in court, city or village; not malign fate or the decrees of the gods or Christianity's sin and punishment but human weakness and pride, basic psychology. Is that why we undervalue it? Because it doesn't pretend to the supernatural but's merely heroic. Like Racine I suppose. And it's so urban, so unrustic and that must make it unpopular with environmentalists. Dido busy building her city:

The prince with wonder sees the stately tours
(Which late were huts, and shepherds' homely bow'rs),

93

The gates and streets; and hears from every part
The noise and busy concourse of the mart.

But I still prefer Tate's version of the story to Dryden's. And
the music, so plangent; the only word for it. What was it
Pepys said, about something of Purcell's making him feel as
he had 'when I was first in love with my wife?' Am I asking
all these questions to provoke you to an answer? There's
another then.

How the city's towers shimmer in the background. Was
Aeneas hedging his bets in his love for the Queen so that if he
didn't make Rome after all he could always fall back on
Carthage? I found myself wanting to warn her: don't trust
him; he's weak. At the first opposition he'll abandon you.
Then I thought: she knows or half-senses, that's why she
doesn't want to let herself love him. His answers come back
too pat: 'Fate forbids what you pursue.' 'Aeneas has no fate
but you.' When he's frauded away he tries to blame the gods
and then, at her anger and misery, he changes his mind. But
now she sees him for the vacillating hypocrite he is. She sends
him away, knowing it will mean her death. What a marvellous
black and gold catafalque it is, all overhung with purple
plumes and the forecast of the burning city for her pyre. We
make epic and opera out of sordid trade wars: Greece and
Troy, Rome and Carthage while out of ideological, idealistic
conflicts we make ephemeral newspeak and bloodless docu-
mentary.

I came down numb and a little lightheaded from overseeing
such events, separated myself from the crowds round the door
to take a breath of cooler air and suddenly I was back in my
hallucinatory self for I saw, or thought I saw, on the opposite
side of the road across a flowing Styx of black cars and cabs
(is Charon's ferry no longer enough to cope with the rise or
fall of the daily dying hordes and has he swapped it for a
hovercraft to get us all to the other side?) Meepers passing by
the park railings with a bulging bag of some sort I couldn't
quite make out. Perhaps he's legion and that's why I seem to

see him everywhere. I wanted to get over to him but the lights wouldn't change and the late homegoing stream was impossible to ford. Soon he vanished, was swallowed up. But how and where? Is he at the mercy of a landlady somewhere, or in one of the sad Bayswater guesthouses with admonitions on every door and under every switch? Perhaps he's a millionaire and hobnobs in the Royal Garden Palace with the blue-rinsed, starved, elderly little-girl American matrons, lorgnettes at the dangle ready to study the bill.

The birdsong was louder even than in his garden hut. It woke him early without need for a betraying alarm. Til the keepers came to open the gates he was monarch on his green island washed by the tarmac moat. He watched from a window as the tall wrought-iron trellises were unlocked and folded back and the uniformed figure strolled away through the dewy foliage towards the flower gardens. Meepers supposed he lived in one of the further lodges that had neat lawns and curtained windows and sometimes a flowered print wife sweeping the steps.

Over a breakfast of tea and hot sausage sandwich in a café that catered mostly for busmen he took stock. His whole strategy needed rethinking. His tentative plan to go to university in order to be no longer the amateur crank disregarded wouldn't work; one unfinished course of lectures had shown him that. Three years of it was unthinkable. The standard was fitted to those who knew nothing. He considered the Open University but for that you needed a suburban home to house your electronic tutor. A correspondence course? He would be able to work at his own speed but there were the essays he would have to submit to the secondrate conventional minds that would mark them. And all this would take precious time. Meepers couldn't wait. The answer came to him quietly but with conviction. He would simply award himself a degree. That was the answer. Why hadn't he thought of it before? It wasn't even dishonest, merely a recognition of the truth: that

95

he had the necessary knowledge and intelligence. He had worked steadily over the years, read and researched in all branches of his subject. Now what should it be? Adequate without arrogance. Meepers reflected that he was probably Ph.D. level but that the verbal jump was too great, like being knighted and suddenly addressed by your Christian name by people you didn't know. A flurry of drivers and conductors changing shift began to call for dripping toast, bacon sandwiches and ubiquitous tea as Meepers in cap and gown struck himself on the shoulder with a parchment scroll bound with blue ribbon. There was safety in numbers so perhaps it should be a London degree. Briefly he considered a foreign award but rejected it, out of a knowledge of academic chauvinism and his own, though perhaps as an extra, something honorary from Leipzig shouldn't be refused. Draining his mug he rose an M.A. (thesis: Evidences of urban survival in post-Roman London). Perhaps the doctorate should come later.

Meepers stepped into the square. The air seemed fresher this morning as if the hot spell might break. It was an appropriate place for a degree giving he thought, remembering Offa of Mercia's contentious synods here where bishoprics and under-Kingships were given, and taken back. 'All his slaves to be freed on the death of a bishop,' but that was later he thought, worrying at it, the day clouding. But here. A bus passed in a red blur on its way to Fulham; starlings chattered in the blistering plane trees. King Egbert, yes that was it, eighth Bretwalda, stalked into the square with his standard borne before him. Meepers turned happily into the tube mouth and began the journey through the tiled gut down into the earth.

He would continue with the course he had decided. His rejector shouldn't be allowed to escape Meepers' deathshead at his feast of learning. For a little longer too he would be a porter because of that nerve centre of manmade intelligence at the heart of the building that he might be able to use. Perhaps with his newly acquired qualifications he could write to the head of the department. What was his name now?

Ponders: that was it. The train thrust its glow-worm head out of the tunnel. Chelsea began to recede. Chalkshythe. A landing place for chalk or limestone he suddenly remembered the name meant, very early seventh century. But, Meepers sat upright suddenly, they built in wood not stone the books said. Then why and what? Kentish ragstone brought by barge as in Roman times still but now to build abbeys like Erconwald's Chertsey rather than villas or the city walls? But perhaps the city was so flourishing by then ... no, too far upriver. Victoria and St James's slid away in his absorption. Westminster forced itself into his consciousness. Mercifully he was alone in the compartment. He was afraid he had been indiscreet, muttering aloud to himself. With Westminster he was safe; only dubious charters until the tenth century which was too late to disturb him. The illustrious tombed of the cathedral, documented and epitaphed in their hic iacets, had no power to move and excite him like the anonymous bones and prints of his lively unknown dead. He slotted the problems of wood and stone away to consider later and swung his way along the rocking compartment from rail to rail like a gibbon in a cage.

It was still very early; the streets were swept and empty. A gaggle of cleaners broke from an office block, exotic and plump as bullfinches in their summer plumage, chivvying each other into loud laughter with tossed-off obscenities, their permed, dyed heads glittering like parakeet crests in the sun. They clustered at the bus stop waiting to go home for breakfast. Meepers crossed the road afraid as a girl below a work-manned scaffolding to pass them by and run the gamut of their invitations and laughter, loud as their sons' as they leant from the frail platforms whistling and calling to make imaginary virgins blush. His parents had been grey all over; colour was vulgar. The undeserving poor dressed their children in cheap satin and patent leather. Respectability showed itself as dinginess; neither voice nor clothes were loud. The women mobbed him across the streets with their cries. At this time it was their city. Without them dust and trash would gradually silt it up. The gleaming offices would film

97

over and dull, the lavatories block, the basins scum, the carpets and floors be overwhelmed in a tide of waste from flowing baskets. Each one carried a version of the same small holdall, big enough for an apron and old shoes or slippers and a headscarf to protect the bright crests against rain or wind.

A bus came up. He heard them rallying the conductor. Then it drew off leaving one or two still waiting but no longer voluble alone. Meepers strolled by the milky river looking across at the great liners of County Hall and the South Bank complex moored on the far side. He might have been on the front at Felixstowe, come out early before his parents were up to lean into the wind. Even the gulls' squall was the same. They had found something midstream and were banking and diving at it with mews and screams like sea vultures. Some planed above waiting to stoop when their moment came. Meepers turned back to the street again. Behind his back it had filled with ambling figures, Peasant Breughel or Workman Lowry. They were coming towards him, for him. He almost turned and ran, shrinking back against the parapet as they began to pass. Then he remembered the morning handout of tea and doorsteps from a mobile canteen parked under the bridge. He shouldn't have come this way at this hour. They passed him slowly, figures in a nightmarescape. He turned away from them towards the river. What were the gulls harrying? Something bulked and dipped as the tide pushed it along. His mother would never buy mackerel: she believed it fattened on drowned men's flesh. What was he thinking of? Something tugged at a memory of ragged boys mudlarking through the pockets of corpses stranded by the ebb. No that wasn't it. The first bank of ooze was appearing with bubbles of gas and trapped air rising, freed from the weight of water to suppurate and pop in the soft wet skin. The dun-coloured mousse was full of treasures: flints, battle axes, shards, coins cast or fallen in, even whole ships. In a magazine he had read of the salvage party that quarried in the mud for them and wondered momentarily if he would join. The layers that lifted the city twenty feet above ground level were here compressed into the river bed, broadening and raising it so that a whole waterfront lay under the waves and under centuries of detritus and excretion. Could he fossick in the sludge even for the mighty bronze head and hand of Hadrian it had once given up? When he had gone for Sunday afternoon walks with his parents he had seen with horror and envy the slum boys leaping like froglings from the landing steps, and grown hot under his grey flannel collar at the typhoid that flowed coolly into their mouths, ears and eyes and ran down their sleek otter heads. If he was sick when they got home his mother called it heatstroke and made him lie down in a darkened room. Statues of Aphrodite and her relations were drawn purged from the warm Aegean seasalt dip with the clean calceous tracery of marine worm and mollusc on their metal flesh. Regretfully he would have to stick to what dry land would yield him.

So we done no more than get up straightaway from where we were sat, left our meat and drink and began to get ready to ride southwards again, wan and wounded as many of us were. Then we set off the way we come not a fortnight before and rode day and night and so wended our way homeward to Lundentowne. But the earls of the North, Edwin earl and Morcar earl, stayed behind to gather their lads again for many of them had been slain or drowned. They said that they would make the North ready and then march South to meet the King. More's the shame, for when we should have had all our might to defend the land we had only the men of Lundene and what warbands could be called up. Near on four days and nights it took from York before we saw Cripelgate Tower and the town walls and the towers of the churches looking over and the sunlight shooting back from the gold on Aldermanburig roof. Then we rode through the gates into the cheers of the townsfolk, glad to see the walls well guarded, the inner way swept clean for the fight and workmen strengthening the gates. The townsfolk had hung their best cloths from the upstairs and the sun showed up the gold and silver thread and bright silks so that they seemed to play in the light weary as we were. Then there were calls for the King and his brothers and for our Ansgar and for the Frenchies the people called: 'Out, out!' I thought then that that Bastard wouldn't never take Lundene.

As St Powles the aldermen had gathered with Archbishop Ealdred and we all went in to the great church and heard mass with the organ playing to burst like. There was nor hide nor hair to be seen of Bishop William. Then we rode everyone of us to his own hall except for them that rode on with the King to Westminster Hall. The town was filled with fieldfolk, some who had come in for fear of the Frenchies and some who had come in to sell. As I rode past Eastcheap the people bought for the sit-in that might come all manner of foodstuff and the shipmen were there to buy for the fleet that lay in the port to go against William. Already the bonfires were lit in the yards of halls, sweet loaves, meat and ale were given to all comers.

Now for five days we mended our wounds and sharpened our weapons the while the King sent out for the warbands to meet him at Haestinga where the Bastard wasted the land all about. Word come that he had a castle of wood with him and from this his horse knights harried and burned, and that he had taken the old forts by the waterside and made them anew and filled them with his men. The sixth morning early I kissed my wife while she clung to me quaking with fear. She put a new gold ring on my arm and told me to come back whole. So we rode out of Lundene as we had rode in with the folk in the streets to cheer us along, horns and pipes blowing and the bright silk webs floating over our heads sewn with signs that marked where a man came from and most the dragon of Wesseaxe above Harold. Then we thundered over the bridge through the portgate and rode on through Sudwerca, towards Haestinga on the old road until noon and there we stayed to rest while the King called his friends and the wise men and priests to him. I was there. I heard the words he said, words I shan't never forget. 'My guard, my help, my dear friends, the kingdom's shield,' he began. 'You have heard that William is in the land slaying and burning. He thinks to bring us under his yoke, to make freeborn men his serfs, to change our laws the which we had from our fore-fathers and from Alfred, to bed our wives, to steal our land. In my father's lifetime, the Normenn found a way wormlike into holy Edward's heart and Godwin my father and all his sons were drove oversea until God should show the truth. Now the Normenn come again with steel-edged swords not words to win the land. You know that I am cursed by the Pope for the oath I gave when William held me in his castle at Bayeux with his kinsman the bishop to put holy relics in the chest under my hand while I swore. Now I am King by Edward's dying words and by your choosing. But if you will, choose another now before the fight.' Then all was still for a short while until sudden like a great cry went up from us all: 'Better war than another King.'

Harold thanked us. I saw the tears stand in his eyes. Then we chose a monk and got him up on a horse to go for William and tell him to wend his way to his own home again oversea with all his folk and leave this land to the rightful King. But we never stayed for no answer but began to gather and gear ourselves to follow him when our weary horses were strong again so that we might outwit the Frenchies and come at them sooner than they thought for.

Now this was at Tonebricg on the Medway where there should have met us all the men from Wesseaxe and Cant at Suthrige and the Denise men from oversea but by nightfall although the seafarers had come in their dragonships and the men of Cant had gathered for Harold there were but half of the men from Wesseaxe. The King's eyes grew hot with ire. 'The lady my sister keeps her men to ward her in Winteceastre while the kingdom falls,' he said. Then come a monk from Certesyg sent by the abbot to say that all were cursed who fought for Harold and then we knew that there would be none from nowhere in Suthrige. And many of them that had come in were lads back from the harvest field in wool tunics with bows and arrows and neither shield nor sword. None the more for that we were glad to see them.

In the morning we went on again but more slow for the folk on foot and for that we were in the deep woods of the Andredesweald, and there was not none of us there that did not wish ourselves whole at home sitting on the bench with a cup of ale in our hands and our wives beside us be they shrew, hag or darling, fair or foul, as we rode through the dark trees and shouldered under the low boughs, knowing that William and his fighting men were before us. Soon our monk met us riding so hard that his horse was darkened with sweat like blood and steam rose from him mist like from a pool at dawn. He almost fell from his horse's neck at the King's feet.

'Where is William?'

'I left him at Haestinga. The fields round about are full of his men gathering food. He says the time of year and the wind at sea forbid him to go back. He offers you all your father's lands if you will be his man.'

Harold called us together. 'Now he will send to know our strength but we shall not sit still for his men to come to us. We shall step out smartly so that when he finds us we can craftily follow close on his heels and take William unawares. He shall not choose the ground for us to fight on.' And so it was. That night as we cooked our meat a monk of his come riding through the trees following the light of our fires. The King came out with his brothers to meet him, a stiff-necked Norman whose eyes were everywhere while he mouthed the Bastard's boasts and lies. The men seethed at his words and I saw fingers go to the newly sharp edges of axe and sword. Harold himself burnt inwardly but he would not never harm a priest. He gave him the golden fee right for them that play go-between as William had done our man, and the monk grasped it greedily. Then he thought to get on his horse again but the King was not done with him yet. 'Today let Almighty

God choose me or William,' he said lifting up his head. 'Now you must eat and drink with us. William must not say I sent you back in hunger.' And he laughed at us. At that men led the monk away and set him down for some eats the while we combed our hair and smeared the sweet oil of roses on it and on our flesh to drown the reek of sweat and blood and death under our helmets, and on our tunics of red silk that would not shew no blood under the locked rings of our fighting gear. Our Ansgar gave a deal of care to his beard for he had heard that the Frenchies were clean shaven priest like and he thought to show them how a man should look, fierce in a fight not fresh cheeked like a child. Each man held up his sword so that the gem stones in the hilt gleamed in the firelight and the silver and gilt windings engraved on the blade flowed like waves in the sea or an adder through grass. They were keen to begin the day's work, to drink hot blood. 'Stay near me,' said Ansgar to me. 'We will fight side by side today.'

Then when we were ready we got the Norman monk on his horse and a knight stung it smartly behind so that it sprang forward. Now the day began to break and the birds to sing above our heads as we went through the wood after him. Not one of us had had no sleep that night but I felt ready for anything and glad to be done with idle-handedness at last. The sun rose red through the mist and some of the men thought it was an evil token until Harold said that the same sun shone on William also. By this time we had reached the edge of the trees on Caldbec Hill. Before us were some little hills on the way to Haestinga. Harold sent me forward as a lookout. I climbed to the top to see the lie of the land. Below the hill dipped away and rose again into another, smaller with a fold beyond and then a ridge. The sight of Frenchie horseknights wandering carelessly in the folds made my heart stand still. And there riding as if his saddle was on fire was their monk on the far rise going towards a group of horseknights. I stayed to see no more but got back to Harold as quick as I might. 'We must win the hill between before William,' he said. Each of us drove his horse back among the trees and let his hawk fly from his hand. Fighting is man's work. Let him who still has life after the slaughter call back his horse and hawk. Now they all fight on horseback and say they are men as did the Bastard's men. My hawk was a young bird my wife had fed with her own fingers and therefore dear to me. But if I lived she would come to my whistle. Each of us drew his sword and lifted his axe, us housecarles before and the others on our heels. 'Now,' yelled the King, 'all together,' and we burst from the trees with horns calling and the clashing of our weapons. The thought went through my head that many of our lads still lay far behind for we had to leave them to ride ahead to come upon William unawares. As we ran downhill we gathered speed for the run up on the other half. For a little I lost sight of the Frenchies on the ridge beyond and only when we reached the top where the sign of the Wessex dragon was stuck hard into the ground could I lift my eyes to see on the ridge a man on horseback who must be the Bastard now with bowmen before him who sent a rain of arrows over our heads and then fell back as the horseknights thundered through up the hill towards us. Then we locked our shields into the wall and Harold yelled for us to stand fast and throw off their first onslaught. Many fell pierced by the shafts from our hands or hewed down by Harold's axe where he fought like ten men swinging the shining blade so that it sang in the wind. It was a great shame to see the horses wounded by sharp-edged weapons leaping and neighing with fear. The Frenchies fell back down the hill.

By now the rest of our lads that could were come up on foot and Harold showed them where they should stand and fight, with himself in the middle to keep the top of the hill where stood one hoary apple tree. Many more of William's men had reached him also, horseknights and bowmen from his fort at Haestinga, Frenchies and Brettas from the islands and lands South of Rouen that the Normenn had won, from Sicilia and from the south of Italia, land and gold-hungry men, wolves and ravens. So the two folk looked each at the other over the fold between and waited who should begin again. The first blood was to us and the Frenchies looked wan.

Now some have said, those who are always wise sitting on the alebench after the fight, that our King should not never have done as he did, that he should have sat still until the Bastard and his men were weary and would go home again. But think a bit. If Harold had done like Fabius Cunctator of old, William would have burned and wasted, and if the King had not fought him then men would have said that he was afraid because he was accursed and forsworn, as did some already, and all his folk had melted from him like snow. So as I see it he had no choice but to fight when he did in hopes of winning quickly. Nor might he wait for the earls of the North to get to him, for as fell out afterwards they were ever slow in mind and deed.

Then a man rode out singing from among the Normenn horseknights, tossing his sword on high and catching it again with a crafty hand, a juggler to witch the eyes of fieldfolk in Westcheap and hearten his own half with his boasts. 'He would like us to run at him and let his friends through,' said Ansgar beside me. But one of our lads stepped forward goaded by his sword play to meet him hand to hand. The juggler rode him down, ran him through with his spear, hewed off and held up his head. The Frenchies yelled.

'Bad that,' whispered Ansgar. 'They go a lot by such things. They tell whether a man is true or not, not by witness and oath as we do but by who wins the fight. Now they will think Christ himself fights on their side.'

And so the Frenchies took fresh heart and their bowmen drew their strings and loosed their darts from their deadly harps so that the sky grew dark with the bitter hail that stung men to death where they stood together like salt herrings in a box. The horseknights come again and we met them with axe and sword so fiercely that on the one side where the Brettas were they seemed to break and fly. Then although Harold called for them to stand fast I saw our men begin to follow, hewing them down as they fled but when they reached the lower ground the horses on either half rode back upon them and began to cut them down.

'We are lost unless we reach them,' Ansgar said. But Harold had already understood their plight and lifting his axe with 'Out, out' he began to move the warhedge forward in a row until we met up with those who had gone before and together we threw the Normenn back and made them fly again.

I wiped the bloody sweat from my forehead and looked for Ansgar. He was leaning on his axe weary like. 'A French son of a bitch sheathed his sword in my guts.' I helped him back to the wood and called for a priest to leech his wounds. Before I went back to the field he took hold of my hand. 'If we should lose, kinsman,' he said and signed himself against that evil, 'take me back to Lundene. Do not, not for nothing, let the Normenn wolves have me to sell.' I gave him my word and went towards the din of weapons and the yells of men. 'How goes it?' I asked of one of our lads for I could see the field was altogether other than I had left it.

'The King's brothers are both slain,' he answered. 'Gyrth nearly slew the Normenn bastard. He speared his horse under him. But William is a fiend. I think he cannot be slain by no man. When we had them going it was him that stopped their flight. Many have fought him but none can best him.' We had withdrawn to the hilltop again and the horseknights were gathered to come at us. Now I fought as never before. I hewed and hacked at limbs until my own ached. In a still gap I looked to see how we did. Now was the time that the weak began to think of flight and to creep back to the woods. I drew near to Harold in the throng. We held them at the hill though they came again and again and the King fought on like St Michel against the droves of devils. As men fell from the hill they were reft naked of all their gear. Not no one was spared not earl nor churl. Then I thought they would deal likewise with the whole land if we let them. But as I stood thinking one rode at me unawares and I was hard put to it to lift my axe again in time and spill his horse's brains. Even so the rider's sword would have bitten deep into my skull if my helmet had not stayed it and I sank down on one knee. But as his horse fell dead and he leapt down I had him within arm's reach and swung unthinking at him cutting him right through the thigh so that he dropped like a stone and the ground grew slippery with his blood. And all at once I saw what we should do. We had given as good as we had got. The Normenn dead lay in heaps. Now we should withdraw as Alfred did to gather our own men and fight again. I would tell the King. I began to fight my way towards him scything a swathe with my axe to where he stood under the dragon of Wesseaxe with one or two of the housecarls.

I never made it. Whether William could read the thought in my mind I cannot tell but I saw him gather three other horseknights in the fore and others behind and ride straight for the King leaving the rest of the fight to go as it might. Four men it took to fell him else they had never done it. They came on him altogether: one struck down through his breast with the speed of his horse behind the spear so that it went clean through his ringshirt and the blood flowed out in a stream; another hewed off his head while a third ran his blade up to the hilt in his belly and a fourth hacked away a leg and his manhood together and bore them off on his sword.

I heard myself yell and a red mist came before my eyes and I began to swear and lay about me. I wanted only to lie in the dust beside him. The word flew from mouth to mouth. 'Harold is dead.' Some fled at once, dropping their weapons. But others grew stronger, weariness fell from them though many wept as they fought on in the waning light. We were maddened by our loss. Let the bastards break us if they could. We would not never budge of our own free will.

But as I heaved my bloody axe again I heard a horn call from the woods through the falling dark and it was like a cloud was torn away and I could think straight again. Ansgar was reminding me of my oath to him. I fell back fighting, calling to the others to do likewise and gain the trees.

They had bound up his wound and sat him on his horse. For

all his weakness he was twice the man of anyone there. 'Can you ride?' I asked him.

'As long as I can sit in the saddle.' He looked at our weary troop. 'I know you would rather have died out there with Harold,' he said. 'But you are Lundene men. Do you want it to fall in flames like Troy because our Hector is slain? We must reach it before William.' The men brightened at that for it gave them something to do. It was dark now and we could hear horns and sometimes weapons dinging among the trees. 'Let our horns tell our lads where we are. We must take back as many as we can.' Our calls rang out.

'It will bring the Frenchies too,' I said.

'So what then. We will kill more of them.'

And men come to us from every side; those who had been on foot on the horses of the dead. I had not thought of my young hawk but I did now as we waited and I whistled her down to me. When we had gathered enough, Ansgar set some of us, the most sound in wind and limb that could be spared, to keep the path while the wounded withdrew. We were to follow as soon as we could. And so it was. Hardly had they withdrawn than we heard a great din of horseknights among the trees. We had put a third each of our men on either hand of the way while the rest made a shield wall in the middle of the path. They come on fast, too fast to stop when they met our wall, driving on to our spears and them behind running into them before. When our lads fell on them from either side those who could fled back again the way they had come. I was sorry that their leader escaped for he was the one who had beheaded the King and I would have loved to seen him brought down.

Not none of them come back for a second helping as we withdrew after our wounded. When morning broke we were through the wood resting when there come an oxcart richly hung. It was the Lady Gytha, the King's mother. It fell to Ansgar to tell her all her sons were dead and the land lordless. Then she never wept but said she would go to William to ask for her son's body to give it a Christian burial. 'Better to send, lady,' said Ansgar. 'He is a hard man. You should not in no way put yourself in his hands for all our good.'

'I would offer him the King's fee in gold. By rights he cannot say me no.'

Ansgar shook his head. 'Them are Normenn and their ways are not the same as ours. They do not deal in fees.' Then she wept. I offered to go for her as would any man worth his salt but Ansgar said, 'I need you at home. We will send a priest. We must go on,' he told her, 'but you should wait here for William's answer. His greed may override his carefulness.'

So we rode away with me beside him. 'What care,' I asked, 'when the King is dead?'

'Lest anyone should say he still lives. Now tell me how he come to be slain.' So I told him and when I had done he said, 'That was the Bastard himself who led them.'

'And the others?'

'Eustatius for one. He always hated both Harold and his father Godwin. I mind the time when he had them sent oversea when Edward was first King and his men slew one of the townsfolk at Dofran before his own hearth. He thought to be a son to Edward and have the kingdom after him. William must beware him. Let the wolves fight among themselves.' He was wan with his wound and loss of blood but he held up.

At last we got to Lundene but there were not no cheers this time only it was bliss to be back home and to have my wife's arms about my neck. She fed me on wine and sweetmeats to get my strength back. So we waited for William to come and got ourselves geared up for the next fight. We knew when he was near for the folk who flocked to the town with the latest news. Now he was in Haestinga. Then he had gone to Dofran and taken the castle driving out the Englisc from hearth and home and giving them to his Frenchie followers. Cantuaerberi gave in and he began to move North with new men sailed in from Franc-land.

One night late Ansgar was borne to my door and set down in my hall. My wife was glad to see her brother but sad to see him so wasted. 'Now,' he said when she had brought us drinks, 'there is not none other I can speak to so freely. The lords of the North, Edwin earl and Morcar earl, are here with their lads to fight beside us so they say. I am a broken man no longer strong enough to bear weapons. Lundene and the whole kingdom are in our hands. What must we do? Tell me who should be our King?'

I looked at him in the firelight. His eyes were bright but not with the fever. 'There is the child Edgar and the two earls and the Bastard, and Swein of Deniscland.' I looked hard at him then knowing that his father's father had come with Cnut and that he was still half Denisc.

'Them days are over. Swein may want the kingdom but he will not have it never. Morcar and Edwin have neither kingcraft nor king's strength. It was Harold who took back their lands for them from the Northmen of Hardrada. Besides the Witan could never choose between them, they are alike as two peas.'

'Then it should be young Edgar.'

'No child can keep Engleland for long without a mother like the Lady Aethelflaed to fight for him until he comes of age. Such women are few and far between.'

'Then it must be William,' I said and my heart sank.

Ansgar did not answer me at once. 'Have you ever thought that the Normenn have no towns? Now why should that be? When you were with Harold in Normandig what did you see?'

'Castles and minsters, great stoneworks but towns no, none except for Rouen.'

'They will be vultures on the land. They will want to bind us all who are not Normenn lords. We have thralls in the fields, men who have done wrong, outlandish men, men who sell themselves or their children in times of hunger and wives too, but in the town we are all free. They call us unruly. Here we are free to come and go as and when we like and it is Lundene that chooses the King. We must keep our freedom.'

'If we fought we might win.'

'When we first came to this land there were great towns

built by the Romane. Lundene was already old. We broke all
that, priests say, for the sins of the Brittas. Would you see
William tear down the town walls and slaughter and burn
or the wives and children dead of hunger?'

'What can we do then?'

'William is greedy for gold and he cannot stay too long
away from Normandige.' He will not want to sit forever outside our gates. He will hope to frighten us. I think he will
make for the bridge. We must beat him there so that he knows
the fighting will be long and hard. First we will choose a
King to hearten our lads and worry William so that he must
come to us. After that we will buy our freedom from him. He
must give it to us in writing so that he can never unsay it. We
must play skilfully to win something out of our loss.' I knew
he was speaking then about Harold.

And so we did, right as Ansgar had thought the whole
thing out. William crossed the Temes at Walingeford and sat
there for a while. Stigand, the archbishop, brought him gold
and gifts from the Queen at Winteceastre so that he should
not never waste her borough. Then he sent his horseknights to
take Lundenebridge and when they could not they burned all
Sudewerc while William sat in the King's hall at West
Minster biting his nails. Meanwhile the child Edgar was chosen
and the call went out to all the land, 'Lundene has a King.'
Then William went wild and laid waste all about him. He
went North to Berchamstede and set up weapons against our
walls to frighten us. But we knew and he knew that he could
not beat us like that for winter was on him, and that he must
make a deal. So he sent stealthily to Ansgar to offer him this
and that if we would give up the child King and the kingdom
to him. By now the Northern earls were fearful that William
would block their way home. But we had what we wanted,
William's oath to rule as Edward had done and sworn on the
gospels in the West Minster before Ealdred would put the
crown on his head.

Nevertheless we bought dear in food and weapons for his
men but most in gold and gems for himself. But our town still

stands. Fire and sword did not bring it down at his feet. He took Ansgar among many others as one of his guards that we would lie still the while he was in Normandige. Soon we may begin to laugh again even though William has built a high tower to overtop our walls and his monks ring us round with their stone minsters girdling the borough. Inside we are still our own men.

William never let his ladymother have Harold's bones. He buried him in unholy ground by the seaside and wrote on a stone that he should still guard the land. They do say he wept at the burying and gave pence to the poor. For he knew he was in the wrong and he hoped in that way to lay Harold's ghost. Be that as it may, and for all men have said after, he stole the land from its rightful King and its own folk and even the tongue we must speak to our lord is no longer our own. God send it a good ending soon.

'William, King, greet William, bishop, and Godfrey, port-reeve, and all the burgeses within London, French and English. And I grant that they be all their law worth, that they were in Edward's dayes the King. And I will that each child bee his father's heire. And I will not suffer that any man do you wrong, and God you keepe.'

III

Respublica Londiniensis

Why does he agitate me so? Does he make me feel guilty? But why should I? He once sent me a crackpot article that I rightly turned down. In a fit of paranoia he came after me and now in some strange way he has the power to blackmail me. But I've never harmed him. Why do I put up with it then? Today I thought I would be tough. I saw him ahead of me in the corridor in his porter's uniform. No one else about. I took a quick breath and called. My heart was hammering away. I thought, This is mad. I called again: 'Mr Meepers.' We've no longer got a formula for calling people, have you noticed? We can't hiss after them like the Italians and Greeks or shout, 'You sir,' or even 'Oi you' as we did when we were kids. He was getting away. I began to run. I heard myself calling again: 'I say, Meepers,' like some cad in *The Fifth Form at St Dominic's*. When he stopped and turned I didn't know what to say and I was panting like some old dog, fat Hamlet 'scant of breath' so that I couldn't speak anyway. So he did. Very calmly, like a butler in a 'thirties thriller, he said, 'Can I help you, sir?'

I had a terrible impulse to hit him, an almost elderly man, not quite right in the head; the impulse of an offended girl or rather fright and anger combined which I suppose is what lies behind the sudden slap. My hand even twitched but I pulled it back in time. He stood quite still. I couldn't see into his eyes because of the twilight there always is in those damned corridors. 'What is it you want? Why are you here?'

'I have to earn a living, like most other people.'

'As a porter, here?'

'The work is clean, not very hard, in surroundings that are fairly congenial to someone of my interests.'

It was absolutely reasonable, irrefutable. I cast about for some other line. In that murky light I'd become a crafty angler, playing a lone equally crafty fish. Just the two of us. And if I managed to catch him, would the air be full of his soundless screams? 'Fair enough,' I said. 'But coming to my lectures; you don't get paid for that.'

'Curiosity. Perhaps I wanted to judge the ability of the person who had rejected my work,' he said with a controlled contempt. Yet I knew this wasn't the real reason. He had too little difficulty in giving it away.

'I'm sorry. I explained at the time. It's not really suitable for *Studies in History*: too early and conjectural. I'm sure someone else would take it. It's only a matter of the right outlet.' I heard myself begin a gibbering justification.

'On that basis you would have to reject another Gibbon.'

'It's the historical obscurity of that period in this country. Classical Rome and Greece fit in because they belong to recorded history even in decline. The Dark Ages are different, more like palaeo and neo and so on. History isn't continuous.'

'Quite.' I'd insulted him again. But he was winning. Oh yes. I was no closer to what I wanted to know. I tried again, a lazy trailer drawn across the surface to deceive.

'Well now you know there's no need for you to keep on. The standard is so far below you, you must be terribly bored.'

'My interest isn't merely academic. You could of course report me as attending without being enrolled. No doubt I should lose my job.'

My hand came up this time as if I was warding off a blow. Now my eyes were more used to the light I could see him better and I thought I saw a flicker of almost sympathy – no, too strong, but doubt; that perhaps he'd gone too far.

'What is it?' I said. 'What is it really?'

'If I told you you wouldn't believe me.'

'I might.'

'Alright.' His face was drawn, taut and fierce daring me to disbelieve or laugh. 'I want to save the city.'

'Don't we all.' I made it too light.

'I'm sorry, I have to go. Mr Emery ...'

'Just a minute. One more thing. The article, I'd like to read it again some time. Not for *Studies* you understand. What I said before still applies. For my own interest.'

He didn't answer and I couldn't tell if this was a further mistake. But I'd got somewhere. Emery was just an excuse because I was pressing him too hard. Will he let me see the article? I believe the answer's there. The truth is I didn't really read it before. As soon as I saw that it belonged to one of the lunatic twilight zones I knew it wasn't for us. Did Meepers sense that?

This afternoon I had to go up to Russell for a standardization meeting. I decided to walk through Bloomsbury. Most of the decent houses are university property now but they still give me a restful feeling. As I passed the Department of Archaeology, a new glasshouse on a corner, I glanced in and saw a skull looking out at me. It was an exhibition of some sort. No one seemed to be going in. There was just the skull quietly looking out as if its eye-sockets weren't full of air and, very shadowy behind, a porter in blue serge who could almost have been Meepers, custodian of the dead. I went on a bit shaken. The traffic seemed for once too far away. I kept on towards the Euston Road. Then suddenly I saw his name on a rather dusty bill stuck to the inside of a shop door, antiquarian books of the more dubious kind; economically dubious, tattered and undusted. It was the programme of some local society, lectures with the vicar working the slide projector. And there the name was staring out at me like the skull: Meepers.

My life the damp. Put another log on the fire. Never mind the cost. A month in this piddling country. I never thought I should miss Rouen. And the seasickness coming over. Every man throwing his guts into the sea as if he never expected to need them again. You were lucky to cross in the summer I tell you. Where was I? Yes tomorrow. Tomorrow you order the stone. What good is a wooden treasury? Fire. My house is my coffer. Now as for the workmen. The English are sullen pigs now but they must eat. What do they know? That it was our money paid for their defeat? No. Only that the Duke, King we should call him, has us under his special protection. For this they'll hate us. But later. We are new to them. Soon the stories will start: that we crucify children; that we steal their matzos from their churches and put them in our filthy mouths; that we bewitch their animals. Keep your eyes from fingering their daughters. Nothing enrages the goyim quicker than that. Then will come the jokes: about the Jew who fell in the privy on the Sabbath and wouldn't be rescued, about the walking nose, about charging the devil interest. Then because they are now the underdogs they will turn on us and trample us underfoot so they can say, 'At least we are better than the Jews.' And one day they too will kick us out. Oy it's a Christian world isn't it? Haven't we travelled all the countries of the earth. When that day comes some of us will stay here, change our names and become good citizens. It always happens. Meanwhile there's money to be made and lent. A thriving port like this; a new king with a subject people. He'll need to pay soldiers, to build castles. Business will prosper. Merchants will want money to fit ships and buy cargoes. Who has money? We have. What else should we have? Because their religion forbids us to deal in anything else. So forty per cent. That's safety. Order the stone. Learn English. French you know already. Why English when the King and his court speak only French? Ai, ai, ai. Because a businessman who relies only on the favour of princes is a fool. It's the burghers we must win, who must come to us for gelt. Now leave me alone. I have to think sometimes.

Dear God, listen. The boy is a good boy. He means well but he isn't tough yet like me. He trusts people. You and I know you can't trust nobody, not even yourself. Look at us in the wilderness; look at Adam and Eve. Even you don't always let your right hand know what the left is doing, between justice and mercy I mean. Let him learn God, not the hard way; the easy way from listening to his father. Forty per cent: that's all he has to learn. Then he can be rich and safe, can buy safety when they break the door and the windows. Here in the Jewry with our friends around us and the new King's protection he can finish his growing up. He's a clever boy too. He could be a doctor or a mathematician or an artist. Anything is possible. Dear God, look after him in London and teach him forty per cent.

He was tempted to whistle to himself as he packed his gear but it wasn't worth the risk. The traffic was still flowing beyond the wall; occasionally a lone car squealed its tyres through his gate, the driver in a Brands Hatch fantasy dare-devilling through the park's warm rank darkness. Lovers might pass his window and hear his haunting. In any case what he wanted to whistle always sounded well enough in his head until he tried to formulate it, to get percussion, strings, brass through his lips. For Meepers music meant instruments. The human voice touched no answering note in him, indeed it stepped between him and the music so that he could no longer hear the harmony only the animal hurt keening or the yap of delight.

Mentally he checked through the things in the bag. He hadn't been out for some time on this sort of expedition behind the lines. Getting back in would be difficult once the gates were locked but he would see about that when it arose. He was almost happy as he headed for Knightsbridge through lit streets that seemed never to sleep but to have been swept of people by some catastrophe. The lifesize display dolls leant elegantly inquiring towards him behind their plate-glass moats as if the age of robots had already come and in the morning at the press of a button they would start awake and begin to ape the perishing flesh and blood that had conceived them.

The footpads had made him wary. Every sense jumped at

shadows and footfalls. Meepers watched in the pool surfaces of the windows to make sure he wasn't being followed. But he had learnt too to carry nothing of value on him, enough for his fares; that was all. His wallet with its precious paper cargo was left behind. The watch had given him trouble. It had been with him longer than most things, apart from the splinters of his wounds, all through imprisonment and demob. He bought a cheap one, shockproof and waterproof it claimed, from a chainstore jeweller and noted with contempt and almost anger that it was perfectly reliable. Tonight he had strapped it on and grudgingly approved the green glow of its luminous hands and face.

The last train going East was full at first of boys and girls in expensive throw-away colour magazine rags, chattering and clinging to each other against the sway or for the mammal comfort of warm touching flesh. Their loud young voices piped and squawked round his head. Meepers salvaged a discarded grubby evening paper to bury himself in. The tattered peacocks and hens chattered out from Piccadilly onwards, their places taken by quieter suburban couples in longer lasting suits on their way home to Southgate. At Holborn Meepers got out and moled his way to the Central Line whose clothes and customs changed again as the train passed under St Paul's and the city. The deposits were stratified thick around and over him; his compartment nibbled its way through them like a mouse through a richly layered cake. He lamented the lost chances of nineteenth-century burrowing, the lack of knowledge and system, the brutality of the rape, the never-to-be-repaired hymen of history. They rattled through the city wall.

Liverpool Street brought him the anxiety of drunks: flushed sweaty young bruisers loud with beer and the muttering, stumbling figure that would take offence at an unintended look. 'Wotcher bossin' at? Gotcher eyefull. I'll poke it out,' an unconscious old unease for the malignant stare. Now the line ran alongside Roman Road and under the river Lea to swing Northeast into Stratford Marsh. If he could have jumped off here, Meepers thought, as they clattered up into the night, it might have saved him a lot of walking. As it was he got meekly out at the station leaving the train to scurry off towards Epping Forest, its deer and sleeping cattle.

Outside he was horrified at how much had been done since he was here last. Would he be able to find his way in? A giant had laid about him laughing, with his sledge-hammer. Then he had come back with Herculean bucket and spade and built great sandworks, bastions and ramps which had set fast baked by the summer sun and mixed with his own piss and spit. Where there had been cottages and barrows in Little Nell proportioned streets there were ziggurat car park and supermarket, launching pad flyovers and moonrocket tower blocks among which clung the old Royal Theatre, a shrunken decayed shabby gentlewoman dwarfed and pitiful. The foundations for all this must reach the earth's core. Nothing could be left. In time Meepers stopped himself from groaning aloud as two middleaged railwaymen in uniform, drivers going home, rolled past him deep in garden lore.

'She'll miss it.'

'For a fact. Many's the time we've had a lovely feed of beans from them over the fence.'

'Some do marvels with a window box.'

'A wooden box to carry her out is all she'll get up there.' It could have been heaven the way they cast their eyes up.

'Always supposing she don't get blown up.'

'They've learnt a thing or two now it's too late. They make them all electric since Ronan Point fell down.'

'Go on!'

Meepers stood with his back against the fence and considered. Perhaps he was already too late. He turned away from the giant's concrete causeway over a humped bridge and down past the old Great Eastern railway works. Long hours with the Ordnance Survey map had made the area as familiar as the lined layout of his own palm. The works were deserted, idle now like the Thames itself. The ghosts of old steam engines still snorted and whistled behind the fence where they had come for doctoring. Soon the moon he was relying on should heave itself far enough into the sky to light his way. Here the fence was gap-toothed beside a solitary crumbling house that had once been an off-licence. A second board was loose and could be swung sideways. Meepers stepped through from the road and pulled it back into place behind him. As he did so the nearly perfect host washed its light over a lunar-scape as desolate as its own.

Now on the ice the boys bind shinbones on their feet, skim like waterfowl stiltlegged on ironshod skipoles. Breath steams. Cries echo across the frozen marsh; bounce back from the city walls. Some slide on icesleds drawn by companions; others tourney for broken heads. Winter.

Scholars and tradesmen, their fathers on horseback watching, play at football. Now springs the spray in the gardens. Young lovers sigh, fowls flaunt. Spring.

Maidens dancing under the moon on the warm, short grass. All day their brothers wrestled and shot winged arrows at the butts. Girls' voices in the round. Summer.

Run to the public cookshop for we have unexpected guests. Among the winecellars soldiers, strangers, poor and rich find for their palates, day or night, coarse fare or fine. Then to the smooth grass of the horse mart. Nags amble, cart-horses plod. A shout. Up on the glossy backs climb the boy jockeys. Ears prick; limbs tremble. Away go the chargers. Fall.

I have been to coffee with my young lovers who ain't lovers at all I find, at least not in the accepted by our generation sense or of each other. At the end of today's lecture (no Meepers) they came up invisibly hand in hand and asked if I would like to see how the poor live. They gave me an address in Hammersmith and a time for their at home: 8.oo. How did they know I had nothing better to do? Perhaps I have that look of a loose end waiting for someone to gather it into a love-knot. Anyway it was a fine evening and an outing would do the car good. It was covered with a glazed spit or shit from the aphids in the lime trees overhead that resisted all rubbing and made the windscreen prettily but blearily crystalline. The aphids seem like most plagues to be pollution immune. Their little green lungs (I imagine a sort of horny bellows for Lilliputians) must be able to transmute carbon monoxide into chlorophyll to leaf out their wings. I believe rats and mice are similarly and plaguily endowed.

So I drove out to Hammersmith with the help of the *A to Z*, the laterday Antonine itinerary. What have been terraces of handsome porticoed clerks' houses let out for dozens of furnished tenants each are being busily gentrified, sold as luxury flats or choice town houses for forty thousand quid, a lifetime of paying for a roof and a few walls to support it. I was amazed at how far it had gone. And the people who used to live there I suppose are on a housing list somewhere, in temporary accommodation or gone out to the fringes of Slough. Yet there's the dilemma: the houses look so much better for it, re-plastered and painted with coy peeps of Habitat curtaining at the windows, even a couple of tubbed orange trees to one. Why couldn't that have been done before? Because the tenants weren't paying enough. But they didn't earn enough to pay any more. And so it carousels with no one able to stop the machine and say, 'Right everyone get off and we'll give it a push and start again.' I begin to sound like Wandle. But it was impossible to shut out. At one point the streets are a simple grid layout, renovation had got halfway down the street to the crossing and the other side was untouched. It looked like a faked up advertising before and after montage. In the retouched there were no kids on the pavement and no walkers either. Across there was hopscotch chalked on the stones, wheeling bikes, neighbours on doorsteps, fuzzy black heads and lank tow heads side by side; shouts, football endangering the windows. Disraeli's two nations were living end to end, the length of a train apart, not speaking and so easily defined that if you'd been god playing with a model you could have picked up each figure in turn and put it in its correct end of the street without hesitation or even hearing a word spoken.

Would Robin and Jenny live in such a street? No, their address led me out of the remediable into an area of workmen's cottages, with a front garden one pace wide, gothic bow window, two doorbells. Robin let me in and I followed him through a door at the foot of the stairs. Jenny was there and a very stunning black girl, Martha. The doorbell had woken a baby, somewhere. Martha disappeared and soon it stopped its wailing. I'd brought a bottle with me and I gave it to Jenny. She produced glasses which were as assorted as I'd known they'd be and an efficient corkscrew. I'd pitched the wine carefully around a quid so's not to give offence either way. The room was very small and I was glad of the open windows to let out a certain claustrophobia of embarrassment. Martha came back with a mite of baby and sat with it in her lap, one palm cupping the cricket ball head, so small it must have been premature. It was a pity there was no Velasquez present to do a black madonna and child.

What could we talk about now that I was there? I wanted to ask about their threesome but that would have looked (a) nosey and (b) not at all cool as the jargon has it. So there are two women, a man and a baby living together and none of them is married or kin (except the baby and mother I suppose). Related they must be in some way. Robin showed no sign of being the baby's father. How to open? 'Nice place you've got here,' would have been thought sardonic. Suddenly I had a vision of assorted pockets like this all over the city. Very few of our students can get into a hall. Most of them have to live somehow like this. Compare and contrast with the convivial fraternity of a Camford staircase with college servant to sweep under the bed. The Paris of Abelard or Villon must have been like this for its clerks warming their hands and ink at a midnight candle. 'Who lives downstairs?' I tried.

'Mr and Mrs Drinkwater. She has bronchitis and coughs and wheezes a lot. He looks after her now he's retired. We've got a bathroom up here but they've only got an outside loo so he's put up a roof so she won't catch cold when she goes out to pee. That sort of thing.' Jenny. 'It always reminds me of that bit in Hamlet "so loving to my mother that", what is it? "He might not beteem the winds ... visit her face too roughly." '

'Like my old man, hell,' Martha puts in fiercely over the baby's head. She has a strong cockney accent, second generation immigrant, probably born here. 'Nothing was as rough as him. An earthquake would have been gentle compared to how he thumped her till her teeth rattled and we kids all screaming.'

'Is it their house?'

Robin laughs. 'The landlord's. We get the bathroom because we pay through the nose. He'd chuck the Drinkwaters out if he could and make twice the money. The other day he came knocking on the door wanting to look around. I stood in the door and said it wasn't convenient: one of the girls was in the bath.'

'He mustn't know about the baby you see.' Jenny. 'No pets. No children.'

'Won't the Drinkwaters tell him?'

'They might if they didn't hate his guts and if they didn't think Jenny was their long lost daughter.'

'Oh Robin,' she protests. 'Their daugher married an American during the war and went to live there. They have snaps of their grandchildren all over the place but they've never seen them.'

I dredged up the term 'G.I. bride' but suppressed it. What was the good of offering it to these children.

'Maybe General Amin would think I was his long lost daughter if I took a trip out there. Some hopes.' Martha is strong and bitter like plain chocolate.

'How long do you think you can keep him from finding out, the landlord I mean?'

'How long is long?' asks Robin. 'You have to live the days as they come.' He pronounces it almost as 'coom'. 'Something will turn up as the man said. It always does.'

Are they feckless, rootless? They're certainly kind and easy with each other as far as I can judge. Perhaps rubbing so close together you'd have to learn a kind of gentleness or roughen each other into running sores. Is that what we really mean by urbanity? Overpopulate the rat cages and the vermin fall to fighting: the future that the think-tanks prognosticate for us. But need it be so? Eighteenth-century London was pretty cramped too. The rich could get away to country seats in the summer leaving the rest to sweat it out on gin to oil the chafe of too close proximity. But it was cultural shock too that had to be deadened by drink: the rush to the city of thousands of youngsters, runaways, unemployed, dishonoured, Fanny Hill and her brothers in crime; the sexual and social mobility that followed the Restoration; the religious cool inevitable after a century of holy warfare.

'When I knew I'd fallen and I'd want to keep it Jenny and me decided we'd have to get someone else to share the rent. Til then we'd had one room each. So we advertised and along came Robin. One day there's a knock on the door and the landlord on the step. "You've got a man living here," he says. "My brother," says Jenny. "Oh yes," says the man. "Can you prove it?" "Prove he isn't." Then he says, "There's more wear and tear with three. Repairs cost more." "How much," says Jenny 'cos suddenly she sees what it's all about. "Four," he says. She beat him down to three. Money!'

'And here we all are.' Robin gets up and stands a moment with a hand on the door, looking hard at me. Something clicks in my head about his look and his stance. He's telling me or asking me something. He has very red moist lips which might be my wine.

'Tell me about the old guy who knows so much,' Robin says when he comes back.

'Who do you mean?' But I know very well of course.

'Meepers-creepers. What's his name?'

'Meepers? You tell me!' So I dodge and accept complicity in whatever it is he's up to.

'Why should he want a course like that? Ouch, sorry.'

'I agree,' I laugh. 'Why should he. Who can tell why people do things. Why do you?'

'I have to keep up with my subject,' Jenny says. 'If you're not on top your classes scramble all over you. I know. I did the same. You get stale teaching. Sometimes you have to stop handing it out and rethink your material.'

'I'm just one of nature's dropouts,' says Robin. 'I can't settle to anything. I take odd jobs and make a bit of bread and then I do a trip or a course. Why not yours. I might go out to Africa next and drive trucks for famine relief.'

I envy him this mobility. What have I done but go from school to university, to research and back to university, at the front of the lecture room instead. I'm monkish and cushioned. Only a natural asperity (waspishness?) stops me becoming the typical portly S.C.R. denizen. And I meant so well. I meant to stay fresh and anarchic, not to be taken over. Yes I know one can do miracles in one's own back garden. No doubt Meepers could furnish chapter and verse on some dessicated Saxon hermit who never moved from a rock off the Hebrides and waited for his students to paddle out in their coracles to sit at his grimy feet while his thought went winging about like a sea eagle. I feel mine has bogged, sog and sag, twin genii of my unrubbed lamp, and I feel it most in my lost passion for this city that's become an old wife I hardly speak to except to complain my dinner's cold and dry.

Death eased himself out of the bristling fur and thumbed a lift ashore in a bale of cloth glad to shake off the monotony of shipboard. He took a refreshing draught from his porter and skipped nimbly away among the wharfside crowd til he found an overseer to take him home to his master's house for the night. He dined under the table on the plump white thigh of the merchant's wife then crept back into the shop where he curled up with a snoring apprentice warm until daylight when the shutters were opened. Death sprang up merrily determined to get as far as he could by nightfall. Burrowing deep he was carried off by a peasant buying a length of woollen to take back to his wife from the sale of their produce. It was a fine hot summer's day. Death chirruped and rubbed the legs of his metallic carapace together as he rode along. He would spend a few weeks among the harvesters gathering his strength; then for the city. So he sported and grew fat with the country folk, danced at their harvest supper, grew drunk with them and was carried to bed. On Sundays he fidgeted through the sermon. Once he got into the pulpit in the priest's robes and looked down on the congregation. He leapfrogged among the choir and see-sawed on the organ keys. The countryfolk thought him a harmless little fellow and laughed at his antics before his black footprints appeared in their faces. But winter was coming and that was no life for him among the frozen fields. He must get into the warmth and safety of a town before the snow fell. So he journeyed more quickly in a pedlar's pack to Goose Fair where a squire bought him in a nest of ribbons and rode on with him to Southwark.

But when he reached London Bridge rumour and fright had got there before him and the drawbridge guards tried to keep his carrier out. Death leapt on to the guard's collar and watched as he shook his pike at the young man. Then Death marched smartly into the guardhouse and sat down to a game of dice where he tilted the bones so that they fell skull uppermost. Now he had the whole city before him for larder and playground.

Easily he leapt from one upper storey to the next across the street, creeping into the bedrooms and the bed curtains. Death held all men in common. He was as at home in the ermine of Guildhall as in the rags of the Marshalsea. He gambolled in the counting house. Sometimes he lay between lovers, fed on their kisses and bathed himself in their sweat. They laughed to see their blood mingled in him. He wandered in the scent-less poppyfields of the Turkey carpet and sat beside the silently gushing fountain in the tapestry Garden of Love.

When his young were hatched Death sent them out along the roads to frolic in other towns saying there was no room for them in his capital where men and women died too fast to satisfy his hunger. No sooner did he set his love bite on them than they sickened and cried out against him and wouldn't feed him on their fevered blood. Now he drove about the streets at night in the deadcart huddled close to the carter against the icy air, drinking deep to keep out the cold til the carter slumped in his seat, the whip fell from his hands, his blood congealed and Death was driven to horseflesh to nourish his cold shell. He became the greatest landlord in London. Rich men bought up acres of fields and gave them to Death who danced at midnight on the common graves. They built chapels and set monks to sing his praises. But he was growing old now. He no longer leapt so swiftly from man to man. For one thing the men were fewer, the streets empty and of those still alive many he had tasted and found too sour for his palate.

As the days lengthened his strength began to wane. Teeth and claws menaced his slower progress. No sooner had he settled down to feed than they clawed and bit at him and gave him no peace. For he was grown fat and clumsy as an alderman. The rats were too sharp for him. Dogs flicked him away contemptuously. Where could he find something that would let him stay still and suck in nourishment. He took a staggering leap from the rushes to a cradle. The woman was rocking it with her foot as she twirled her spindle, her eyes on the lengthening thread. Death sighed happily and prepared to pierce the tender young flesh.

'Filthy thing,' cried the woman and seizing him between finger and thumb she cracked him between her nails. There was hardly enough blood in him to leave a smear.

Who would bother to guard such a waste? Even so he must be careful at first til he was sure. Meepers stood quite still and listened. Far off there was a sound of singing backed by traffic on the main road and the occasional clangour of the underground. Perching himself on a severed chunk of masonry he unslung his duffel bag and began to take out his first needs:

a pencil torch, a map, a pocket compass. A glance at the load-stars of Ursa Major and the polestar helped him to align his compass at once so that he could swivel the map to marry with what he saw around him. This industrial desolation had once been marshland cut through by the rivers that turned the many mills on their banks. Through here the Roman road had run before the railway drained the marsh for works and sidings. He was sure of it. The projection from the ford where the road stopped just before the river led straight across here. He stared into the dark and then down at his map and compass, willing the contours to appear. The huge sheds that had housed the engines were all gone, together with their tracks and turntables, defunct as the watermills. Would the marshland bear the weight that they meant to lay on it now? Foundations would have to be sunk deeper than ever before, destroying all former traces as they plunged down. The rows of nineteenth-century workmen's cottages were going too, replaced by estates of flats and maisonettes. An exploding gas-main had ripped the desirability out of the few highrise towers and no more had been built. But the scale of the borough had been destroyed. It was the first of the Essex villages, two-storeyed where the city rose to three or four, a natural halt on the road to the barbarian capital and later miller for the city's flour. The millwheels were too recent to turn in Meeper's head but he looked up towards Llugh's town on his river and saw its waters leaping in the jewelled dragonfly sunlight.

No sound had come to alarm him with discovery. On this side work wasn't far enough advanced for there to be anything of interest to vandals or robbers. Tractored earthmovers brooded under the moon, abandoned dinky toys for giantlings or illustrations for a science fiction where machines had replaced humans. But Meepers had no fear nor blame for the huge toys. They were merely overgrown shovels and he would use them himself if he needed to, though carefully of course not to destroy the delicate artefact time had built up in the earth, the memory bank that would give you the answers as long as you asked the right questions in the right way but whose subtle structures could be so easily and irrevocably destroyed.

Now that his eyes were accustomed to the moonlight he could pick out landmarks. First he must get across the line. It was so peaceful under the moon that he was almost unwilling to begin to disturb the night. Then he thought of the earth-movers starting up in the morning, the men in orange helmets and mud-stained overalls who would direct them to sink their teeth and take great bites of the layer cake. The picture of them crunching through a metalled track, chewing up shards and coins with the pounded gravel, obliterating ruts and runnels, wheel and hoof scars, smashing through a stone coffin to devour the bones, got him to his feet. Meepers slithered down the embankment and stepped neatly between the rails, his calves jellying as he poised over the live one pencilled in by his torch. Everywhere features were being flattened so that the new face could be built up; even so he had to follow the thin beam very carefully.

It was a mile and a quarter to where the road had last been found. Between ran the Lea itself, Pudding Mills River, City Mills River, Waterworks River, all easily forded, and Carpenters Lane. Meepers worked his way towards the furthest corner of the waste where his projected line should cross and came up against a fence. This was the end of the old railway works. He travelled along it, feeling the dead begin to stir under the soles of his feet, his torch the dowsing rod that divined where they lay. The main road was very close. The two roads must have met here and then divided again for their separate journeys. The clank of armour and the swirl of chariots drowned for him the hum of cars on the dual carriage-way. Careless with excitement following his pin-point of light, he didn't see the pit that seemed to open to engulf him. The torch flew out of his hand as he fell but he hung on to his bag and fetched up still holding it, on his back, his head muzzy from a bang against the pit side, winded but with nothing seemingly broken.

For a moment he lay there recovering. By some jog of

memory he thought that he was wounded again at the bottom of a trench and that if he looked up the light would catch on the po-shaped helmets and gunmetal covering him. As his head cleared he saw there was nothing but a pale inkwash of sky. The pit was full of shadow. Meepers stretched his arms above his head to try to measure how far it was to ground level. Miraculously he seemed to have fallen about twenty feet with no great hurt except for a strange sensation in his mouth he couldn't account for. The torch was still alight, shining under a puddle he had been lucky to miss. He moved the beam over the earth faces. He had fallen into something remarkably like a game trap, nearly big enough for an elephant but probably meant for concrete footings or a sunken oil storage tank. There was no way out that Meepers could see.

The odd sensation in his mouth bothered him. He hadn't tried to open it since there was no one to speak to. Now he did and felt a sudden collapse. His top plate had snapped, no doubt as he banged his head. Gingerly he manœuvred out the two halves, wrapped them in his handkerchief and put them in a pocket. Then he opened his bag and took out his trowel. Steps would have to be cut in the earth wall so that he could climb. It would be long painstaking labour and he had better begin at once. First he would pick out a handhold as high as he could, then the first foothold at knee height. The torchlight passed over the face and picked his spot. Meepers began to chip away at the hard earth, slitting his eyes against the flying fragments with the torch held in his mouth. After half an hour when he was spreadeagled against the wall his trowel struck with a different sound and dislodged a fragment with a jerk that nearly tumbled him off. Meepers followed it to the bottom and hunted it down. It was a sizeable shard of red pottery that only needed a rinse in the puddle to bring up its fine Samian gloss. His hands trembled as he dried it. Here was proof of a sort and now there was no opportunity to follow it up. He was tiring rapidly and he still had to get to the top.

When he reached it after an eternity of picking out foot and handholds with the beaked trowel, he hauled himself over

the rim and lay still until his heart stopped thudding and the
sweat had soaked up into his clothes. Now he had to go down
again for his bag but first he lowered the torch on a string to
where the shard had come from and knotted the depth. It
needed his last strength to send his weary body down into the
pit, to sling the bag round his neck and haul himself up from
clay rung to rung, cut deep so that the edge wouldn't crumble
and drop him down again. Even so he felt one shift under his
feet and moved quickly up to the next while his belly sickened
and the sweat poured in rivulets down his skin.

The moon had set. Meepers' legs were trembling so that he
dared not cross the line again but struck up North, directly
through the deserted yards. He heard running water, another
branch of the Lea, and followed along its bank where it
ducked under a bridge carrying a branch line. A rat scurried
away as he passed and plopped into the stream. At last he was
beyond the works in a playing field where only goalposts stood
up without menace against the sky. For a while he lay under a
tree on the soft grass with his bag for a pillow. Then he
struggled on again. A dog barked from behind a hedge.
Meepers paused at a gap and peered through. Caravans were
parked. It was a gipsy camp site. The dog ran out from underneath one and shouted at Meepers to go away. The caravans
were luxurious motor trailers with ruched and frilled curtains
in the open windows. Enviously he pictured the families
asleep in their bunks before he plodded on. He was too tired,
even if he could get to the other side of London, to try to
break in to his lodge. He turned back again towards the playing field to sleep under the tree. He was nearly there when the
headlights gunned him through.

Then I took my old cloak about me and loped long legged
down Cornhill and by little lanes to Westminster. I climbed
upon a cleft in the wall and lifted my limbs among the leaves
that overhung the garden where ladies' garments glowed with
gold and young lords' locks lingered to their shoulders. They

have meat at every meal and their breasts are white as blanc-mange. The poet came to the pulpit and preached above them. Envy nudged me to listen to his lines. He was mild in his manner and gave them sops to soothe them. The gentlefolk laughed gaily, sitting in the sunshine. He lisped his lines, jolly in his jingle learnt in foreign lands, in snippets and gobbets too small to make a whole coat, but enough for a purse full of pence at his belt.

Perilous it is for a poor poet who lives upon London, hardly staying his hunger with bitter ale and bread while he prates of the poor. But he who follows fashion, rhymes instead of reasons, shall feed upon white flesh, be furred in frost and foul weather. So Envy prods me, singing psalms for my living, no better than a beggar, making and remaking, stitching and patching my shroud all my dark days til Jesu sends me his summer.

I was up late working on Francis Place, the London Corresponding Society and the development of eighteenth-century radicalism. Got very excited over London's support for the American colonists in the War of Independence, 'no taxation without representation', London refusing to let the press gang recruit in the city, all going on while capital's empires were being built up at the same time. Suddenly it was gone one and I thought I ought to go to bed. (The suspense is killing you but don't look at the end.) Would have liked to play some music to unwind but remembered the lease. Oh where's Ranelagh and Vauxhall Gardens, and perhaps most evocative of all the Cherry Garden in Rotherhithe now a warehouse, where you could wander til dawn, dancing and drinking or just being seen? Now the Sunday sober city shuts down at midnight apart from those seedy down-at-heel haunts for tourists round the Dilly. I bet Times Square is just the same, bedizened with empty Kentucky Fried Chicken cartons, coke tins and neon lights constantly spelling out their runic message of missed letters, exhortations and stop press news in

Hottentot click language, unintelligible as speaking with tongues. No wonder most of us Cinderella home from that ball. Anyway no night music small or great, after eleven o'clock so I got a small Scotch and a paperback and stood for a moment breathing in the draught from the window and listening to the street turning in its sleep, glad I hadn't got an early lecture but another whole day to tie up the radicals. And then the bell rang.

I was so thrown at first, I wasn't even sure if it was phone or door. I stood there gawping at the phone thinking (I suppose simply hoping) it was you from across the ocean to say you were on your way home. Alright, I know that's blackmail. Then I realized it wasn't a double ring and that it must be the door. I went to the intercom lifted it and said 'Hullo.'

A man's voice said my name with that inbuilt rising question mark. 'Yes.'

'Oh it's the police, sir. I'd like a word with you.' Again my head was full of thoughts of you but this time of terror, accident, plane crash, broken flesh stabbed by twisted metal. I ran down to the door. Just one uniformed bobby on the step.

'Sorry to disturb you, sir.'

'That's alright: I wasn't in bed. What is it?'

'A Mr Meepers sir ... '

'Meepers? Good lord. Where is he? Is he alright?' I was so relieved it didn't occur to me to query why Meepers.

'You do know him then, sir?'

'Yes, of course. Has he had an accident?'

'He was picked up in suspicious circumstances by a patrol car and taken to the nearest station. At first he wouldn't give his address but when he realized he would be charged he gave this.'

'Where is he now? Does he need bailing out or something?'

'Well that depends. First we'd like you to identify him as to who he says he is.'

Then I saw what I'd missed before: the patrol car at the kerb. 'I'll come at once of course.' We drove through acres of empty streets. Anyone looking in, I thought, as I stared out of the windows would think I'd either committed a crime or was a plainclothes man. St James's Park was a lovely lit scenario for a dream, Midsummer Night's or Acis and Galatea's, the ducks no doubt making their drowsy duck notes if I could have heard. The roses in Parliament Square were all sucked of colour by the lights and the Houses looked more like illustrations for a sauce bottle than ever. County Hall exhibited a sort of foolish podgy dignity like a matron overblown in pastels with its green and pink floodlighting. Then it was a discreet flash of his elegancy Paul's once we were past the concrete droppings of a monstrous clay cow that's the National Theatre and next city cliffs, fascist classical of bank and brokers', and the carrion-eating insurance businesses that make us shit with fear (what would your family do if ...) then gobble up our gilt turds. We ran through Jewry where the orthodox were able to put on the light now if they couldn't sleep, down a long straight road of handsome terrace houses badly gone to seed with weedy front gardens and crops of bus tickets in front of classical façades that would fetch 50,000 in this area, and then we began to twist and turn among ever smaller, darker, more deserted backchats where the subscribers to Place's corresponding society, or anyrate their inheritors, were snoring towards tomorrow. And all the time I was trying to think what the old fool might have been doing. Did he live out here? Why wouldn't he say where he did live and what should I say? Had he been caught cottaging and indeed could you be done for that anymore? I couldn't remember. The car squealed on the still warm tarmac: the young driver fancied himself as Jackie Stewart or Stirling Moss. Perhaps he'd missed his true career and should have driven ambulances.

Finally we screeched to a halt outside a lit building that could have been a wing of the municipal baths or a Bethesda. The copper sitting in the back beside me whose sweat smell had enveloped me like an animal threat all the way along got out smartly and held the door for me, a courtesy or a way of making sure I didn't bolt though I'd have had to be Houdini to do so scrambling along the back seat. Only now it occurs to me that I could have tried to open the door on my side. We pushed through a swing door with a murmured, 'If you'll come this way sir,' to urge me along and into a white tiled lavatory without tiles or runnels but a table and chairs, with Meepers in one of them. He stood up when he saw me and holding his hand in front of his mouth he mumbled something I understood as 'Good of you to come'. I looked at the table. There were papers and a couple of tea mugs down to the dregs, a collapsed duffel bag and what I thought must be its contents, among them a brush and a trowel, a chunk of red glazed pot and what seemed to be a snapped set of false teeth.

She was called Flower de Luce because she was found on the doorstep of a pub called that, wrapped in her swaddling clothes against the cold and carried off like that, a bundle of soon needing washing, to the nuns' orphanage whence she fled at the age of nine to live off her Becky Sharp wits as beggar and petty crook. For three years she dodged the gallows until at a blossoming twelve Fleming Froe seized her as she was making off with a pie and brought her back to her stew house called the Cross Keys from the sign painted on its front wall looking out on the river. The river stink and that from the beer garden nearby seemed to be healthy for the child grew in beauty like her name. Fleming Froe had pointed out to her that she could be sent back to the nuns where she would most certainly be shorn and vowed in a twinkling, or caught thieving and hanged, or lose a hand or die of gaol fever in the Fleet or Marshalsea. Or she could learn the easy life of a whore. The threat although veiled was clear enough and in any case life in the house was secure and friendly after the life of the streets and softer than the chores of the spital. She was made to wash and Fleming Froe examined her to make sure she had no burning sickness. Her rags were burned and she was given new clothes. For the first couple of months she was handmaid to the older girls and learnt her trade by listening to their gossip between custom. Fleming Froe kept a good house and so her prices were high, her clients rich merchants or young gentry who often came in drunken gangs together to finish off an evening. Sometimes Mayor Walworth himself who owned several of the houses would bring a party of friends. Flower handed round drinks and sweetmeats at these occasions and on one such, a little drunk herself, lost her chastity, as the nuns called it, while hardly noticing it go. She became quite a favourite with the Mayor who slapped her bottom and pulled her ear and said she was a good girl. Luckily she didn't seem to become pregnant easily. Some of the girls fell regularly every year and were exhausted into retirement at twenty. In winter in the evenings they sat together in the upstairs parlour waiting to begin the evening's work with their skirts flung back from their spread legs to let the warmth get to their thighs and cunts and chattered while Alisoun who had a voice as sweet as her lute sang them some lovesongs. Then they aired their dreams and told fortunes: who would marry a rich old merchant, who would be a courtier's mistress, (a pity the King was still so young and it would be years before another Alice Perrers could become the royal concubine lending prestige to the whole profession), who would get a returning soldier with a French noble to ransom, who would die in the street. Sometimes on fair days they would be taken by the young sparks to the bear baiting where muzzled bruin with his hind legs in a bag would be set on by a dozen yelping hounds and rend and growl in rage and misery until they wore him to death. Other times they would cross the bridge into the city to watch the street plays or to see the new mayor sworn. It was at the swearing of Sir John Philpot who had taken a fleet from London and scoured the sea of pirates capturing all their ships that Flower found herself being preached against. 'Make way for Lady Meed,' cried a mad old fellow in mock humility and the people began to laugh. But as he went on with his ramblings their laughter turned sour and they began to pelt her with filth from the gutter. When Fleming Froe heard she said the girls weren't to go abroad unattended and hired a returned soldier, with one arm and a half of his own and the rest a spiked wooden stump, to escort them. Twice a year a friar came to bless the house and to hear confessions. Fleming Froe paid his fees and the girls entertained him with wine and Alisoun's singing. They were all shriven clean, did their light penances dutifully and the following Sunday went demurely to Mass and made their communion together, shepherded by Fleming Froe who swore she was lucky and that they were the best and cleanest girls in the world. She took no more for their board than statute allowed and only half what they made for she said that money to spend on trifles made young girls happy and the happier, the prettier, the more they made for themselves and her. Some of the older girls when they had saved enough, moved out to lodgings of their own where they could set themselves up and when their more permanent arrangements fell through as they did from time to time they would send to old Froe to tell her they were available again. But Flower liked the communal life which was so much like a happier convent. She had known beggary, fear and hunger and had no wish to get acquainted with them again. In another way too she was different from the rest: she didn't fall in love. The others were in and out all the time, sometimes unsuitably with penniless apprentices or clerks and then Froe scolded them for giving away their goods free. That was all very well for married women who could afford to be generous to their lovers. Flower was never tempted. She listened to their yearnings with amused incomprehension. In bed with a customer she was amiable but uninvolved and when more was required of her she could simulate passion or fear as required. If women had been allowed to act or had a guild of their own she could have played the virgin or the magdalen equally well. Yet perhaps because of this, young men and old too professed themselves in love with her. Flower laughed, not unkindly, and took their presents. She began to forget that she had ever been hungry, for Fleming Froe was a good manager and there were no lean seasons for her household as there were for most of the rest from New Year to summer. Then it was best to stay home for the hungry roamed the streets and sometimes came in a gang to beat on foreigners' doors and shutters. The war was going badly now and a new tax was to be raised to pay for it. When the tax-gatherers came to count heads most of the girls had gone into Kent for the day leaving only enough for show.

They rode past St George's towards the village of Camberwell in the forest like ladies going hawking, with Onearm as their squire. They would buy milk, cheese and cherries to supplement the spitted fowls and wine they had brought with them. The girls ambled along under the trees on their borrowed nags, glad to be away from the stinking streets for a day.

It was some time before they realized that they seemed to have the countryside all to themselves. No one was working in the fields that supplied the city with most of its food. When they reached the village there were the usual hens and pigs in the street but at first no people until they became aware of women and children watching them from windows and doorways. Onearm was sent to knock and ask for milk.

'And for the men,' called Alisoun and giggled. The men were all gone down to Dartford he told them when he came back.

'They said John Ball had rung their bell and the men had gone to free Truth,' said Onearm. The girls rode on for their picnic a little dampened until Alisoun led them in a chorus of 'Merry it is while summer lasts'. When they had eaten in a clearing they stripped and splashed in a stream while Onearm kept watch and after they fell asleep together under the trees on the grass taking care to keep out of the sun for fear of an ugly brown skin. When they awoke the midges had raised weals like lovebites on their white flesh. They jogged home still a little sleepy and some cross with the June heat.

Flower had enjoyed her day out but it caused her to listen more carefully to the whispers in the streets. The tax-collectors hadn't been pleased with Fleming Froe's almost empty house and had threatened to have her flogged through the streets at a cart tail for a bawd and a foreign witch. The close air was thunderous with discontent. Rumour said that the rebels were marching on the city from every side. Flower de Luce felt a trembling like that the other girls described as love. An army of them was at Blackheath by the Wednesday; another was camped in the fields beyond Aldgate. The King had taken refuge in the Tower. Crowds gathered in the streets outside the gaols and shouted at all who went in and out. Fleming Froe called the girls together. Bad times were coming and they should go to friends, relatives, lovers til it was all over and they could come back again. 'I shall stay,' said Flower. 'I've nowhere to go anyway.' But she wanted to drink this strange excitement. With Onearm she went out on Thursday morning down to the river to watch the boy King sail up in his barge to meet the rebels. Before it could land at Greenwich it went about and sailed back to the Tower with the King still on board. Flower heard the roar of rage. Around her they said it was not his fault, him being only a boy, it was his advisers. 'But you'll see: John Miller will grind them small, small, and there shall be no more gentlemen, nor bishops neither and all their goods shall be given to the poor.'

Flower hurried back to the Cross Keys. Onearm had vanished, to the alehouse she supposed. Fleming Froe shook her dewlaps when she heard. 'It was bad to disappoint them. It will only make them mad.' Flower wanted to go out again but the old bawd held her back. 'Let's eat and drink. Who knows when we shall again. Who will pay us if there are to be no more gentlemen.' So they were sat to eat when Onearm came in swaying on his feet. 'They are coming,' he hiccupped. 'They have opened the Marshalsea and the prisoners are leaping in the streets.' Now they could hear a roar of voices. Old Froe fled to the attics. Onearm tottered away. Flower was alone. She could hear them enter the street, the steady tramp, the splintering of wood as they began to go from house to house.

The door was torn open. 'Here's one,' called a voice and half a dozen helmeted heads looked through the door. She turned to run up the stairs but a hand clamped round her ankle and dragged her down. The men were all armed and armoured as if they had come from France. 'Is this Walworth's house?' asked their leader. 'Aren't they all?' answered another. 'What shall we do with her?' asked a third. 'Let's see how the rich feast,' said a fourth and spilled out his genitals while the others held her down. He flung back her skirts and drove between her thighs quick and hard till he spent himself and fell back limp and another took his place. 'Good flesh. Rides well.' 'Come on Jack!' they urged each other. A trembling took hold of Flower's thighs. She began to buck a little. 'Hold the hot bitch,' cried their leader. 'She shall make her vows to the Great Society and cry for us as she has cried for her lords,' and he thrust himself in to the hilt, drew and thrust til moans and at last a long scream of pleasure forced open her mouth as she arched and squirmed against him. The man let her go and she fell back. They laughed and clapped their leader on the back. 'Take her outside,' he ordered, 'then fire the house.'

As the flames licked up the bottom storeys Flower saw Fleming Froe at an upper window but there was nothing she could do. The crowd cheered as the old body flung itself from the fire's hands to the waiting cobbles. 'You come with us,' said the rebels and hoisted Flower on a horse. Later she was to remember only a series of pictures: faces thrust under hers, the bodiless head of an archbishop that floated on a pole, the bridge flung open and the crowds beyond, all in any sort of order, flames ravishing the great Gaunt palace in the Strand while the gaolbirds from the Fleet danced free, and the screaming figure of a looter who had dared to sully their cause with stolen silver in his pocket as he was thrust back into the flames, ('We are seekers of truth and justice not thieves or robbers') and the cries of 'Treason' when they thought the King was cozened. She slept somewhere in straw and in the morning was put on her horse again, 'for you are our meed and that is all we ask,' and climbed up on a balcony to see when her old master Walworth pulled her new Wat from his horse and they stabbed him, and how the boy King deceived them all with his fresh looks and his pardon, saying he was their captain and spurring in front of them. Flower came down from her vantage and slunk her way home for she knew then how it would go. There were the still-smoking ruins of the house. Somewhere old Froe had kept her silver. She poked among the remains till she found the pots twice fired fallen from the attic with the pennies in them run molten into a lump she could sell. It was enough to set up her own business as bawd and bring up the boy who should be no man's Jack.

He flung up his arm against the lights as against a blow. The car skidded to a stop and doors opened and shut with a metallic slam. Boots crunched shadowy bulks towards him. Meepers' first instinct, like that of any other animal, was to run, reinforced for him by memory. With an effort he kept still and lowered his arm. They were young and fit and they had a car. He saw it mount the pavement after him and pin him against a wall.

'Bit late for a walk isn't it?'

'Where've you been Dad? What's in the bag?'

The knowledge of his toothlessness stopped him from answering; in any case it had been too quick: he had no story ready on his tongue, the tongue that would lisp wetly without his top plate, making him a figure of fun, Gummy Adams, sadly obscene. A torch travelled up and down his muddy clothes and settled in his eyes.

'Lost your tongue. Let's have the bag then.' A hand came at him out of the torch light and he gave it the bag which was passed to the other uniformed, capped figure.

'Here's a funny old lot. What's this for then?' The trowel was held up. 'Bit late for gardening or were you going to lay a few bricks?'

'Name and address ... ? Alright, play it the hard way. Let's have you in the car.' A hand took his elbow and propelled him along. The door was opened and he was stowed inside with one of them beside him. The driver got into the front and radioed his summary of the happening and the time. It was useless to try to jump out. There was nowhere to hide. He must think of a story, an alibi as it used to be called. At worst he was a trespasser but that he thought was a civil crime and any prosecution would have to be brought by the owners of the land who were, he supposed, British Rail. And it would have to be proved. There had been handsome stamped metal notices on the railway embankments when he was little saying that trespassers would be prosecuted but they never were. Meepers in grey flannel shorts, shirt and school cap with a red badge had hung about bridges and stations with his contemporaries collecting the names and numbers of steam trains, creeping through wire or hedge to get a better view and chased off by station staff which had only made it more exciting. Now the steamers were as forgotten as stage coaches. He must try to concentrate. They were drawing up in front of a police station that was old enough to have a blue light.

Inside he was given a kitchen chair while the patrol made their report. His bag was emptied on to the table. The duty sergeant picked among the contents as if they might suddenly speak. 'What's this lot then squire? What's it all about?' Meepers said nothing. The sergeant whose blue shirt was deepened to cobalt by sweat in halfmoons under his arms and the neck of his vest at the back, reddened angrily. 'Name and address?' His biro poised for Meepers' answer. 'We can still charge you, you know, even if we don't know who you are. We can charge you as a suspected person, as a vagrant, as loitering, as being in possession of suspected housebreaking equipment,' the trowel again, 'and so on. Now turn out your pockets. Let's see if you've any I.D.'

Meepers could have laughed as he did as he was told. He knew there was nothing. Surely they didn't expect to catch an old soldier like that. A few coins were all that he placed carefully on the table, and the handkerchief. The sergeant picked up the trowel and unfolded the handkerchief with its point. 'What's this then? Well, well, well! Lost your teeth have you? Is that why you won't talk? Well let me tell you

144

Grandad we don't have any pride here. Besides this is only half a set. You've still got the bottom lot. And if you can't talk perhaps you can write, if a scruffy old tramp like you can write, the which I doubt. Now, what is it to be: a bit of verbal or a cell and the magistrate in the morning. You must have been up to something you're ashamed of.'

Meepers felt his mouth open to protest but the broken teeth looked up at him and he shut it again. He must think. 'Right. Vagrant. No fixed address. Sling him in number three.' Meepers reached forward his hand for the pen. Misunderstanding the nearest patrolman knocked it down sharply so that it struck the side of the table. The stinging pain brought tears unwillingly to his eyes. He couldn't stand there weeping. Again he stretched out his hand. The sergeant held down the handkerchief with the trowel. 'Name and address.'

Perhaps they wouldn't check very closely. The accommodation address was too risky. They probably knew them all. Kept a list in fact. He would have to chance it. His right hand sketched writing. The sergeant slid pencil and paper across the table. He wrote. The handkerchief was pushed towards him and he wiped his eyes. Already the bruised vein on the back of his hand was dark and swollen. 'That's a start. Chalmers check this out.' A patrolman took the paper into another room. His bluff was to be called. 'Now what about this lot?' the sergeant indicated the bag and its contents. 'What were you doing and where?'

Meepers was silent; the tears were wiped from his cheeks. But he mustn't be charged and put in a cell. Not that. He gestured for the writing materials and when he had them wrote simply: *I don't remember*. The patrolman stuck his head round the doorframe.

'Sarge. Could you come here a minute.'

'Look after him,' said the sergeant, nodding at Meepers and went out of the room. Suddenly he felt very tired and closed his eyes against the station lights. Behind his eyelids he could see the broken pink plastic bridge with its too regular, too white, small tombstones. What could happen now but further humiliation? Time passed. They seemed to have forgotten him.

'Somebody claims to know you,' the sergeant had come back. 'He's on his way. Feel like talking now?' Meepers closed his eyes again and leant his head against the wall. The room was in danger of turning slowly; the walls and floor had a tendency to flow up towards the ceiling as if he was drunk. Without opening his eyes he tried to identify the sounds that came to him, to stop himself from slipping away completely. Sometimes the door was opened and policemen came in to report. Once the sergeant sent a couple off to look into a reported disturbance: the world was beating his wife or breaking up his happy home after a skinful. Someone knew him and was on his way. But who? Meepers knew no one.

A fresh commotion made him open his eyes: a patrolman followed by a figure he recognized and another patrolman. So this was it and he was to be humiliated again but worse now. And then there would be the charge and the cell and the man would be rid of him at last. No doubt he would see to it that Meepers lost his job as well. He got wearily to his feet and with a hand over his mouth he tried to speak. The man's eyes had gone to the table: he would see everything.

'My dear chap, are you alright?' The voice was slightly higher, the accent more affected than Meepers remembered. 'What on earth are you doing here? I thought you were giving a lecture somewhere this evening.'

'You identify this man, sir?'

'Yes of course. What's this all about? He looks in rather a mess.'

'A patrolcar picked him up in suspicious circumstances and he refused to co-operate. Wouldn't explain himself or give his name and address. Naturally the officers thought he was either a vagrant or up to something. We found these tools on him.'

'I see. Well it's all quite simple really I expect.'

'When asked to explain himself he wrote this.'

'I imagine that's the true explanation then. Mr Meepers is a distinguished specialist in archaeology. He frequently gives lectures to local societies. The tools are what's used for digging, remains, you know Roman walls that sort of thing. Nothing sinister about them. And indeed if I'm not much mistaken that's a bit of pot.'

'Are you an archaeologist then too, sir?'

'Good lord no. All too early and fragmentary for me. No I'm a historian as a matter of fact.'

'Could I have your name and place of employment, sir?'

'Well you've got my name already or you couldn't have found me. I'm employed at Queen's College, University of London, like Mr Meepers.' The sergeant wrote carefully as a man used to a heavier implement than a biro.

'So you confirm his identity and address. Now what about this?' He pointed to Meepers' message with his pencil.

'I confess I find that rather puzzling. He went out, as I said, to give a lecture, taking those along for demonstration purposes. Now clearly he's had an accident of some sort and that's caused him to suffer a temporary attack of amnesia. What we don't know, and neither does he, is how that happened. Was he attacked, or knocked down by a car or what? That's the question. You can't remember old chap, can you?'

Meepers shook his head. The fellow was chattering like a magpie but it seemed to be working.

'Have you been living together long?'

'Only while my wife's away in America for the summer. It seemed a convenient arrangement.'

'But you've known each other for some time?'

'Yes indeed. Quite some time. Now I really think we should get him home. After all he's not a young man and he's clearly had a nasty shock of some kind. I think he should see a doctor.'

'We could fetch the police surgeon.'

'I wonder if that would be best. Or whether I should let him have a night's rest, what there is left of it, and let the doctor have a look at him tomorrow. There could be a spot of concussion.' He had contrived it, Meepers thought, so that he had become an object and therefore of lessened interest. It was hard to imagine this inanimate bundle with the initiative to commit any of the crimes that had been possible for him an hour before. 'After all you know where to find him if you need to talk to him again. Perhaps with a rest and some tablets he'll remember what happened. If the car that brought me could take us back ... ' Miraculously he was being eased out of their hands. Meepers almost held his breath so that no one should realize he was alive. His things were being put back in the bag and handed over. 'I'll carry that.' A hand was under his elbow helping him and indeed he felt old, tired and a little ill. He had just enough will left to take up the ridged halves of his plate and put them in his handkerchief. The coins had been given to him to pocket. The hand dug into his elbow in unnecessary warning. There was nothing he wanted to do or say. Once again he was stowed in the back of a police car with a claustrophobic presence beside him but now whirled back towards the city walls, along the Roman road that lay vibrating under the modern tarmac skin of the burning tyres, over Llugh's river, by the bowed bridge past the abbey where bony prioresses lisped in provincial French to their lapdogs, through vanished Aldgate and the blizzard ash and flame of a thousand fires long out, by cheapened London Bridge broken down for ever, with the chunk of red Samian invisible in the bag yet warming him like a ruby.

PANTOMIME

Enter Richard Whittington in his house in a carved oak chair, very old and shrunken, in a furred robe with a puss upon his lap which he strokes constantly. Enter to him Robert and Hugh apprentices. They go upon their knees.

WHITTINGTON. Stand up lads, stand up.

BOTH. Thank you, sir.

WHITTINGTON. Now what can I do for you? Speak up and don't be afraid.

HUGH. We have come to ask your advice, sir.

WHITTINGTON. My advice. What about?

ROBERT. We want to know how to become rich, sir.

WHITTINGTON. And you couldn't ask a better man.

BOTH. No, sir.

WHITTINGTON. Well now. First you must choose your parents carefully.

BOTH. Yes, sir.

WHITTINGTON. The country gentry are best. That will give you a coat of arms and some breeding. Then you must get a rich uncle, preferably a merchant adventurer with interests in foreign trade and a marriageable daughter. She needn't be pretty but best if she's not positively foul. You'll need to entertain Kings, ambassadors and people who'll be useful to you and nothing turns the stomach like a sour face at high table. Then you must run for office in your guild and begin to lend money at a reasonable rate. These two courses will make you powerful and bring you more money. Now you must begin to give money away.

HUGH. Give it away, sir?

WHITTINGTON. Certainly; where it will be noticed and enhance your name. You must build and endow for charity, both lay and clerical foundations so that no one feels left out and you're assured of treasure in heaven and a good name when you're gone. All this will show confidence and that breeds more money. Look round for something permanent to leave like a library or a college. Meanwhile of course you mustn't neglect your trading and wheeling and dealing over the wine cups with your fellows. That should do it I think.

ROBERT. But, sir, what about the poor boy who's bullied by the cook and runs away to London with nothing to his name but a cat and hears the bells telling him he'll be thrice mayor of London and marries his master's daughter and sends his cat on a trading voyage and makes a fortune ...

WHITTINGTON. ... and ends in Bedlam or Newgate as a madman or a rogue or both. Mark you I've always had a soft spot for cats, particularly pretty young shes.

*

I lied of course but I was/am prepared if they inquire to claim you in common law. The patrol car dropped us at our door. I said thank you and good night and loudly: 'Soon have you in bed,' to Meepers, got out my key, opened the door and steered him inside and up the stairs. All the stuffing had gone out of him. I think he wanted to argue but he hadn't the strength or the teeth. I sat him in a chair and got us both a large Scotch. I needed mine, I could feel myself starting to tremble with reaction, and I was damn sure he did too. It was hard not to go to the window and peer through the curtains to see if they were still there waiting at the mousehole. Meepers downed his drink and hoisted himself to his feet. 'Look,' I said, 'you can't leave. If they're still suspicious they could be watching, so you might as well sit down and have another drink. I'm going to. It'll do you good.' And I sloshed us both out another big one. He took the drink; then he got up suddenly. I'd been a fool not to think of it: the release of tension and the drink must have gone straight to his bladder. I told him where the bathroom was and he was away some time. When he came back he was much more composed. He walked to the different lamps and switched them all off except the one where I was sitting. For a moment I thought he'd gone quite bonkers. The thought even crossed my mind that he might try to murder me, but when the rest of the room was in shadow he sat in the deepest part so that I could hardly see him and then only his profile. 'You'll forgive me. This is the only way I can talk,' he said. 'I feel I must explain unless you want to go to bed.'

'No, no,' I said, 'say on. I'd like to know why you picked on me and why you had to and so on.'

'I was born in this square,' he said like an oracle out of the dark. 'In the house next door. That's why I was able to remember your address so easily. When you sent back my article I wasn't sure whether to try to see you at Queen's or at your home. I looked you up in the phone book. When I saw where you lived I couldn't come to see you here. It was too risky. I was living in the garden hut at the time. You never go into the garden do you?'

'No, I don't seem to have the time.' The whole conversation was so bizarre I didn't quite know how to keep up my end of it. At the same time it seemed impertinent to ask questions. I just had to let him go on. I supposed it was all true. It would have been an incredible thing to make up.

'At present I have some temporary accommodation but not an address I could give the police. I didn't intend, when I gave them your address, that they should come and disturb you. I thought they might simply check that there was such a street and number and let me go, or not even do as much as that. Therefore I feel under an obligation to you.'

'That's alright. I've never cared for coppers. I don't like to think of anyone in their hands unless they've become such a homicidal menace that there's nothing else to be done with them.' It was odd: as we talked all our past strange conflict was present with us, making us choose our words very carefully, animals proferring ritual appeasement gestures because of the animosity still crackling in the air. I knew there were things I positively mustn't ask. He was handling the lack of tooth very well, no doubt helped by the drink.

'I'd been on a little expedition looking for some pieces of archaeological evidence that were in danger of being lost by redevelopment. Technically I suppose I was trespassing. I'd had an accident. I fell into a pit, very careless, and it took me some time to get out. Amnesia seemed the only explanation but it wouldn't have stood up very well without your help. Again I must be grateful. I found this.' He rummaged in his bag and brought out the bit of pot. 'First-century Samian. It proves the early date of the settlement and the road. Beautiful isn't it.' He burnished it gently with a fingertip. 'Yet completely commonplace, mass-produced in Gaul. The Romano-British equivalent of grey Minyan. Not at all what I was after. A bonus if you like.'

'What are you after?' I risked.

'This is the beginning,' he said touching the piece of red ware again. 'I'm really interested in the end as perhaps you remember.'

'Yes,' I said hastily. 'I do remember vaguely but I don't really understand.'

'The real question is in the future not the past. Or perhaps I should say it's the same question with a gap of fifteen hundred or two thousand years between the asking. Does it survive?'

'I don't follow quite,' I said, feeling a fool of course. 'What?'

'The city, this city. This concept or medium of civilization. Did it survive? Or did it collapse and the rats and rabbits nibble among the ruins of an unburied Pompeii, along with a few impoverished squatters? Or did it hold out, make terms with the barbarians, carry on, modifying itself in the process, maintaining a high degree of civilization? Was there in fact no break in continuity?'

'Is that what you believe?'

'I think the evidence points that way. But I want to be sure.'

'How can you be?'

'I think a computer could do it. If it was fed all the information I think it could say yes or no.'

'But what difference would it make?'

He got up and went to the window but didn't touch the curtains. 'If the city survived then I think it will again. It's threatened, you must see that.'

'By pollution and the collapse of its internal workings and services?'

'Yes, but much more by lack of faith. We are out of love with it because we're out of love with ourselves. What might really destroy us is human self-disgust.'

' "Where every prospect pleases and only man is vile." '

'Something like that. There's still a belief, largely unacknowledged in this half of the century but powerful, possibly even more so for being unexpressed, that the Roman Empire was destroyed by decadence.'

'*The Last Days of Pompeii*, and Gibbon's fault too for inventing such a marvellous title as *Decline and Fall*. Most people don't realize that for him the fall was Christianity and

152

think he must mean orgies.'

'Suppose for a moment that the Dark Ages hadn't been so emotively labelled, that they had been called something neutral, post-classical or early medieval, would we have found them so hard to understand?'

'You think the division has been overstated, that it was possibly no more traumatic than the British loss of empire.'

'Exactly.'

'But we have lost something. We no longer know who we are or what we should be doing. We don't seem able to stop the process going on and on like an amoeba constantly splitting. Now Scotland and Wales want to go. Next I suppose it'll be Cornwall. They've certainly got as good a case as any of the others. Shall we split North and South, Severn to the Wash? Little countries the size of the smaller African states jostling each other in one tiny island and getting more and more ingrown and insular. Perhaps all the dialects'll revive and we'll become unintelligible to the rest of the English-speaking world. And the miseries will sit around saying it's a judgment on us for our moral decadence. What you're implying is something very un-English, that ideas matter, that we are what we think we are.'

'That we may become what we think we have been. But also that if we have misinterpreted once we may be doing so again.'

'We must go to bed,' I said then. 'Can you make do on the sofa? We haven't a spare room I'm afraid.' Was that lousy of me? I suppose it was after what he'd been through but somehow I didn't want him sleeping in our bed, not because it's Meepers but anyone.

'You've been very kind,' he said in his rather formal way. 'I owe you a great deal.'

It didn't come easy to him to say it, not just because of our row, if you can call it that, but because of a stiffness in himself, as if all the normal means of communication have rusted up. 'There's something I'd like,' I said.

'Oh yes?'

'That,' I pointed to the red fragment. 'Not necessarily that piece, another bit would do. I want to think about it.'

'Of course. Take this one. I have a note of its find spot. By itself it isn't much use to me and in any case I know where it is if I need it.' He almost smiled.

So I have the piece in front of me as I write. It has the ambiguity of all polished things or people. The curve of it is almost a smile of its own. If landskips can laugh why shouldn't artefacts?

Shall I grave my name in glass or on the stone walls of this bell tower? Do I stand in danger of death for love or politics? Such questions occupy me by the hour for what else should I do except sometimes walk a little on the battlements but inside the wall so that no friend is tempted to my rescue. Perhaps I stand in danger for hate not love, and envy that I should still be loved of he if not of she. And this is the bitter irony of my case that she for whom I am accused has long since had no thought for me but laughing affection as for a puppydog, a species lower than man that gambols for his amusement and is fed tidbits at ladies' hands. She loved me once or said she did or let me say so when we stood together in rank and age but the way up is on a man's shoulders treading him down and so from rung to rung rising to the topmost until all tumble down like children who play ring-a-roses. Now a bloody dance has joined their twelve hands together for their fall and I was forced to watch it from this grating and feel for my own neck if it should be the next. Then I saw her fair face which I had loved so long and long ago drained of its blood by the leaping veins. Poor country mouse that the city cat caught on his hip and overthrew. My heart is broken, my youth and lust died together so that only my body remains as if living which may itself soon be dead. Yet even in this danger I will not crouch or kneel, admit tyranny to be the right of a prince's reign nor lie that black is white or the lecher a lover. Cato loved the commonwealth so that he escaped by his own hands out of

Caesar's rather than live where liberty was lost. So I might escape this prison rather than suffer out my life in chains or with the memory of that bloody sight that sticks in my head. Shall I ever see May again or with any joy? Shall I love again? Love should be a commonwealth, and the lovers its fellows but only in Utopia which is indeed Nowhere, the island, perhaps shall such things be and no more falseness but only honesty. Yet the hunt is not so easy left though the deer is down. Once as she sat sewing she pricked her finger til it bled. Then I wrote that she thought she had my heart under her hands but now I think it was her own self-wounded that must love Caesar and no less or rather perhaps be loved by him. We say women are changeable but princes whose every whim makes law wax and wane as the moon and draw the foolish waters after them that have no will of their own. The fickle common sort too who would not cheer her when she was crowned but called her whore loved her at death because she died bravely and they saw that the lechery was not only hers as the barge went out each night with lute and song and dancing until dawn while she paced in terror within these bitter walls. The King's wrath is death. There are wolves among the silly lambs but I cannot praise them. And yet I too have hungered after honour, have been touched by the fire of glory and even now swing between desire only to be safely out from here, retired to the country, and fear to have no more part in the world's business, between resolution never to love again for the pain it brings and fear to have no more pleasure. My falcons fly up; they take the dove and bring her to my feet. They will return to my wrist while my friends crawl from me like lice from a dead body. As I walk on the walls I hear the sailors' cries, the watermen calling while my ship steers between rock and rock and I despair of any port. Yet I suffer less than my father did for his honesty, racked and imprisoned in this same Tower. God keep my son out of our footsteps and if I die give him a quiet life retired from London and the danger of courts.

*

He woke early as usual, startled for a moment to find himself on a strange sofa under a blanket. His memory of the night before was full of holes. He had got drunk and talked too much in a confessional dark but he couldn't remember what he had said or given away. He had made a fool of himself and must get out quickly before the other awoke. He dressed as silently as possible. On a table lay the piece of Samian. Meepers reached out to take it. Something moved in his mind. He thought he had given it away last night though he couldn't remember why. Well it was a kind of payment and made him less in the man's debt. He wished he could remember what he had said. With his shoes in his hand he crept to the door and let himself out. It was quite late for him. He put on his shoes outside the flat door in case anyone should be about and notice his stealthy behaviour. He must walk out confidently in case the police were still waiting. His clothes were a mess of dried mudstains and he must do something about his teeth. He was hungry too. Meepers set off for Charing Cross and his suitcase wardrobe. A bath and a breakfast later he shut himself in with the yellow business section of the telephone book and ran through the list of ever open dental repairers until he found one that was prepared to make him an immediate new plate on a Saturday. Oh the convenience of a city: first that it should make false teeth at all and then that it should renew them in a twinkling when broken. Meepers joined a waiting room of furtive unfortunates like himself all trying not to be looked at and when his turn came tendered the pink and white halves wordlessly.

'Take an hour,' said the white-coated technician. Meepers nodded. It must be a strange job; like those other strange jobs, undertakers, grave diggers, makers of glass eyes and wigs. So many things were needed to hold the human psyche together, to camouflage senescence and keep us in apparent working order as long as possible. Sometimes he was thankful that his wound was only invisible, except to X-ray eyes, shrapnel and not a lost limb or fire-scarred face. He waited outside the nearest public library for it to open and then made his way to the stale newspaper room where he could prop himself behind the news for an hour. There was the usual collection of sad job and flat hunters, a few genuinely in search of information and those who had come in to rest their feet. One or two of them smelt with the undefinable sourness of the uncleaned, unwashed. A woman in a black hat and coat with thick black shoes and grey anklesocks muttered her way from one obituary column to another looking for someone to mourn or the magic phrase that would unlock silver caskets 'something to his advantage'.

Meepers wished he could be sure what he had said under the influence of shock, fatigue and a dose of Scotch. He thought back to his fall and traced the sequence of events. Why had the man come to what could only be described as his rescue? Surely Meepers' hold over him wasn't that strong. Would the police bother with him any more? Probably not. But he was on file, in their books, perhaps even being keyed to disc at this moment to be stored in a computer memory bank, an electronic impulse somewhere that a stab at the nerve ending in a helmeted blue figure could re-kindle. He could change his name he supposed but that would be inconvenient and in any case he was attached to it, had managed to keep it all his life even when everything else had been sheared away. It had been strange to be taken in a double sense home, to see inside an identical house to his parents' and realize how it must be now. They had climbed the handsome staircase to what had been the drawing room. On Sunday mornings he had gone with his parents and little sister Florence, who had died of diphtheria in the year of the General Strike so that for some time after he had a half belief that it was General God who had stricken her like a plague of Egypt, to the nineteenth-century perpendicular church in its flowery yard in the next square which supplied most of the hatted and gloved congregation. In spite of Florence he had joined the choir, mingling fear and sexual repression into devoted attempts to climb the mystical ladder into perfection. It had come as a shock when his parents were killed away from home taking shelter in the underground from an air raid to learn that they had never owned the house merely rented it in those now incredible days when agents were only too eager to press the keys into your hand in return for a week's rent in advance.

They made good flats he conceded. In the end he had rattled about in the empty house and would have been happy to give up part of it. But the rent for such a flat as the one he had been in last night was beyond him even if the landlords hadn't been determined to get him out. To Meepers it had seemed over-furnished to an excessive degree of comfort. He detected a recent female presence he thought though no doubt such a man would be lavish in his tastes even without a woman to egg him on. A faint perfume had still hung in the air and there had been bottles and jars in the bathroom whose labels had proclaimed that they were for women. Whatever else he thought of him Meepers didn't think he was homo though quite why he couldn't explain to himself, more what used to be called a ladies' man. The remembered fragrance moved some atrophied member in his personality. He felt its tweaking with surprise. The last time he had had a woman had been on embarkation leave over thirty years ago.

He had given him the shard but how much else, what power over him with his confidences? Well he would soon tell by the man's behaviour. He had seen Meepers three times now at a disadvantage; once more and Meepers might lose his hold over him and with it his job and the opportunity that Queen's offered. The hour was up. He would go and get his new plate and spend the rest of the day in the Reading Room. Somewhere there must be accounts of when the first station was built on those marshes and what had been found then.

King Elizabeth turned himself sideways and edged his skirts through the narrow door to the privy stairs that led down to the waiting barge. Mother of Parliaments what a day to go by water! Still it was better than the slow progress through the stinking streets with the litter jolting and the stockings of the gentlemen pensioners spattered to the thigh with muck after the rain. Well there was nothing for it, if he wanted more funds he must show his bosom bravely and hope it wasn't too goosefleshed in the cold or the Spanish ambassador (or was it the French?) would be sending home secret despatches again that it was growing wrinkled. Sometimes it was a pity that Walsingham's spies were so efficient. After all their prince was only asking for the money on loan. His people should have it all back after his death. He wouldn't leave it to that puling maiden James; it was enough for her to have the throne. Here was young Blount to hand him aboard; a hand to kiss and a little dalliance were called for besides he liked to feel the soft brush of a youthful moustache on his skin that was still plump and white through the efficacy of powdered chicken bones mixed to a paste with mare's milk. The third oarsman's blade was a little askew spoiling the symmetry of the present oars: a trifle but it irritated Elizabeth out of his usual public graciousness. 'The barge she sat in burned on the water,' indeed. Today it was as sluggish as a pregnant sow and they would miss the tide at London Bridge. Elizabeth shuddered. Going to the city always called for his best performance, the heart and stomach of a King. This morning his womb felt like a shrivelled grape contracted to a knot of pain. But he mustn't show it. He must put himself about, smile, give kind words to every old soul with nosegay and petition, praise the halting Latin of the Colet's boy who would quake through his eulogy and be first gravely gracious to the Lord Mayor and after a little flirtatious. He was definitely out of sorts and must send to Buxton for a flask of medicinal water. The barge shot the bridge to the cheers of the citizens who had braved the weather. Yesterday the Commons had been tiresome and he had had to woo and command alternatively, with swooning and flashing eye, to bring them to heel. The cheering was growing louder and there was the Tower which he never entered without a shudder of remembrance. From there he would ride to Guildhall where he would get the traditional cup full of coins and must repress his fingers' itch to count them at once and give thanks from a loving heart instead. Elizabeth stood up and let his ladies arrange his skirts becomingly. With any luck there might be a new song upon his virtues: 'Bonny Bess' or some such. He was feeling a little better already and wasn't that the sun? Perhaps the fresh air had done him good after all.

So in the morning he was gone, as I should have guessed he would be, while I snored my head off. Indeed he might never have been there at all except for the piece of red ware which I saw in the morning light has a raised design on it of flowing animals and plants which could be some sort of hunt though it's hard to tell with only a fragment. I've tried to remember all we said but I must have been a bit sloshed because everything's a little hazy. Then I decided to go into Queen's even though it's Saturday. There were some things I wanted from the library to prepare Monday's lecture. The place was even more like a morgue. Emery was sourly holding the fort. No students were in of course. I sat in the library for a while until it began to get me down. It must have been the influence of last night's conversation plus a bit of a hangover but I felt like the last man in the world, holding up civilization alone in a dusty library at the heart of a huge empty building with a city running down around it; much the same feeling you must have had I imagine as the district officer in some distant outpost of Empire, wondering if Queen Victoria was dead or not and the only white man for miles around, nothing but bush or jungle, flies and monsoon at midday, with a touch of some variegated fever to excuse your nightmares under the mosquito netting. We mustn't be ungrateful for the Empire: it brought us that black madonna Martha and her baby who'll grow up, with any luck, as a cockney and give us a shot of the thick warm blood we need since ours was thinned and chilled by Depression and war. The thing that Meepers said that most runs in my mind was the bit about self-disgust, being out of love with ourselves. The dregs of Christianity. By that I mean the last to go, the muddy bitter lees in the bottom of the barrel after anything that might have been palatable has been drained away or evaporated by science, reason or experience. Centuries, nearly millennia, of belief in original sin and the corruptibility of the flesh must have eaten into the communal psyche and been culturally passed on from generation to generation so that we still believe that the pursuit of happiness and reason is wicked, though we call it selfish, and say it lacks moral fibre or spiritual depth or some such and shows no concern for others, as if you can't have parity of happiness as long that is as it's yoked with reason.

I left the library and poked my head into the common room more for something to do than expecting to find anyone, and there was Wandle and Ponders. With me we made up the three wise men of Gotham spinning in our bowl with a ballast of old wine since the sherry was out. I took a hair of the dog and felt better. 'I hate the place when it's like this,' I said. Then to Ponders: 'How's George?'

'We're switching him on again today. That's why I'm here.'

'I've got a barmy student,' I heard myself saying and then couldn't stop, 'who thinks George could solve a problem for him.' I saw Wandle begin to give his full attention and Ponders was hooked at once.

'What sort of problem?'

'Did London become uninhabited at the end of the Roman occupation or not?'

'That's rather off your usual beat isn't it?' Wandle asked.

'It came up in the course of discussions about the eighteenth-century's contribution to civilization,' I lied easily.

'But there's more to it than that surely?' Wandle probed.

'Just a minute, I'm afraid I don't quite understand. Do you mean there's some doubt about what happened?' Ponders puzzled.

'Apparently,' I said. 'As Wandle says it's not really my field but it seems to be one of those questions that was always assumed to be settled and now people are asking it again. Could George tackle it?'

'He could come to an informed conclusion if he was given all the available pros and cons.'

'Like the doomwatch people: the committee of Rome or whatever they're called. Only in reverse.'

'Yes, that's it. It would make a good exercise for some of my more advanced students to have a crack at. Get your chap to set it all out and then we'll decide. Lots of detail. Comparisons with similar happenings. His suggested weighting for the various elements and so on. If he can be bothered to do that much work. I usually find that they like the idea but when it comes to the hard graft they're not so keen.'

'I think this one'll be bothered. He's a patriarch, one of the very mature students.'

'I still scent a mystery,' said Wandle. 'Why should he want to know? I'll grant you the value of pure knowledge and all that but I'm not convinced this is just research. Is it?' He was grinning away at me, waggishly, insistently, and I found myself for some unaccountable reason unable to lie coldbloodedly or barefacedly, or however it's done, but anyway straight to him, out of respect for his curious perpetual innocence. 'No, not quite. He believes that it's a prognostic. From it we can judge our own future.'

'Aha!' Wandle pounced. And then he said: 'Well it may be no more unreliable than any of the other attempts at prophecy. Mind you I don't promise to accept George's findings as a lodestone for the future. There's human will and knowledge and they're always variables aren't they?'

'Oh yes,' says Ponders. 'If they weren't there wouldn't be any point in prediction would there?'

Next was brought in the Ranter Coppe who as soon as he was in the chamber began to throw fruit and empty nutshells about to signify his opinion of the Committee of Examinations and to swear horribly. He rejects the digging – levellers as he calls them, who dig up and plant the wastes for common use but not their doctrine of purity, equality, community, and is against all property saying, 'Have all things common.' He says God is in tobacco and righteousness in lewd kisses. His *Fiery Flying Rolls* are condemned to be burnt and he committed to Newgate. These Ranters have no name for their sect but 'my one flesh' and they call each other 'fellow creature', and God, 'reason' or 'nature' or 'the high-leveller'. This is the result of those who petition Parliament to allow the presses to print seditious matter, to undermine the Commonwealth and the true faith of the people, that lack of respect for property, that idleness and lewdness which spread everywhere and in particular flourish in London among masterless men and vagabonds of acute wit and voluble tongues such as visited this Coppe in prison, with smoking, swearing and laughter.

Part of his mind registered that they must have earned overtime to drop that lot on his doorstep on a Saturday. He had been away less than twenty-four hours and now there were baulks of timber, bags of concrete, planks, a heap of sand, fortifications moating the lodge from the public and from Meepers if he lingered. Order had caught up with him again. The lodge, his princely tenement was to be done up for a park-keeper and his wife. Meepers had one more night in it. He couldn't even risk that the workmen wouldn't be back on Sunday. In the morning the hermit crab must drag its vulnerability to find another shell. For the first time too for weeks clouds had eaten up the sky. The damp presage of autumn came on the wind. Then it would be winter and where should he go? If he kept his job at Queen's he might afford a room somewhere. No, he wouldn't give in, not just yet. Some Russian whose name eluded him had lived out all winter, and a Moscow winter, in the base of Lenin's tomb he thought it was.

But in the morning when he began his search with his possessions rucksacked on his back he found it wasn't so easy. The Albert Memorial had a solid marble base welded to the earth. No little door opened Alice-like into a refuge for him. Meepers sat on a bench while the Serpentine ducks gave themselves a meticulous morning preen and ran his mind through London's monuments. There were the rooms above Admiralty Arch whose windows flared in the sun setting down the Mall but it was madness to consider them though the flow of traffic under his feet and the view of the Square with its fountains and columns caught at his imagination. He might live for a time in the tower of a blitzed city church if he could get in through the barred heavy doors but stairs and floors had probably gone and the flags of the ground level would be green with damp. Worse, there was only one way in. He was too old for the liftless heights of Nelson's Column or the Monument. Cathedral and Abbey were heavily populated with staff and tourists all year round. There was the dome of the Imperial War Museum but he wasn't sure if it had been repaired since that attack of arson and in any case Meepers felt himself shudder a little at the thought of the history of bloody death that would lie under him at night and the dreams it might engender in his private memorial of shrapnelled braincells. There seemed no lodging for him in London; no tomb that would take him in. Even to lie in the Tower these days was an impossible feat with its ice-cream and hamburger stalls, hotels, children scrambling on the cannons, fancydress tourneys in the moat. What empty unvisited monuments were there left? He stared across the lead skin of water under the changed weather at the cityscape on the skyline where the unclassic symmetry of the glass and concrete office batteries were drawn two dimensionally on grey cartridge paper. Meepers got up and heaved his pack on to his shoulders.

IV

Babylon

A postcard. 'All well. Love as ever.' A hatful of rain in a
desert. What am I to make of it? I turn it all whichways to
fathom out some coded message. And then the picture: a
visual parable of Venus and Mars their legs bound by love's
ribbon while another love disarms and teases the proud war-
horse to look coyly down his sleek nose. Behind, gorgeous
bedclothes have been draped over the ruins, with Venus' white
shift. From the Metropolitan Museum. There I've sucked it
dry unlike Venus' breast that drips a liquid pearl for love. I
tear again at the words to wrench a double meaning from
them. How can such a card come back from my storm of
pages? I prop it up in front of me hardly knowing which
side's message I like best: your calligraphy or Veronese's.
Both are equally mysterious and seductive. Together they
make an unbeatable double-headed coin I must win with.
Enough of that for the moment. Something I didn't tell you.
I don't think I consciously suppressed it. If I did it was from
myself not you. Anyway now I remember that on the way
back with Meepers in the copcar, and maybe on the way over
too but I didn't notice, we drove past the street where I was
born and that I haven't seen for years. I don't even know if
it's important. The city is a twenty-mile diameter cake. We
live in a wedge of it, travel into the centre down our narrowing
triangle, know the base of our portion, the bits to right and left
of us but no further as if it were indeed boxed, sliced into
these segments by uncrossable chasms. Immediately opposite
this wedge beyond the centre is the bit where I was born,

where Meepers was fossicking about for his Roman remains. Yet it's further from me than Paris. And there we were driving through it. No, we couldn't have done on the way out. Surely I would have seen. We must have come back a different way. I've never taken you there have I? I wonder why: I'm not ashamed of it, at least not consciously. But it had become irrelevant and perhaps that's wrong. I haven't been back, to tell the truth, since my father was killed. I went back for the funeral and didn't know what to do or say, not out of grief but because I'd lost the idiom and the fact that it was a funeral made my tonguetie worse because they all thought it was grief, and I was taking it bad but brave as I should and my own sham upset me. His mates had had a milkfloat made for him all in flowers and I thought it vulgar being at that stage of self-consciousness where only the visually chaste and elegant is acceptable. But if you're going to mourn why not do it with a flowery popart rather than the non-committal but dreary wreath of dusty laurel. He didn't win any laurels except from his workmates and the one that should have come from me. He was run over going to work one morning with only a few years to go til retirement. I've told you about my Nan, his mother, who brought me up. After she died we lived alone together for a couple of years until I went to college. Since then it's been buried in me. What a strange thing for Meepers to give back.

I met him today in the corridor. He seemed alright; none the worse for whatever it was that really happened to him. He wants to take me to some exhibition. I've told him about the computer you see and I think he wants to thank me though he's such a strange chap it's hard to be sure. Robin and Jenny listened dutifully to me on attitudes to the American War of Independence in London but after all my preparation it wouldn't take off: I was dull and I knew it. When the lecture was over and I was making a business of collecting my things I saw them talking to Meepers who was rolling his eyes as if cornered. I laughed to myself, knowing how hard even he'd find it to evade that awful innocent persistence.

And now I take up your card again to see me to bed: my cupful of water, my nourishing drop. There's one thing I don't understand, I mean another. It's posted in the wrong city. Were you down there on a trip? But why take a card from New York elsewhere to post? Is America so destitute of cards? I can't believe it. Then it is indeed special and a picture with meaning. Lay aside war and you'll give me your naked self again. But I don't know who I'm at war with, except perhaps myself and you. The ache for your body and I mean that, not your mind or anything platonic, is intolerable tonight. I shall go to bed with a Scotch and try to resist the urge to join all the other sad wankers jerking off in their bed-sitters, moaning into the pillow lusty fantasies as they rub and sweat over a pin-up, pull-out, scrawled sweetmeat, remembrance of things past or today's pleasure.

Ah, Cremorne, what pleasurable anticipation dwells in your name alone. Let us enter the gardens just as the evening is beginning when the daytime denizens have gone East in calico and the penny steamer taking with them both the too old and the too young. Not that some of both do not find their way here. There goes old Lord B, seventy if he's a day but not dismayed in his search for a handsome companion and there cluster the blackamoor children begging with their dogs and monkeys who cling to the silk skirts of dressy females until their victims throw them a coin. Here are casbahs, alhambras, harems set amid the plash of waterfalls, the shimmer of flower-beds, under the canopy of the sky, lit by a thousand sparkling gas lamps. It is the magic garden of fairy tale. Here the gay ladies, the prima donnas, Cyprians of the best sort, gather to stroll and dance to the waltzes of Strauss on the elegantly arcaded dancing floor strung with coloured lights. They greet each other with cries of 'My dear!' compare toilette and coiffure. Silk and pearls are de rigueur for them and their escorts are wealthy men in top hat and tails. As midnight approaches they hasten like so many Cinderellas into the waiting hansoms to drive to the supper rooms, the most favoured to Kate Hamilton's where business and refreshment may combine, then on to Mott's for a little light gambling. There they may be joined by a seclusive or two with their paramours. These are the highest ranks of the profession and it is because of their charms that the torch of Hymen frequently burns dim among our aristocracy. Theirs is the box at the opera, the carriage in the Row, the handsome apartment and sparkling jewels that a man should lavish on his new wife. They provide our English courtesans equal to those of the Second Empire: Nelly Fowler of the divine fragrance, and the inimitable and vivacious Skittles who may be seen by the fortunate roller-skating with such grace in the new rink or riding her steeplechaser in Rotten Row.

We left our Cyprians at Kate Hamilton's whose mistress reclines her twenty stone on a dais amid her favourites, sipping champagne and shaking with laughter but with a constant eye on all comers to her establishment to see that only the best are admitted. For the others there is the parade of the Haymarket and Regent Street where according to the hour of the day and the state of the pocket the girls and their gallants may step aside for a cup of bohea or glass of gin. These girls will have spent the morning gossiping in dishabille in some house in Brompton or St John's Wood or with their bullies or fancymen in a furnished apartment in Soho. The fancymen are their lovers and bawds while for business they are visited by those with whom they make assignments at the music halls or outside the fashionable clubs.

Yet our wanderings are not done for there are girls of every price on the streets from the amateur dollymop, the shopgirl supplementing her earnings who is usually clean and content with a modest price, to the girls who live with their young pickpocket lovers in a thieves' rookery where they become as adept as their partners at rifling a gentleman's coat, and the miserable diseased wretches who will retire to a back alley with a labouring man for a few coppers.

Whence comes this army of gay women, some married some

single yet all equally degraded? All are seduced governesses or the daughter of clergymen so they will tell you. An untold number of British women are ever in passage through prostitution. Each year over two hundred infants are found by the coroners to have been murdered in London by their parents, aside from those who are made away with before birth whom no man can number.

This is not the limit of the Paphian resources of our capital for there are the Margeries or Poofs to supply more depraved tastes. It is hard to believe but that these are driven by vice rather than want of employment. Like the seclusives and prima donnas they are the playfellows of the rich and frequent the cafés and theatres among their female counterparts. Others gather near the picture shops, flaunting their fashionable clothes and offering their services by waggling their fingers under their coat flaps.

Whatever you desire then may be supplied. Should you have a passion for virgins there are those whose maidenheads have been twice nightly taken and sent the next day to a quack for repair. Should you wish to be caned as you were by the big boys at school or by governess the cat is ready to the hand of a lusty guardsman or a nun in the habit. Would you improve your French or German at lessons with a native you may do so. If your taste is for the coarse featured and dumpy our Irish cockneys will supply it; if for a genteel milliner, dressmaker or shopgirl, flitting along Pall Mall like a bright bird of passage, she may be yours for a few guineas. There are ebon skins too for those of exotic taste. Perhaps you may wish to gaze and press a hand. Enter one of the cafés in the Haymarket where a gorgeous creature sits behind a counter. She will call to you, compliment you, smile and flash her eyes for you, let you inhale her rich perfume and bring a blush to her delicately rouged and powdered cheeks and ask nothing of you in return but ten shillings for a paltry glove box. Where is the harm in that?

Yet as you pass along Panton Street with a dear bright companion on your arm on your way to the supper rooms and the night's promised pleasures, a Dantesque figure may catch at your gay lady's silken skirts imploring her for sixpence to rid you both of the obscene shape, a base coloured woman riddled with the Dry Pox that the Malays, Lascars and other orientals bring among us, shooting out her disgusting tongue between her thick lips with a horrid leer. Then see your darling fumble quickly for a coin lest the lewd spirit should scare you away. Look into her eyes and read her fortune. It lies there more surely than in her soft palm: the last days in the arms of Madame Geneva, the only white satin she may gather about her for comfort, no longer distinguishable from that hag she has sent away except for the sable skin though hers may be by then darkened with filth and neglect, her fine clothes long since pawned, herself forgotten by the friends she claims wait at home in the country. But do not falter in your step or cause the dear creature on your arm to stumble for we have reached the Haymarket where all circles of this world meet. The broughams are already drawn up before the Alhambra and the Argyle Rooms. Hurry your progress and you may be in time to bow as Harun al-Raschid enters with the divine Scheherazade.

It was good of them to ask him he supposed but unfathomable. He had spruced himself up at Charing Cross and set out in good time. Now he perched uncomfortably on the edge of his chair holding a tumbler of undistinguished red wine and trying not to wonder too much why he was there. He had been invited for supper and wafts of it trailered into the room whenever the door was opened. The house was very small and cramping, a workingman's cottage of about 1880, Meepers thought. He wasn't used to such confinement and had to fight down an urge to duck his head. The house he had been born and brought up in was large-roomed and high ceilinged. This wasn't much bigger in its individual rooms than the gardener's shed that now seemed so long ago.

Red wine on an empty stomach went quickly to his head. He forgot to sip and his tumbler was refilled without his noticing. They were called Robin and Jenny. If he'd married he might by now have children this age or older even. He might be a grandfather. Meepers sat back in his chair and smiled. They were amiable children, particularly the girl. The boy was a little casual and his hair was long enough for a wig. It was hard to do away with one's prejudices. Really he of all people should know better. He ran through the list of long-haired warriors. But the girl was speaking.

' ... so I hope you don't mind if it's rather basic.'

'Since I eat mainly in cafés I'm sure it will be delicious,' he said with a gallantry rusty with long disuse. A daughter would have been best. What a pity men had to have women before they could have children. Athena sprung from her father's head was an excellent idea.

'Are your parents in London?' he asked her.

'My mother's in Rugby. My father's dead.'

Meepers was shocked to find himself glad. He presumed that she and Robin were living together and then tried to bury the thought. If she were his daughter he wouldn't allow it, would make the chap marry her. He was asking Meepers something now while the girl went out to the kitchen.

'Why are you doing this course?'

'Why are you?'

'It passes the time.'

'Exactly.'

'We didn't think you needed to. What do you think of the Prof?'

'I think he knows his period. It's a new one for me. Much later than I'm used to. My interests are more archaeological.'

'Old bones and stones.'

'That's right.' Meepers laughed at himself, and was surprised again.

'I'm interested in Indians, red ones.'

'Ah yes,' Meepers yearned a little. 'If I could afford it I'd like to go to the Americas before I die.'

'Maya and Aztec and all that?'

'Yes, yes.' Perhaps he wasn't such a bad young man. 'Then

there's the big question of when they crossed.'

'The Behring Straits?'

'I've always had a feeling it was much earlier than is generally assumed.'

'I'm more interested in them later: the end rather than the beginning if you get me.'

'If it is an end.'

'Well they've been given a terrible beating for nearly four centuries.'

'Exactly. You see how long it's taken and now I understand their populations are starting to rise. They're beginning to make themselves heard politically.'

'Four centuries is a hell of a long time.'

'Yes and then no. People are remarkably resilient. We are remarkably resilient.'

'You can make that an excuse for anything: what does it matter in such a time scale. But individuals suffer. They're the units of pain. Unless you believe in another life or lives.'

'Transmigration? Economically most appealing but no I don't believe in any other life but this, not any more.'

'But you did once?' asked Jenny coming in with the first of the food.

'Until I went into the army. I was wounded and spent a long time as a prisoner. Since then I've never felt quite the same about anything.' Meepers marvelled at himself. He was chattering away like an old woman over the fence or on her doorstep. Words, whole sentences popped out of his mouth revealing him, his own self to almost strangers. They had moved to the table, to an earthenware casserole of some species of stew and chunks of hot garlic bread. He found himself eating with pleasure, accepting more wine. Perhaps they weren't living together and the boy had merely been invited round too. Jenny seemed to be a teacher. Meepers approved: a stable and valuable occupation for a girl.

'Do you live in London?' she was asking.

'I'm a squatter,' Meepers replied to his own astonishment.

*

On coming to London he had no money nor any friend to assist him. He went to Kensington workhouse to get a night's lodging, and lived for about a fortnight at different workhouses about the city. They used to give the lodgers a piece of bread at night and in the morning and a night's lodging on straw and boards. He spent several years living in the low lodging-houses. About nine years ago before they were reformed both sexes, boys and girls, men and women of all ages slept naked on the floors side by side. On Sunday evenings the only books read were such as Jack Sheppard, Dick Turpin and the Newgate Calendar they got out of the neighbouring libraries by depositing a shilling. He was about ten years of age at the time and in the evening the boys would pick each other's pockets for diversion and training. Soon he began to go out with a mate as look-out for he was quick to learn, with a light touch. When they had had a good day they had steak and pickles, eggs and bacon, plenty of porter and ale and cigars to smoke. But when times were bad it was nothing but a pennorth of bread, a ha'porth of tea and sugar and a ha'porth of butter and a game of hunt the slipper to follow.

When he was about fourteen he began to dress better and wander further and to live with a woman about ten years older than himself. Between them they did well for she was a good worker both at picking ladies' pockets and shoplifting. She was very handsome and dressed well so that she could mingle with the fashionable crowds and get up beside a lady without attracting attention. However when he was taken and sent to Tothill Fields for six months she left him. When he came out he took up the life again and was lucky enough to be in time for the Chartists' gathering on Kennington Common. He took several ladies' purses there and then he saw a gentleman place a pocketbook in the tail of his coat which, when he had fingered it, he discovered to contain a bundle of banknotes: seven £10 notes, two for £20 and five for £5. He bought himself some better clothes, a suit of fine black cloth, grew a moustache and set up as a swell mobsman. Because he had taught himself to speak politely he passed easily among fashionable people. Some thieves give themselves away by their vulgar address or by a shifty look, but he cultivated an open frank appearance and looked the world boldly in the eye. He had been transported once for seven years and spent another three years on and off in gaol. He had a son by a young woman he met at an Irish penny ball in St Giles. He was a good dancer and she was much pleased with him. They went out and had some intoxicating liquor which she had not been used to and exchanged love tokens of two silk handkerchiefs. After, they corresponded for some time and one night he took her to a penny ball, kept her out late and seduced her. She did not go back to her friends any more but co-habited with him until at a public singing room he got jealous of her taking notice of another young man and the next morning sent her back to her friends. She cried a great deal. She was pregnant at the time with his child but her friends got her a situation as a servant in the West End where her young master soon fell in love with her and set her up in fashionable style which he has continued to do ever since. Her boy, his son, is getting a college education but he does not take any notice of either of them now.

Meepers took me almost by the hand Ancient Mariner style though he's neither skinny nor bearded. (Not fat either, I don't mean that.) We set off up Kingsway and plunged into Bloomsbury. It was then I began to get a distinct feeling of déjà vu, particularly when we turned into the square where I'd seen the skull looking quietly out at me. Further surprise: Jenny and Robin were on the Institute doorstep. Meepers was childishly delighted like a trainee conjuror who's just pulled his first rabbit out of a hat. We all went in to look at his dead. It was hardly a winning collection. To start with nothing was left whole apart from a couple of limestone coffins and even one of those had a broken lid, broken once in antiquity and again when it was dug up. There were four distinct skeletons, distinct because of their four skulls, one of which was my friend in the window, though three of them had got their other bones rather mixed up and they'd needed a lot of sorting out. Two of them had been co-habiting in one stone coffin that had been put on top of the other chap's which, unluckily for him, was of wood. (How do they know? They found the nails.) Anyway Meepers wasn't so interested in those three. It was the fourth who had a coffin all to herself.

He said hers was a rich burial. There were a couple of fine stone and jet pins that had dressed her hair and a strange object they can't identify yet made of iron that looked to me like her doorkey. It was lying by her side as if it might have hung on her belt. Her hands were folded over a long vanished belly, a bone girdle full of air.

'How do they know it's a woman?' asked Jenny. Meepers explained about pelvic and cranial differences.

'You can see the shape of the skull,' he went on with a kind of clinical necrophilia, 'it's typically Romano-British: long and low with a sort of bun at the back. That coin,' he pointed to a fragment of rusty metal suitably labelled, 'is third or fourth century. She's very tall by contemporary standards, with a strong right arm longer than the left. But both arms were very muscular. See the slight bowing of the fibula? Malnutrition; lack of calcium, Vitamin D, sunshine.'

'She's got good teeth,' said Robin. 'How old was she?'

'It says about twenty-seven,' Jenny read. 'They don't know how she died. Here's a marvellous bit: "most fatal diseases leave no bony marker of their existence." '

We put death away; we don't look at it as a rule and here we were chatting over her remains as if she was the Sleeping Beauty under that glass case and would wake up one day.

'She was found outside the walls on the main road going Northeast. The Romans didn't allow burial inside the town walls.'

'The Italians still don't,' said Robin. 'You see the walled cemeteries, like towns for the dead away by themselves, from the train.'

'It's hard to tell whether she was buried near a settlement

because that's where she lived or whether she was taken there from London,' Meepers explained. 'But then she's all mystery. Consider her. We don't know her date precisely. We know she was a tall wealthy woman who had suffered from malnutrition when she was young, led a physically active life and died in her prime. What was happening about then? The commander of the Thames fleet seized power and called himself Emperor of Britain until he was murdered by his second-in-command. Then the Imperial government sent an army and took back the island. There's a gold medallion that shows Constantius Chlorus, the Caesar, on one side and on the other the Thames with a war galley and the city of London with a citizen kneeling outside the gate and Constantius, the victor, riding up. Round the edge it says in Latin: Restorer of the Eternal Light. Was she involved in all that? Could those muscles have been developed guiding a chariot? Perhaps there were still descendants of the old British royal families, living in poverty, who might get swept up into such events, a late third century Boudicca?'

From his bright-eyed enthusiasm it was clear that Meepers had fallen hard for her. Like all fairytales she had to be princely, no blowsy drab in a daub hut for him as he mindfucked her ghostly cunt. I begin to wonder about the tale he told me, whether he wasn't really bodysnatching. Probably for Meepers the flesh has to be well picked away by time down to the clean bone before he can get his pecker up. 'Here lies a most beautiful lady; white of thigh is she, her breast is sharp, her eyes are deep and she says nothing to me.'

'Haven't I seen you somewhere before?'

'Not me. My grandson Rowe. You picked his brains as no doubt you want to pick mine, you and that other old geezer who was round here the other day with his questions and notebook and pencil.'

'You must be the watercress girl.'

'That's right. Wouldn't think I'd ever grow up to get

married and have a grandson would you, to look at me? But I'm tough for all I look so frail. First off he tried joking with me as if I was a child, asking about toys and then about the parks. "What's a park?" I says, all innocent. Then I tells him how I lives don't I, and he can see there's no room in the day for toys and parks. What do you want to know?'

'Nothing really. What you're doing here.'

'Where else would I be? Thought you'd leave me out did you? Well you can't because my song keeps going round in your head.

> I always rise up early
> my creases for to sell.
> Oh no sir, I'm not lonely
> They call me the watercress girl.'

'Why does it keep going round?'

'Because you know if you'd been born when I was most likely it'd have been you standing here in carpet slippers at eight years old with your fingers dropping off from bunching up frozen creases. I'm not giving you any soft soap am I?'

'Not much.'

'The other geezer I give a lot to 'cos I thought he might have give me a shilling back but all he done was offer me a dinner I didn't want. Still it was worth a try so I was a dear little innocent for him. Well now are you satisfied? I can't stand about all day gassing to you. I've got all these to get rid of. That's all we are to you raw material. Get us up when we was having a nice rest to ask us a load of silly arse questions and set us to our trades we thought we'd done with forever and all for your own selfish satisfaction. How's he doing now my grandson Rowe?'

'I don't know. We've lost touch.'

'Had what you wanted from him no doubt. Ah if only I could read and write I'd tell me own story and then where would you be. He's a good steady boy, grandson Rowe. I'm glad if he got a decent job away from the creases. But he won't have had it easy. We never do in our family; all sorts of bad

179

luck. It'll have touched him somehow. Take more than a generation or two to work its way out that will. What sort of lodging has he got?'

'A council flat, I think.'

'Council?'

'Like the parish only bigger.'

'Look after them better do they?'

'I think you can say that.'

'Well I don't begrudge him. Does he work as hard as his little granny?'

'Nobody works that hard any more. That's why we call them the Good Old Days.'

'You're pulling my leg.'

'No, not yours. Tell me what you told the old geezer.'

' "I ain't a child and I shan't be a woman til I'm twenty but I'm past eight, I am. I don't know nothing about what I earns during the year, I only know how many pennies goes to a shilling, and two ha'pence goes to a penny, and four fardens goes to a penny. I knows too how many fardens goes to tuppence – eight." '

'Not any more they don't.'

In the evenings he worked steadily at the project, shut in one of the spacious washrooms in the well of the building high up on the eleventh floor. Here he could have a light after the sun was gone without it showing up on the outside. He had even allowed himself a few permanent books ranged along the back of the washbasins over which he had laid a sheet of hardboard for a writing desk. There was water but no electricity in the building. Meepers improvised with a small Calor Gas stove and a battery lamp. He could wash and shave in the morning and only needed to go out to Charing Cross for a bath. His washing was draped over the cold radiators to dry. He had removed the lock from the washroom door and replaced it with one to which he held the only key. True they could break the door open if they really wanted but any watchman on a tour of inspection wouldn't be likely to bother, unless the rooms were going to be let and there seemed no danger of that. Since there was no electricity there was no lift and the watchman never bothered to inspect above the fourth floor. Knowing his times and days Meepers was able to impersonate him, walking boldly in through a service passageway in his porter's uniform and losing himself from sight in the underground car park whose door he now held a key to. The building still smelt freshly of concrete and plaster. Some of the office suites were unfinished, the floor tiling unlaid or fittings not in place.

The climb up to the eleventh floor made him pant and his heart thud but ensured his safety. He didn't know quite why he had stopped there rather than at the tenth or twelfth but now he was installed he returned to it methodically every evening, resting from time to time. It was a temptation to go to the windows and look out to see the view changed from his last stop by a subtle gradation. But he resisted, standing well back from the sheet of glass that might reveal him to anyone glancing up. The horizon dipped slowly below him dropping roads with insect traffic, houses, Wren churches, their spires, office roofs one by one under his feet until he was level with the air only and could look across at other distant monoliths. He had thought himself too old for the Monument and Nelson's Column but now he was nearly on a level with the stone admiral and his pigeons.

Already the evenings were beginning to draw in. Would he be safe here all winter? The wind and rain would beat at the block as at a lighthouse; even now the gentlest airs soughed round it in the night. Sometimes to check a point he didn't come straight back but made his way to another part of the city. Standing on a findspot he was often able to reconstruct better than from a map. So he found himself one evening wandering through the Barbican in search of Cripplegate Fort where St Giles was caught, an ambertombed fly in a complex whose buildings were the offspring or cousins of what Meepers now thought of as his own highrise but on such a vast scale that he was as stunned as if he had landed on a moonbase where the earthrocket docked once a week. And seemingly deserted. Above him soared stilted terraces with flowers looking over each balcony, hanging gardens that indicated that a way of life still went on divorced from the ground for each family in its gilded cage. No children hopscotched between the legs of the buildings. The pavements were sterile, unchalked, undogmarked, litterless and forbidding. In one corner was a pub with medievally evocative name but that was all: a name above a door, no windows marking the pavement with light; soundproofed, no warming noise of voices or singing; no gush of beersmell on to the street to suck you in. Robin's Cuzco, Teotihuacan must have looked like this but it was foreign to Meepers' Western eye whose standard of measurement, he thought, was the home rather than the public building, hut and villa-sized for domestic comfort more than ceremonial, sacrificial statuesque. Then he remembered Stonehenge and looked again. That was it. That was the scale and men had lived in the shadow and simplicity of the stone circle these concrete pavings emulated. Up there were homes for people, perhaps like Meepers. He should be glad. Yet he felt insecure, unsure. Even with his knowledge of other cultures, Sumer, Thebes, these structures distressed him. Tools evolved: the stone or bone notched with menstrual or hunting days became the computer. Why not the hut? But he didn't want to live there. Aloft in his block index fingering the sky he still remained related to things he knew. He could look South as far as St Paul's riding floodlit into the night, serene as if incendiaries had never menaced it. But in this split level Ziggurat he felt himself dwarfed, overpowered, become less than a Lowry imp gangling matchstick limbs through a satanic factory townscape.

Should he add it to the complex equation he was assembling for George? It went against his theory that civilization was irrepressible. He must be blind justice adding without prejudice to leaden and golden scale. It weighed heavily down in his own mind. All such concepts had perished under advancing individualistic barbarisms that had brought anarchy and misery. Would these dwellers climb the thousand steps to the morning human sacrifice or merely stand and look up in return for the people's car, that tough gutsy little beetle, ignoring the spindle shape high up where the golden knife plunged catching the sun's rays or the barbed wire beyond the paddock and the occasional drift of sweet smoke from the incinerators when the wind was in the wrong direction. In purging them the world had lurched each time into a sickly wane as the sickle was pared and sharpened, the tides sank, women grew listless, men looked out only for themselves, grubbing in the middens.

The harvest moon rode up full orange behind St Giles cheering him. It wasn't possible. He wouldn't believe it or it might affect his judgment and, as he understood it, this could unhinge George, make him spew out a doombrief the facts didn't warrant. 'Let her live,' Meepers found himself whispering as he risked a sight across the city from the flat roof of his eyrie and surprising himself again, this time with the vehemence of his incantation.

'I am sorry for you: it is harder for the likes of you than it is for the likes of us.' There, I have said it, what has been on my mind to say for days as I've tramped round behind him seeing his misery. Not those words of course. I didn't know how it would come out but only that come out it would somehow. Just pop out of its own accord out of the side of me mouth without the lips moving as you learn to talk on exercise. It is worse for him and I'd tell anyone for why if they ask me. Because for all he's a grown man of forty, in these matters he's a little child doing his first sentence and I well remember when I was that same child, am reminded of it every time I see a new one brought in and hear him weep in his cell. For there are shocks that come to you that first time that can never be the same again. First there is the losing your own clothes for a suit of coarse broadarrows. Now that will itch his gentleman's skin terrible being soft as a child's from silk and looking after. Next there is to be locked up alone twenty-three hours out of the twenty-four which can drive any man to madness or at the least to great nervousness for it is not natural for human beings to be so alone all day and locked in cages like monkeys at the zoo. This causes the children to cry and call out in terror. Now the grown man won't call out for he knows it is no good unless he is already silly in the head but he will cry and there is no shame in that. For the first time he comes in he never knows from one minute to the next what further misery or punishment may be laid upon him so therefore he is apprehensive all the time and that and the dim light and the loneliness prey upon his mind. And here too he will feel it more as being a man used to control his own life and one surrounded by laughter and friends as theatrical people always are.

Next as to beds there too he comes off worse, for us who are used to sleep on the floor of lodging houses with a coat over us or in a room of our own not much better will make less of a three plank bed than a man who has always laid down on a mattress, and nothing so undermines a man as not to sleep well of a night, night after night. Except perhaps not to eat which I lay twenty to one he cannot do as yet for the prison dry bread and dish of stirabout porridge for dinner will cause any man except a starving beggar to refuse it at first and when he do begin to eat it out of necessity, will give him the runs so that his cell is always full of the stink of his own shit from the slop pail. To a man used to smell sweet this foul air must be ranker I'd say than to the likes of them that live in stinking alleys.

Last I would tell them of the hardness of the labour to one who has never done manual toil, of the broken and bleeding nails and cracked muscles, the ache to the very bones when a man whose body is soft already as a child's, is weakened by hunger, sleeplessness, terror and diarrhoea. So I said to him, 'It is worse for the likes of you,' and he answered me, 'No, my friend, we all suffer alike.'

*

184

This is a letter I shall never post. Why am I writing it then? Because I must. Because I have to tell you even if I won't actually let you hear what I'm saying. All writing has these two parts: expression and communication. I'm like the poet who won't publish; John Clare hiding his poems in crannies in the wall. I think it was Meepers' necrophilia that cracked me; envy perhaps that he should get such pleasure from the dead while I got so little from the living. Instead of coming straight home I dropped in at the pub and began seriously putting away the pints. Jay Black came in and joined me. 'What do you do,' I said, 'when you want a bird? In my young day Curzon Street was a parade. You could saunter along past their pitches and take your choice. The bigger the bag the higher the price.'

'My dear old chap,' he said in his best fake Joe Gargery, 'while the cat's away eh? I know just how you feel. When Beryl went off to her mother's for a fortnight last year with the kids, I had a glorious time screwing everything in sight and out of it, and then was I glad to see her back. Set me up for the rest of the year that fortnight did. I go round the clubs. The Overseas is about the best. Lots of sweet young crumpet all fresh from Down Under like hot new rolls if you get me. A couple of hours, a few long looks, buy her a drink and you're set up.'

'Suppose she doesn't want to?'

'Soon let you know. No hard feelings. Try another til you score. Mostly they know what it's about and make up their minds as quickly as you do. All sorts, any colour or shape you fancy.'

'Amateurs!'

'Oh nobody pays for it any more. Sometimes it's someone you've seen around for months. Suddenly tonight's the night: you connect and there you are. You're making me hungry and I've got to go home. I'll give Beryl a going over. She's the most wonderful woman in the world, you know. I really respect that woman. You try the Overseas.'

'I'm not a member.'

'Who is. Just go along. But for Christ's sake don't offer a girl from there money. All done for love or kindness.' I thought he was going to slap me on the shoulder like an uncle or the vicar. 'I am the vicar.' 'I'm only thirteen.' 'I'm not superstitious.'

All colours and shapes: Martha and Jenny. Should I try to ring one of them up and to make something of that? Martha has enough problems and Jenny struck me as the sort who'd take it very gravely. I didn't want an involvement. I wanted you. But did you really exist and if so what were you doing now? Lying down under someone? I nearly cried out loud the pain was so sharp.

Oh the ladies of my youth, last of the Lautrekkers, wicked as cami-knickers, high steppers, low kickers. You knew where you were with them. You didn't have to pretend to be a telly director in a bedroom with two-way mirrors. Shepherd Market should have been Shepherdesses'. One year the fashion was for poodles and they all had a little bit of fluff dancing on a lead in a rhinestone collar. Then it was umbrellas, bright silks and pasha handles and stiletto heels would stab through your eyes straight to your heart if your wallet was lying over it; handy in a fight too or if anyone didn't want to pay for service. There were raven rinses, henna heads and bottle blonde beauties; three colours to choose from and all with the Macmillan motto: You've never had it so good. Their lips were carmine, their eyes black-rimmed after Elizabeth Taylor's Cleopatra, their eyelids thickly blue or green jaded; their breasts had a martial jut in rubber reinforced cups. They smelt of dress-shields overlaid with Evening in Paris. Their hearts were alloy whose chief element was tin or brass. They seemed cheaply immortal until they were wiped away. I remember one at the height of her profession, a mature thirty, black-haired, red clinging dress under an ocelot mac, black-bowed winkle-pickers with heels so sharp angels might consider them for a dancing floor. But how to convey the virago, the heavy Max Factored pancake features, the swing of hips and handbag, the thrust of her calves in their fishnet so that young as you were you felt her beckon would take you over, slap you into life, that you could do her no harm and she do you nothing but good. She was the prototype for today's drag queen, Madame Fifi La Rue, for the fast transvestite who doesn't want to play a dowdy mum, spangled Rogers and Starrs in your eyes.

I am not yet Donne for, there's a dance in the old don yet, I thought after Jay Black and another pint had gone. There was no one else I knew in the pub, no one I could confide in or simply talk to about the weather and if we'd ever have a team to win the World Cup again, to take away the ache. I went out into the early evening, cool after yesterday's rain, and a grey day in half-mourning already for summer, and began to walk towards the Lord Nelson, passing the three Asian delicatessens, one driving school and one betting shop that are supposed to supply all our worldly needs. The tourists were snug in their hotels eating cardboard and plastic dinner. The locals were unwrapping their take-away suppers in their bed-sitters. The street was Sunday morning bare. At the traffic lights I stopped to look in the tobacconist's window and there they all were, coyly hidden by French lessons and Swedish massage and of course the new one I'd read about, the sauna. Not that anything is ever new. Baths of various sorts and prostitution have always been in business together: the stews, the hummumi for the boys (where do they go now the old Russell's gone?) Should I get myself birched and tickled in a cloud of healthy pine steam? The lust went out of me. I wasn't drunk enough. The Lord Nelson should see to that. It was dim and smoky. A juke-box was playing the latest pops which are all golden oldies of the 'fifties and early 'sixties. I couldn't decide whether it made me feel incredibly older or younger again. I wasn't drunk enough. Got into one of those interminable conversations about where is Old England, that never was except on Christmas cards where the snow-trimmed coach draws up with a flourish of horn to let Mr Pickwick and friends stamp into the inn for a hot posset. No one ever sees that they're lamenting for a lost childhood where it never rained but it calendar snowed and cats sat smug on mats

187

instead of having tin cans tied to their tails by nineteenth-century Eton yobs. I have come a long way haven't I? Some things I yearn for still but not without some discrimination any more. He was going out to advise Africans on electronics. Individuality was finished here. Yet looking with open eyes at the Nelson's customers Hogarth wouldn't have been at a loss for raw material. It doesn't get the middleclass dollies and their lads but the sad and the mad, the workmen on their way home, the trans-European emigrés. 'Shakespeare,' a man in a thin black suit shiny with grease declaimed, 'it's all in there. He said it all. You read him and you won't go far wrong.' Another myth, but a more attractive one. Did you ever sing a patriotic setting of 'This royal throne of kings' by Parry when you were at school? No one ever remembers how it ends 'is now leased out ... 's now bound in with shame with inky blots, and rotten parchment bonds ... hath made a shameful conquest of itself'. I will not die pronouncing it or only to note our long tradition of self-flagellation, the sterility of showing our sores and refusing a poultice or balm; nothing but a moral mustard plaster, painful and ineffectual, will satisfy us. Only the eighteenth century saw with balance and we lost that in the gothick morbidity of the next hundred years that still over-hangs us, would have us go naked with whips lamenting through the streets in a mass penitential. By then I was drunker. Del Shannon from the juke-box cried out of my adolescence (late and protracted) for his little runaway, backed by an electric organ. A couple began to fight in sharp whispers with daggers flashing out of their eyes. A tall black boy in a group laughed too loudly and put his arms round everyone in turn to show he was in and at ease. The robot man left for Africa. I stayed on through another couple of bells til the dreary shrilling of time even the Rev. Elliot couldn't drain of potency. Then I lurched into the street to be slapped by the fresh air. There was the tobacconist's, Goodnight ladies. But why. Why not good evening for one of them. I closed one eye and read through the cards again. Not Swedish massage: too strenuous. French lessons would be all whips and black garters. Something simple. There she was: Sylvia. 'Sylvia, fair in the bloom of fifteen.' 'Who is Sylvia?' 'Except I be by Silvia in the night, There is no nightingale.' I had nothing to write with so I memorized the number.

I fumbled the door open, nearly tripped on the stairs, came in, went straight to the phone and dialled. It rang three times and then the receiver was lifted. 'Sylvia?'

'You've got the wrong number, mate. And you're pissed.'

I wept, I howled and cursed and beat the walls and fell on my knees and spewed my guts down the pan. Over and over I called out aloud for you to come back until I must have passed out and woke shivering, though still fully dressed, on the floor and crept to bed. Today I'm calm and weak as if just recovering from a long and perilous illness.

V

Cockaigne

When he was a boy

and worked for Mr Jollins who owned the coffeestall in Sally Lane, short for the salutation of the angel on the signboard of the hostelry on the corner, they would get up behind old Daisy, the two of them in the trap, man and boy, 'cos there wasn't room for any more and jig away to where the fields and lanes began through Wanstead. Mr Jollins would do business with a Mr Colegrave the greengrocer, including something for Daisy, apples and oranges for the boy and whatever was in season for Mr Jollins to carry back to town. Then they would jig along again, Daisy farting wetly all the way so that the boy would have to wash the cart and her down when they got home. There would be several stops for Mr Jollins' whistle to be wetted. By the time they got back to town, with the boy's eyes stuffed with the greens of grass and leaves and his ears clattered with Daisy's hoofs and shrilled with birdsong, the gaslights were coming on and the naphtha flaring on the stalls. They would buy soft-roed bloaters for Mr Jollins' tea, and when the boy had finished with Daisy and the cart and given her feed and water he would run home to his mother and sisters with his apples and oranges.

After tea he would go upstairs to Stormy Jack's room and watch him clean his rifle. Stormy Jack claimed he had shot quail on the mills' marshes. His mother wouldn't let him go out shooting. She had been in service in too many houses where there had been talk of accidents with the guns and bloody figures brought home on a hurdle with a limb unnaturally adangle. But on Sunday mornings she let him go with Stormy Jack, if he wasn't shouldering his gun, to watch the gippos and the gamblers and the ratcatchers put a rat and a ferret down their trousers for bets, for the dustshoot was alive with rats and birds of every kind and men who would gamble on anything.

When she was a girl

she was a terror, always playing football with the boys and over the mills' river with her brother where they would find a long pole and vault across the water, her button boots dangling an inch above the wet. She wasn't much good at history or writing but top in sums and music. She loved the tick of the metronome and mistress's hand signalling them through the tonic-solfa. She could play anything by ear on the front room piano. At the Band of Hope they sang 'Jesus wants me for a sunbeam' and her voice rang out clear above the others, true to the note. It was lovely to open your throat in a jolly good sing.

But most of all she liked it when they were all dressed in their best and put on the train for Granny's, to wander through the fields and pick flowers, fruit or nuts in season, to be passed from house to house of their country cousins and told they were peaky from the town, needed fattening up and stuffed full of grub til they were bursting and the little girls fretful and likely to be sick. She played on the dustshoot too among the birds and the rats, not when the gippos and gamblers were there but only a bent figure of a man or woman totting among the refuse. Big green and blue bottles buzzed there, the size of bees, helping the work of decay in the heat. A train called from the sidings beyond the dump, a train that might have taken them to Granny's. 'Come on slowcoach,' said her brother, 'dawdling along. Watch me jump the little brook. Then we'll look along the lines for coal.' If you found a piece you spat on it for luck and put it in your pocket to take home for the fire. And when a horse and cart went up the street you followed it with shovel and pail hoping it would drop a steaming heap of manure to nourish the thin soil in the back garden and mother's rows of runner beans that would give them a good feed for days in the summer as long as they all remembered to throw their soapy washing water over them to keep the blackfly away.

Once again their technology made him gasp. He looked at the drawing of a reconstructed floating wharf that rose and fell with the tide and hadn't a nail in it to rust and rot the wood but was all barefaced dovetails, false tenons, half-laps, solid carpentry that had resisted nearly two thousand years in its grave beside the river. The materials of their technology obscured their achievements, connected in our minds as stone and wood had become with the decorative, with aesthetic rather than functional values. Plastic and concrete were somehow less real because we had made them not nature, and imbued them with our own self-disgust as cheaply impermanent. Yet iron we had made too and that had become morally acceptable, perhaps because it had been largely superseded by other metals and was identified with bridges and railways, Brunel and the Great Eastern. Meepers pushed back his chair from the washbasin desk. His study was almost complete. Tomorrow he would hand it in. A student team from the cybernetics department would reduce it to a programme and key it on to tape.

In concept that floating wharf was the ancestor of Mulberry Harbour and the oil rig. How long would it have been before the Romans had got round to that if they hadn't been interrupted and how important were such interruptions? Perhaps they slowed down the pace of progress so that the human psyche could keep up with it. Perhaps we had got ahead of ourselves too fast this century. He was suddenly weary of his own questions. His guests would be arriving soon and he must be ready for them with open bottles and clean glasses.

They were there as arranged when he crept out to let them in but three figures instead of two. 'We hope you don't mind,' Jenny whispered, 'but we brought Martha too.'

'Not at all, not at all,' he said mentally checking the number of glasses and things to sit on. Meepers bolted the doors behind them and led them up through the building in the small spill of light from his torch. 'Hold on to the banisters and keep in touch with each other. It's a long way up I'm afraid.'

'Jesus, it's spooky,' Martha whispered.

'We can talk out loud,' said Meepers, 'there's no one to hear us. It's quite safe.'

'It's like being in church,' said Jenny, 'that's why one wants to whisper.' She half remembered an old picture seen at the National Film Theatre where someone was always trying to get a dead airman on to a moving staircase that slowly escalated to heaven. No that wasn't right. He wasn't dead, that was it, but he would be if he ever reached the top. Where was Meepers the old magician leading them up, into the dark? Hell might be up instead of Dante's down since space travel, out further and further towards the sun, each planet a refinement for a more terrible evil, the top of a tower block the launching pad where hope must be abandoned, with Meepers for guide.

But they didn't go right to the top. Panting Meepers pushed open a door into artificial light, a washroom with cubicles and basins which served now for a bar. He had obviously gone to some trouble. There were dishes of salted peanuts and biscuits and cheese, sandwiches and cakes.

'I'm afraid cooking for so many was beyond my Calor stove. I hope you don't mind everything cold.' He ran from one to the other, sitting them down and giving them each a glass of wine.

'This is the weirdest place I ever came to a party,' said Robin. 'I like it. Gee, it's kinda different,' he mimicked.

'Aren't you afraid to live here all alone?' asked Jenny.

'It's too young for ghosts.'

'But someone might break in to steal.'

Meepers shrugged. 'There are always risks. Crossing the street is most dangerous.' It was good of them to worry about him at all. He began to explain the progress of his programme.

'Then where will you go?' asked the girl called Martha.

'I'm not sure yet. I've become a nomad,' he laughed, 'when one well goes dry I look for another.'

Robin took a mouthorgan from his pocket and began to play a sad little tune on it. The air was veiled with his and Martha's cigarette smoke. 'I'm just a poor wayfaring stranger, a-travelling through this world of woe,' wept the metal reeds.

'May I?' asked Meepers. Robin handed it over and he rinsed it under the tap and dried it on tissue wrapping from one of the bottles. He began to play a medley of music-hall songs and Irish and Scottish dance tunes, ending with a virtuoso performance of 'She Moved Through the Fair', a longdrawnout keening that made them want to cry and then to clap.

'Keep it,' said Robin when he tried to hand it back. 'It belongs with its master,' and wouldn't be gainsaid.

'I'd like to see the view from the top before we go,' said Jenny.

'It's as far again.'

'I'd like to see it all the same.'

'I've never been to the top of anything,' said Martha.

They climbed once more, not noticing the steepness now because of the wine and giggling a bit in the dark. Meepers unbarred the door on to the roof and they stepped through into the wind that always whirlpooled around the top. There were no stars but fast-moving clouds, perfectly shaped for the conveyance of gods and cherubs, divinities in a baroque opera. In every direction the sky took on a city red shift into which towers and spires jutted and everywhere were lighted window squares behind which people made up their lives as they went along.

'All those people improvising while we watch,' said Robin.

'And we haven't paid a penny,' said Martha.

'Here come the ticket collectors,' Jenny pointed. They stared down at the street below where distant klaxons had begun their nerve-racking, hysterical hee-haw. Two cars with flashing blue lights drew up.

'They're not coming here, they can't be.'

'Someone must have seen or heard us.'

'I'm sorry,' Jenny said to Meepers. 'It's our fault.'

'That's alright my dear. It had to happen sometime. The only thing is I'd rather not be arrested; that's all.'

'What do we do now?' asked Martha.

'I don't think they'll rush in. They'll reconnoitre first. Then ask for orders or help.'

'Downstairs,' said Robin. 'We have to stall. We'll need a sheet or a big piece of paper and a way to write big. Jenny, you and Martha get to a window above where they'll try to get in and drop things on them, water, bottles anything. But to miss. Down now as fast as you can.'

'I don't understand,' said Meepers.

'We have to be a protest movement, make a big fuss. Pretend there are more of us than there are. Then they won't rush us. We'll say we're occupying the block until tomorrow and then we'll leave peacefully. With luck someone will pick up their transmissions and put the press on to it. Then we can take our time. You must pack your things in four lots so we can carry one each. What about a sheet?'

'Just one, that's all I have, and to write with – some shoe-blacking?'

Old man Moloch picked up another soldier and bit his head off before stuffing the still wriggling limbs into his maw. A leg twitched over his chin and tickled him until his red tongue lolled and sucked it in. He could never decide whether Tommies or Gerries tasted better, or the rank sauciness of half a dozen poilus. Some days he fancied one, some days another. Austrians he took in a string of sausages, a mess of Alpini bolognesi, a flock of Turkeys. But best of all he decided was a sauerkraut of Russians and Germans. Nearly two million each of them he reached down for and smacked his chops over as he plucked them from their barbed wire pens or the deepfreeze of the snowfields.

He

sat behind his machinegun and waited for Moloch to get him too, tit for rat-a-tat-tat. But when the great hand lifted him up to the rank mouth it opened in a belch and the hand dropped him back, blinded, seared, gasping for air; still kicking.

She

looked up and saw the air which was now Moloch's blood bathtub darken with his new playthings that dropped their load on the streets, and sometimes themselves in a slowly descending inferno, smashing houses and people and nearly a thousand years of the city's invulnerability. The queues stretched for hours while the profiteers and black marketeers got rich quick. Now there was margarine, guns and no butter.

Moloch laughed and pissed all over Europe turning the trenches to mud so men slithered and rotted, became his sewer rats, and between the lines he set his land, Noman'sland where nothing lived or stirred among the craters he had stamped or blasted with his barrage of farts.

So they fed him year after year in the hope that one day he would be satiated and fall asleep. Then the rats who were left could creep out of their holes, run a stake through his heart and bury him forever. But when they tried they found he had no heart and all they could do was lock him up with treaties and leagues until he grew strong enough to break them or one of the rats grew bold enough to let him loose again.

'It's our responsibility, I think,' said Wandle, 'as the only senior staff here.' He had that bright-eyed, eager-to-be-off-on-crusade look. His hair positively glowed with righteousness.

'What's up?' I asked.

'The police have rung to say some of our students have taken over some building.' Ponders seemed puzzled.

'Hell,' I said, 'We'd better get over there and see if we can stop them being arrested. Have the police got any names?'

'Not yet. I agree with you. The sooner we get there the

better. I was just leaving. They don't seem to know how many there are either. Shall we all go?' Wandle of course.

Ponders and I followed him out. For once there was a cab that wasn't just going off for elevenses or changing shift or booked by a hotel. We all got in the back and were whisked up Kingsway and along the Euston Road to where there are a couple of those sore-thumb tower blocks. It was easy to see which was ours by the crowd of photographers and police. There was a good-sized mob too of unmistakeable students, come to cheer and see fair play for their kind. The police were keeping them back and there was a lot of barracking going on that reminded me of Saturday morning pictures, all boos and cheers. A tatty banner hung from a couple of windows halfway up one block with the smudgy legend: QUEEN'S HOUSING DEMO. There were faces at other windows looking down. We pushed our way to the front. More cheers and catcalls. Wandle gave one of his most limpid smiles to one of the policeman in a flat cap who seemed to be in charge.

'Good morning. We're from the college. We wondered if we might help. What's the position?'

They don't salute; not like coppers abroad; an ambiguous blessing.

'Well as you can see they've taken over that block. Some sort of housing protest. They got in last night and we weren't quick enough to stop them. Then when the word got round this morning some more managed to get in through the back way. They sent one chap out with a statement saying they didn't want to cause any damage and they'd come out at midday. The owners have asked us to keep it cool. Don't want any damage to their property. They say they won't charge them if they don't break anything. There's not much we can do about getting them out. If we try to force things there's sure to be something smashed.'

'We could try to talk them out a bit sooner if you like. It's hard to tell from down here but we probably know some of them at least.'

'You can try; if they'll let you in. The sooner they come

out the sooner that lot with the cameras will lose interest and
we can all go home to breakfast.'

'Right,' said Wandle, 'we'll see what we can do, shall we?'
Ponders and I nodded.

There were a couple of pickets inside the main glass doors.
Wandle grinned and made signs that we wanted in. One boy
in a teeshirt marked CHE held up a piece of cardboard saying:
No Fuzz. I gave the thumbs up. 'I thought Guevara was out,'
I said as they unbolted the door.

'So he is. That's the Campaign for Homosexual Equality.'
Wandle smiled at my ignorance. Poor Ponders was looking
ever more puzzled. They're a quiet, dedicated lot in cybernetics. Some of them still wear suits. It's always sociology, arts
and humanities that cause ructions.

We climbed the stairs, endless stairs, after one of the pickets.
Wandle would've like to chat him up but he had to save all
his puff for the climb. At last we came off into a room full of
jeans and assorted shirts, boys and girls I didn't know but
some I did by sight, and Jenny, Robin, Martha mercifully
without the baby and, you could have floored me, Meepers
sitting on a box.

'Well now,' said Wandle laughing, 'who's the captain?'
They all looked at Robin.

'I think I'm elected.'

'What's it all about?'

'It's a sort of housing protest. You know, empty blocks when
people need houses, all that.'

'The police say you're coming out at midday?'

'That's it.'

'Any chance of bringing that forward?'

'It's difficult. We don't want to look as if we're giving in.
But Martha here has to get home.'

'Suppose we took out most of you and left a token force to
sit it out?'

And that was how we settled it. I turned to Meepers. 'Are
you one to stay or go?'

'He goes,' said Robin, 'definitely. Clive and Liz take a

bundle each. You carry this.' He pushed a small suitcase at me. We made up our caravan. Jenny and Robin and the two pickets were left behind. There were cheers and groans as we emerged. Wandle slipped away to explain to the police. Ponders and I led the crusade past the cameras.

Beyond the limelight a collection of bundles was dumped round Meepers. A cab came past and I hailed it. I put Martha in. 'I think I should send these two home,' I said to Ponders. 'What will you do? Wandle will stay til the other four have come out.'

'I don't feel I understand any of it,' he said. 'But the worst seems to be over so I think I'll walk back to clear my head.'

In the taxi Meepers put out a veined, freckled hand towards Martha. 'I'm so sorry for all this,' he said.

'It'll be alright. Sandy's good. She wouldn't leave him alone. She'd have been worried until she got the message but she wouldn't leave him.' We dropped her off at their door.

'Where to?' I asked Meepers.

'Anywhere will do.'

'But where do you live? Where are you going with all this stuff?'

'Nowhere; nowhere in the world.'

They were married from the Works as you might say. He'd finally got a job there the year before after three years unemployed and she'd been there since she was sixteen. The first day she went into the big workshop she marvelled to hear all the girls singing together. The jobs she'd had before, in the laundry where her thin fourteen-year-old's arms couldn't lift and straighten the heavy sheets, at the tobacco company and the printers, they'd been allowed to talk but not too much. She loved the new work, polishing walnut and mahogany for the firstclass carriages and lavatory seats til they were like silk or velvet depending on which wood you started out with.

He wasn't so keen, except that he was glad to be out of the scramble for jobs but it was filthy hard slog with a flogging hammer in the cinders and soot of the cooling boilers. 'His poor hands all broken with great lumps knocked out of them and he had such beautiful hands.' But it was safe in the works. Trains were always needed to take people to business or down to the sea, to shift the country's goods about, even though most had no money to buy them. They were the princes of the workingclass, railwaymen and postmen, so that made her a princess and theirs a royal wedding.

She was sad to give it up: the singing and the gossip of the workshop where they took it in turns to tell the story of the last picture they'd seen but you couldn't go to work when you were married. Besides it wouldn't have been right as the dole queues lengthened and there were no jobs for men though polishing was women's work of course. Then there was the baby and screwing and scraping to keep their two rooms decent and the three of them well fed and clothed and a bit left over for beer and fags and the pictures that were talkies now. They'd have been happy as sandboys, were too, if it wasn't for her sisters all falling ill and dying of consumption and his poor chest that hadn't quite recovered from the gas and now was filled with dust and soot. If he could only have picked up where he'd been when he volunteered (though she was proud of course that he hadn't gone with a paper in his hand), but it meant that now he would be classed as semi-skilled for the rest of his life where he could have been a craftsman if he'd finished his apprenticeship.

They were lucky though, so lucky. The papers and the streets were full of terrible things. What could you do but give eye to your own, be a good manager and lose yourself a few hours a week in the starry dreamworld of the darkened picture palace.

It was like coming home. There was the sofa he had slept on. He hadn't intended that his remark should lead to this. It had been a statement of fact, almost a joke out of the curious new serenity that he had felt lately. But he was relieved all the same to have a little respite, not to have to begin looking at once. Perhaps he could stay a day or two to get his breath back.

'I'm sorry I haven't a spare room. I expect I said that before. Anyway we can probably make do for a bit.' He had shown Meepers where to stow his things neatly and then announced that he must go out to do some shopping.

'I'd like to finish the study. I'm nearly there. I wonder if I could use your desk. With luck I might be able to hand it over tomorrow. Fortunately today is my day off.'

'Do. I shan't be back til this evening. Help yourself to anything in the fridge. Make some tea or coffee, whatever you like.' And he had gone. Perhaps the shopping was merely an excuse to remove himself from proximity and this embarrassing new relationship. If so Meepers was grateful. He knew he should think about the future, plan what he would do, but he couldn't. The only thing now was to finish his work. That had been the cybernetics professor this morning and the sight of his tangible presence had filled Meepers with an inspired impatience. He unpacked his papers and notes and sat down.

After the Great Fire a plant had grown up amid the charred ruins, as rose-bay willow-herb had covered the bombed sites. London rocket it was called. Did nature always cover the scars, move in when man moved out? If so a sifting and soil analysis on sixth-century London sites might show one plant taking over from all others and man if the city had been largely deserted. He wondered what sort of plant it might be, whether it would wave a tall roseate head or creep a little yellow succulent like stonecrop over the walls. Perhaps a London Gildas had gone about the streets proclaiming the last days like Daniel in Babylon reading the writing on the wall. There would have been no princes to castigate for their luxury. The princes ruled in the tribal capitals. London was free like a Renaissance Venice. Bede had mentioned one who had the status of a tribune. Perhaps the shadowy Ambrosius Aurelianus was the city's governor. He must have been a Christian general. Bede was obviously wrong about his parents being of royal birth and title. The Aurelians were all of common rank although they might rise to be emperor. That was it, he noted: confusion with the Emperor Aurelian caused him to be given royal parents. Aurelian himself had started as a common soldier. But his other saintly namesake, Ambrose of Milan, came from a senatorial family just to muddy the picture further. Certainly the two together were enough to account for the original confusion in Gildas, passed on to Bede. What would make sense would be if a Christian soldier had stayed on when the legions were withdrawn in 410, had children and grandchildren who had perhaps become local notables leading a silver-age patrician life in a villa or as governors of the city as others were still doing in Gaul. The Chronicle said the Romans buried some of their treasure in 418 before going to Gaul. That must have meant they were intending to come back. Obviously the government and the Church continued otherwise the British Church wouldn't have asked the Gallic bishops for help against heresy. And the appeal to Rome for aid against the Picts and Scots suggested a Romanized government that expected the empire to be concerned.

He could see it all. The messengers crossing the sea and taking horse to ride through a Gaul still enjoying a golden autumn only to find Attila occupying all Rome's attention. 'Britannia? My dear chap, he's in Italy. You'll have to look out for yourselves.' But St Germanus came for the second time to beat down the British heresy only a few years before the ageing Vortigern invited in the Angles. It seemed a good idea. They were used to German troops among the imperial forces. They knew them for good fighters. They might even be doing the empire a favour in employing potential enemies as mercenaries. Instead they had let loose their own destruction. First Kent where the barbarians had landed fell to them and the British Army was forced back to London; then prow after prow was driven ashore along the Southern coasts; Ælle, Cerdic, Port, Stuf, Wihtger, Hengest.

And it might all have been different, Meepers thought, if Pelagius had won instead of Augustine. He saw him disputing in Rome, a Dark Age Dr Johnson, heavy in body through eating too much Irish porridge Jerome said maliciously, with the same ability to make mere common sense glitter into aphorism and with Coelestius as his Boswell pattering behind him; Morgan the Britain, so in love with things Greek that he translated the seaborn of his name into Pelagius and went to Africa to talk Augustine out of the unreason of original sin. If he had won and human dignity had been the official doctrine of Christianity instead of despair, the struggle against the Saxons might have been prosecuted more keenly; the whole history of the West could have been changed if we had believed his If I ought, I can. Meepers sweated with the effort to visualize a society that could bring forth such a man. Augustine was the product of urban civilization. Wasn't it reasonable to imagine that his great opponent might be too, that he might have been brought up in London as Augustine was in Carthage. It would help to account for the popularity of his teaching in Britain and the frantic efforts of Germanus to stamp it out. Meepers bent over his notes and began to add this new imponderable X to his equation.

'Dolly will have to go.' He rocked a little on his feet in front of the fireplace. Since Florence's death they hadn't really needed her but she had stayed because to send her away was to admit finally that the child was dead and there wouldn't be any more.

'You've been expecting it haven't you? I know I have. And it could be worse. What's ten per cent less compared with the sack, after all.' She lit a cigarette.

He frowned. He didn't like her to smoke even in their own drawing room or to use slang. 'It's not just that. There'll be the fares, and the long hours travelling to a new job. Perhaps we should move.'

'Darling not out there, South of the river. We'd vegetate. No one would come to see us. It'd be like living above the shop.'

There seemed no way to make her understand. She didn't care about him, how tired he'd get shunting from end to end of the city. She could never forget she'd been a bright young thing even though she was a mother now and a bereaved one at that. 'We shan't be able to afford a decent school for the boy. He'll have to really get down to it and win himself a place at one of the grammar schools.'

He stood there looking so grim and dreary. Already he reeked of the suburbs. Well she wasn't going to be buried alive in Bexley or Sidcup.

'Perhaps we should buy a car and you could drive to work.'

'My dear little featherbrain where would the money for that come from?' Almost he was beginning to look forward to it. Although it was a cut in salary it was promotion of a sort, and it would be closer to the real thing than Whitehall, following in old Sam Pepys' footsteps as an Admiralty clerk. 'You'll have to stop smoking and buying new hats.' A jolly fine set of fellows the Jack Tars. He'd do his best for them.

'Rule Britannia and England expects,' she sighed. 'I could get a job too or open an antique shop or something.'

'Don't be such a duffer. What on earth do you know about business?'

'I could learn to fly and be the first woman to win the Schneider Trophy.'

'Oh Lord, here we go. Now be a good girl and stop making a fuss and maybe I'll take you to see *Cavalcade*.'

He takes her hand. 'Kiss and make up.'

'I suppose so.'

They join hands and sing.

HE. Oh you're such a little duffer
SHE. But I'm really rather sweet
BOTH. So though times are getting tougher
    We can both stay on our feet
    If we really pull together
    We can reach the distant shore
    Of peace and picnic weather
    And prosperity once more.

MAID (*entering*). 'Scuse me madam, sir. You're a-wanted on the h'instrument sir. They do say on the wireless as the navy's on strike.

    (*Blackout.*)

We're like Cox and Box or the old man and woman in the barometer rainhouse. When I got in Meepers was about to go out. His computer study is ready to be put into Ponders' pigeonhole first thing in the morning. I shall give my last lecture of the course. I haven't told him yet, or anyone else, but I bought my ticket today. Without you my veneer of civilization breaks down. I become brutish and stupid. You are my city and I'm coming to find you. That's all. It's so simple I don't know why I didn't think of it before.

And at its worst that night they thought they would never see another day. But it was a shame to waste the gin. The bottle and glasses jumped on the table from the repeated concussions. If they were going to die it would be in their own home not in a hole in the garden they had decided. He poured another glass. Whenever there was a lull they went to the top of the house, put out the light and pulled back the blackout to see the sky above the docks angry from the fires below. Then another wave would follow, the unsynchronized engines beating their dead pulse through the sky, and the distant nearing crump of the bombs would drive them back to the kitchen. You can't take it with you but they could. She poured another glass. At least Hitler wouldn't spill good drink without spilling them first.

    It was all around them now. He remembered other bombardments when all you could do was keep your head down. She wept for the daughter she would never see again, tears of pure gin and as crystal clear. Drink up, mustn't waste it. This was it. This time they wouldn't escape. The whole house trembled with each blast as if it was the last left standing at

Armageddon. They waited for the glass to splinter out of the frames, the roof to cave in. There it was. The lights went out. The shock wave shook the little house til it rattled. They were goners this time. In the dark the tears streamed down her face.

It was quiet at last as if that final explosion had deafened them. Perhaps this was being dead. But the lights were on again. They were still there either side of the table with the bottle and its drain of gin between them. They looked at each other and began to laugh. And the tears ran down her face through the blackout of soot the blast had swept from the chimney and flung over their faces, making white rivulets across her cheeks. Later, arm in arm, they picked their way along the street through the debris, their faces still smudged, to the tumbled walls where men were digging for broken bodies in the mound of rubble while the all-clear wailed up another day. They needn't have drunk all the gin after all.

At first he hadn't believed it. Then he had felt that he shouldn't accept. Gradually the man had worn him down til it seemed the most natural thing in the world. To walk up to a front door in daylight and put a key in a lock was the most extraordinary experience. He expected a hand to fall on his shoulder. Now it was evening and he was crossing the familiar square. It would be too dark to see into the garden he had never thought to walk in again and that he now held a new key to. One day he might meet the gardener and ask him how he found it. It seemed so long ago. There was the coffeestall bus. He would stop for a cup and a sandwich which would save him tackling the fridge when he got in.

'Well, well stranger. I thought you'd gone for good.'

'I've been away for a bit.'

'After your accident. A good thing too. You was more shook up than you thought for. Come inside for a minute. It's quiet tonight.'

Meepers let himself be persuaded up the steps into the Turkish bath interior.

'The first couple of nights I put up your Thermos. Then I thought: he's not coming back. It's still here. Look. Quite safe.'

'I must pay you for that. I should have let you know.'

'Lord love us what's a drop of coffee. I must say you look more handsome than when I see you last. Here, try that.' A laced and steaming mug was put into his hands. 'It's good to see old faces. Cheers.'

'Cheers,' said Meepers. A moth plane with white landing lights picking its path for Heathrow swam towards them across the black bay of sky.

'I don't like to see them so low; it reminds me of the war.' Meepers watched it sipping at his mug. It was only the most recent extension of the line that led from a handaxe. 'Noisy sods they are too, pardon my language.'

'They're getting quieter though,' he offered. 'I don't think I mind the noise really. It reminds me of trains. That's all they are: flying trains.'

'I suppose so. I've never been in one and I don't imagine I ever will.'

'I used to think I saw enough of them when I was in the army but just recently I've thought that I might go to South America one day.'

'I'm off to Clacton next week for a fortnight. My nephew can make the coffee for a bit while I sit on the beach.'

'But you'll be back?' Meepers inquired putting down his empty mug.

'Oh yes. You're the stopaway not me,' she laughed. Meepers went down the bus steps. At the bottom he turned to look up at her framed in the doorway as if like a Byzantine portrait she had been painted on a timeless golden backdrop. Her face was dark and featureless against the light which caught at her pepper-and-salt hair and turned it into a flaring halo. The long white overall covered her completely except for a few inches of calf and the black boots she wore summer and winter for comfort. He almost waved.

*

No one ever told you there was cold as this in the world, not a cold hard and bright, sharp-edged like icecubes in a tall glass or mint cold frosting round the lip but a soft, a creeping cold like a worm where the marrow of your bones should have been. No one told you you would need special clothes to keep the cold damp worms out of your bones or they would eat you away, make you tremble and ache, your skin knot into goose pimples and grow sore to the touch. When you got off the boat the teeth chattered in your head so you could hardly speak. There was the Red Cross with cups of hot slop you couldn't taste that they called tea and a blanket to wrap round you so you looked like some damn American or that stooge Rochester who spent his whole film career with his eyes rolling in his head in terror. Don't shoot til you see the whites of their eyes. There you was all refugees from the sunshine fetched up in fog and damp, all as foolish as each other, all blind men when it came to leading each other to where the money was and a roof over your heads.

That was in the beginning. Then you began to look about, get the feel of things, the lie of the streets to the labour exchange where you joined the lines for jobs or to the doctor for pills against the chills. All god's children got chills. They gave you money so you didn't starve while you looked for a job. Hadn't they said back home the streets of London was wall to wall papered with situations vacant. All you do man you just buy the paper and see where they's all hollering out for you.

But that's not how it's done not nohow. What you need is a friend of a friend who knows someone who's heard they're taking on at some place or best a friend who'll recommend you to the foreman. It's better for the women because this city is so sick with the cold and rain that most of all in the world they need nurses to smooth away the fever. See them girls in their crackly starched uniforms making like they was all Doctor Kildare with a thermometer and a watch while we're standing in line to collect our dole. So you learn fast to get yourself a woman to shack up with to keep away the cold.

You forget the sad girl you leave behind. What could she understand about how you live now since you stepped ashore with your British passport in your hand.

Now one day the sun shines some, thin and pale but it's still up there and you put on your teddybear overcoat and your porkpie and swagger down to Brixton market that's all yams and pigstails as if it was Georgetown Kingdomcome, and racks of bright dresses for the girls and fish and chips and the latest from the steelband or Belafonte calypsoing over the stalls and suddenly you've got yourself a piece of this city. Next day you driving you bus like Jehu and the old ladies bawl you out and shake they skinny fists 'cos they falling in the aisle and the spectre adds his bit 'cos you're behind schedule and you lose it again. And the whole world is Coldharbour Lane on a wet night without a minny of rum to put between you and refrigeration. But back there for a moment the street lamp was a banana tree with a yellow bird on its arm. Even here they got to have a touch of summer sometime.

He was very tired now. The stairs seemed endless which was strange after the eleven storeys he had become used to. He was glad to sit down at the desk cleared of his papers. At once he began to think of all the things he had left out. It had been a rush job when it should have been a life's work. Even so all his care and thought, a lifetime of both, had gone into it. But he wouldn't accept its conclusions as final, more an interim report. An exercise for the students was the way to look at it. He began to arm himself against the answer he didn't want to hear. London Bridge is broken down piping voices sang in his head.

Meepers pulled a clear sheet before him and noted a question about dancing on bridges in the Middle Ages, cult or social activity. There was so much to be done. He had been sitting awkwardly and had pins and needles in his left arm. Had he made enough of the letters found in the Wallbrook? Dead voices radioed to him out of the night. 'I believe you know I am very well; please send list ... turn that slave girl into money ... ' 'Dis manibus. MacAur ... aged fifteen years six months. Set up by his mother.' 'London at the shrine of Isis.'

They were pushing up through the ground, standing on each other's shoulders and calling to him not to leave them out as if he was their last hope of immortality. The waters of the Thames shrank back to show wharves and quays with ships riding the tides. Feet thudded on wood, backs strained under bundles and bags. He couldn't keep track of it all. He had failed and they knew that he had. Shadows seemed to brush his face. A figure with a spear came towards him, a pirate, a mercenary and rammed it hard and straight into his chest. The pain took his breath away. The sweat broke out of him soaking him through. His right hand clenched on his breastbone trying to pluck out the spear. There was nothing but the pain and there had never been any like it not in all his wounded days. It squeezed his gut til he vomited over the desk and the dancing figures. At last the shape tore the spear from his chest with a final savagery and flung it away. There was a moment's pause; the eye of the storm. Something he had to do. He closed his fingers round the thickened pen and scrawled 'Sorry so sorry'.

Martha leaned Ben's head supportively against her shoulder and let them both be washed in at the porch. 'They'll think I'm a tourist too,' she smiled to herself. Already there was a slackening in the summer migrants so that it was possible for them to stand still inside the doors while their entering wave moved forward to break on grey walls and black pillars and fetch up against the pale marble limbs of the two magnificent Rysbracks fringed by the lace doily of the choir screen. What struck her first was the delightful gaudiness of it all. Since the days of the cleaning dean it had become a riot of gilt and enamel on white stone and polished marble. Gone was the dust and soot that had made it a mausoleum for late Victorian broad church and state. The perpetual light of huge chandeliers glittered like a ballroom. The thicket of marble and stone figures was poised as if frozen by an uplifted baton. Any moment it would fall and statesmen, generals and admirals would waltz away up the nave. Aside from Battersea Funfair it had rightly become the most vulgar baroque attraction in the city, all the more so for being impossible to guess at from the chaste turf and darkly gothic exterior. She would buy a programme and then they would know what order the dances came in.

At once she realized that with Ben in her arms it was impossible. He was very happy to be carried about and shown his inheritance. The crowds of other sightseers didn't bother him as his black eyes stared unblinkingly around with the consciousness of his own worth and beauty that loved children share with animals but Martha needed both hands to hold him. She would just have to read the inscriptions and give him a running commentary.

She didn't linger over the unknown soldier wanting fiercely that Ben should know and be known, not die anonymous. She remembered the words they had sung in her school choir that she had at first been cajoled into and then had enjoyed a passion for, for the chance to sing out loud so many things with the support and cover of other people if you went wrong and the making together of such a rich dense sound of layered notes. She couldn't remember who the music was by but they had lowered their voices on to: 'And some there be which have no mem-or-ial, who are perish'd as though they had never been.' It had made her shiver, particularly the 'perish'd'.

In such a concourse there would be a percentage of rogues; that was only to be expected but Ben wasn't to take notice of them. They might seem to have prospered to be here among the industrious, talented and numinous but it was no sure way. There were a great many bullies posing as generals but she hoped that wouldn't be his bent. It was the complexity she wanted to point out, the variety of things he might be. However the first thing they noticed was a slave kneeling at the dying feet of Fox and she was glad to make one or two things clear. Don't overdo the gratitude; remember anyone who does you a favour is getting his own satisfaction out of it and likewise you when you think you're doing good. Always query motives.

The stones set in the floor raised an embarrassing problem. It wasn't always possible to go round them and Martha found they were standing on Ann Oldfield, the first woman they had come across. 'Well, at least you won't have that trouble,' Martha said to Ben and immediately felt guilty at envying her own child. They passed on. Here was a poor sailor boy become admiral murdered for his emerald ring, and a rich man in his coach with his three assassins at the window. Now came the poets, many of whom had died poor and were buried here in recompense 'that he who had been denied almost everything in life might not in death be denied a tomb' as one epitaph had it. 'Spenser the prince of poets in his tyme,' at whose feet other poets had begged to be buried, Martha had read for A-level. Sweet Thames ran softly into Ben's ears. Novelists and playwrights crowded up. Ben could choose, she murmured, between the gloom of 'Mortality behold and fear' and the good manners of 'Life is a jest and all things show it'. She wouldn't stop him of course, but for his own sake she rather hoped he would pick some other job.

They looked into the choir to admire the stalls and then moved on to the Chapel of the Kings. Martha was looking for the tomb of the Black Prince, who was so much written about, to show Ben but his only appearance was among his brothers and sisters on his father's monument. It didn't matter. There were enough kings, queens and princes for Ben not to feel without antecedents. Martha turned her eyes resolutely from the deaths of royal infants: 'The Princess Sophia aged three days in her cradle.' Back in the North aisle she took him up to the nurses' memorial chapel so that he could see that his mother wasn't left out, but his little weight was growing heavier by the minute and she hurried him past the stiff queens only allowing him a quick glance at the assembly of immobile politicians. A cassocked shape fluttered towards them. There was going to be a service. She must either leave or sit down. Martha sat, glad of the excuse. Out of sight in the choir they began to sing. She looked across to where Handel, unwigged in inspiration, paused in his larghetto. The choir was making a lullaby for Ben. 'Kings shall be thy nursing fathers and their queens thy nursing mothers.' For Martha they carolled: 'Instead of thy fathers thou shalt have children whom thou mayest make princes in all lands. Kings' daughters were among thy honourable women.' 'King's daughters ...', the boyish sopranos trilled again, 'King's daughters ...'. Ben was asleep.

'We shall have to start without them if they aren't here soon,' said Ponders. 'I thought I made the time quite clear.'

'It was certainly clear enough to me and indeed here I am,' Wandle soothed.

'I can't keep the group waiting much longer. They'll think I don't care after getting them to do the project. I'm surprised neither of them is here. They seemed so keen. I must confess I'm a little bit frightened. I've never tackled anything like this before.'

'So am I. But it's a rational fear surely. To look into the crystal ball, even when it's a technological one, must either reassure or make one afraid.'

'Suppose George tells us we're all dead?'

'Then we shall have a drink and celebrate or go down with the aspidistra flying to a chorus of "Land of hope and glory". Or we shall pretend George got his wires crossed and that he didn't have enough information to deliver a correct diagnosis.'

'That could be true anyway.'

'There you are you see. Whatever it is it will have to be lived through.'

'I don't think we can wait any longer.'

'Shall we go down then?'

*

They sat together in the departure lounge. Soon Robin's flight would be called and he would go out to the waiting plane. It was unlikely that they would see each other again. Lives apart moved on. They would probably both find lovers and become absorbed into new patterns. It didn't mean that they hadn't for a time strangely loved each other or that this farewell was a meaningless formality she shouldn't have indulged in.

'Does Africa really want you?'

'Does anywhere?'

'Yes, I think so. Everywhere really. There's so much to do.'

'You have to do it where you can. I can always come back.'

'Zimbabwe,' she said, drawing the Nile in spilt coffee on the table, 'was that a city?'

'Perhaps I'll find out. It means stone houses. What else is a city? Then there's Meroë in the lost Kingdom of Kush, and Timbuktu.'

'And Thebes.'

'Will Martha be alright?'

'I think so now the landlord can't put us out. Thank God the politicians did the right thing for once. As soon as she can find someone to look after Ben she'll go back to the hospital.'

'And you'll go back to school with a new look at the eighteenth century for the kids.'

'His last lecture about the enthusiasts; I wonder quite what it was about.'

'Some hang-up of his own, something about the limitations of reason. There she blows.' He got up; picked up his bag. 'Take care.'

'And you.'

They still grow roses out of the thin top soil above the brick earth that the house is built from, pied yellow and black London brick, to hand over the fence to the neighbour's children, roses and the apples they bring back from a visit to their daughter moved away to the coast. Streets are torn down around them to be replaced by complexes of flats. The dust blows across from the marshes. Container lorries park where the sidings were at night in the little streets like the carcases of tin dinosaurs. Behind their front room curtains they watch the comings and goings of the street: the children playing out, the workmen renovating number 2, Mr Goodenough taking his first steps to stand at the front door after an operation, a car drawing up, returning men and women from work. 'We always say to them when they go away: Come back to civilization.'

Epilogue

The chopper bounced a bit in the warm updraught. The huge blades swished quietly with a sound of wind over high downs. 'I can put down a bit lower so you can get some better pictures but we have to be careful: they don't like anyone to overfly their air space. Most of all they don't like pictures. They're liable to take a potshot at us.'

'You do this often?'

'Fairly. There's usually someone every six months or so wants to take a look.'

'And how many of them are there down there?'

'Around two million they reckon from aerial closeups.'

'Two million people all living together like an antheap!' He thought of his own house, like all the others he knew, detached in its own plot with solar heat plant on the roof and recycling for waste and water. 'It's Hongkong man, or Calcutta. They must get terrible epidemics. Think of the organization needed to run a place like that, the energy and resources it would consume. I mean like not just fossil energy, human nervous energy, psychic energy.'

'I reckon you have to be born to it. That's why they don't let no one in unless they can prove they're genuine refugees.'

'To that? You want to be a refugee out.'

'You seen the old Paris area?'

'Yeah. I got pictures of that too. Really weird. Kilometres of weeds and rusting iron between broken walls like a filmset. That's what they use it for mostly, location work. I know it so well now I can tell exactly where they shot the hero or the villain, doesn't matter which, running in the final reel or the girl giving you human vanity before she gets laid. You wouldn't think you could tell one bit of weed and stones with a burnt out heap from another, would you. But I can. They get an individual look to them if you work at it. Course there's a bit of science to it too. You can always orient yourself on the line of the Eiffel Tower. You know how that lies there like the spine in a skeleton leaf.'

'Yeah, I know. You don't have to bother about busted instruments over Paris, you can always line up on that. When that all rots away then we'll be left with nothing but technology. Right now. This is as low as I'll chance it, just out of range of their weaponry. You see that there? That's some kind of communications tower.'

Or Hierusalem ...